Café Tempest

Adventures on a Small Greek Island

For ONUR

a fictional memoir

Barbara Bonfigli

Thank you for your loving care..
June 2019

illustrations by Gaia Franchetti
classic Greek recipes remastered by Ana Espinosa

tell me

New Haven, Connecticut

Copyright © 2009 Barbara Bonfigli
Recipes copyright © 2009 Tell Me Press, LLC

Library of Congress Control Number 2009900109
ISBN: 978-0-9816453-1-5 (hardcover)
ISBN: 978-0-9816453-2-2 (pbk.)

Printed in the United States of America
First Edition
10 9 8 7 6 5 4 3 2 1

tell me

Published by **Tell Me Press, LLC**
98 Mansfield St.
New Haven, CT 06511
www.tellmepress.com

Editorial director: Lisa Clyde Nielsen
Editing: Laura Jorstad
Proofreading: Anita Oliva
Production and marketing: Jeff Breuler, Jeff Eyrich, Ian A. Nielsen
Publicity: Gail Parenteau

This is for Sam
my mother

Namaste

All the world is but a play
—Be thou the joyful player

—Robin Williamson (from "Maya"), The Incredible String Band

Contents

1

No one else's behavior makes any sense.

That's it! The end of a continuous struggle for meaning since the third grade. That's when I took a long look at the Brownie pledge. "On my honor I will try . . ." noble and uplifting; ". . . to God and country . . ." I feel like saluting. But then the ending . . . "especially those at home." Sappy and rambling. I sent off my rewrite to National Headquarters and told them they could use it *gratis*—a word I may have misspelled. No reply yet, but you can't expect an organization that sounds like chocolate cake to make snap decisions.

The site of this revelation is the charter terminal at Heathrow, where we're spending the morning en route to Athens. Icarus Air warns you there's a price to pay for flying on a shoestring. "Be there three hours before takeoff," they command. *Three hours!* Whatever happened to "catching a plane"? (I have a little problem with time, which I blame on skipping first grade. "She can already read," they told my parents. They forgot to mention that first grade is where you learn to tell time, and maybe even understand it.) Nor am I thrilled to be flying with a company named for the only air disaster in Greek mythology. Icarus was the fearless god who flew so close to the sun his wax wings melted. I'm not afraid of flying either. Landing, maybe.

I look over the check-in choices and pick Anthony, sympathetic and snappy looking in a uniform that blends nicely with the ticket counter and carpet. With my French roast and Viennese beans, my pepper mill, yoga mat, and summer reading, I'm probably way overweight. As I get closer to Anthony, I do some tai chi balance shifts and practice sending waves of love in his direction. I also run my fingers through my unruly curls and drag a few over one eye in an attempt to look more vulnerable. And I pocket my sunglasses so my grandmother's startling blue eyes can destabilize him. Meanwhile my lower mind takes in the drama unfolding between him and the slim-limbed miniskirted French bombshell in front of me.

"May I see your visa for Greece, madam?"

"See my *what*!?"

Anthony blushes and clears his throat. "Do you have a visa for Greece?"

"Ah . . . *Oui*." She nods her blond sheaves vigorously. "I 'ave one *partout*!"

He smiles a weary, lost-empire smile. "You have a *passport* for everywhere. A visa is something else."

"Something else?" She turns to me bewildered. "*Comment?*"

"*Autre chose*," rises from the ruins of my eighth-grade French.

"*Pourquoi* something *autre*?" She turns back to him, impatiently clicking her fingernails in time with her stiletto heels.

He reflects, scribbles something, and announces: "I think your French driver's license will be acceptable."

Yes! Anthony's my guy. What's a little overweight compared to illegal entry?

"Accept a table?" she turns again and practically shouts at me.

"*Acceptable?*" I try, though I know French cognates are the undergraduate's Waterloo.

"You are American, no?" she demands. Rude, and crushing. Lots of people think my accent is Parisian. Admittedly they all live in San Francisco.

"I just want to help you," I say in a soft tone I reserve for crazy people.

"So do I," Anthony chimes in, picking up my technique of short simple sentences.

"*I* just want to check in!" says Alex, right behind me. She turns her wheely bag around.

"Where are you going?" I ask in perfect English.

"To a line of my own."

Alex (*Alexandra*, if she thinks you're not taking her seriously) decided to come along at the last minute. But it was Julian's idea that I take this unscheduled vacation. Julian is my partner in a West End theater company. Our affair ended the same week our play closed. I knew the play had a limited run, so that wasn't a surprise. As for the Sarah and Julian show, I ignored the critics and willfully overlooked the dwindling returns. Which brings me to the painful conclusion that I'm better at acting than at casting.

Julian thinks it's a happy coincidence; we can take a break from each other without hurting the business. I think it's karma, and karma is a rolling stone; better to roll with it than stand in its path. So I've been planning a few weeks of *uncluttered* renewal on a remote Greek island. Uncluttered as in empty beach, cloudless skies, time alone to meditate, work on a novel, and finish an overdue magazine article. *Renewal* as in retsina. Plus I thought I'd made it clear to my friends that Pharos doesn't rhyme with Mykonos, Jackie O never slept there, and the nearest martini is a five-day sail. No burgers, no discos, and as for getting a torn nail repaired, claws would grow first. Whereas the incomparable charms of Pharos I've been keeping to myself. So I'm not sure what's inspired Alex to come. Could it be she's more tuned in to my state of heart than I am? Asking would only introduce logic into our relationship—a cheap tactic I abandoned long ago. Is there any chance she'll last the month? No way, say our friends, who've never agreed on anything before. I suspect they're placing bets; I just wish there were some way to get into the pool. Thanks to Icarus Air, she now has time to plunder in Duty Free. I find her swinging a full basket.

"Why are you buying all this stuff you don't need and so cleverly didn't pack?"

"C'mon, Sarah. I thought this was a vacation?"

"It is."

"Fine. See you." She slides away.

"And raise you . . ." She doesn't hear. It isn't the first time I've talked to a wall. But it *is* the first time the wall replied: *GIVE UP trying to understand other people.*

(It's an odd thing about revelations. I've meditated at the best places: Ashram in India, hot tub at Esalen, beside the lake in Pokara . . . and I can't recall the great Aha! hitting me at any of them. Here I am at Terminal 4. Why go anywhere?)

Alex reappears, an outbreak of plastic bags blooming on her carry-on.

"Did he say Gate Fourteen?" she says, chewing on a giant duty free Toblerone bar. "I think they're calling our flight."

"I wish I knew," I say, breaking a piece off the end.

Heathrow's the summer school for places that teach English as a second language; articles are optional and, interestingly, there's no future tense. Plus its PA system is a holdover from the Blitz. So the odds of making your plane are roughly the same as colliding with a neutrino. We find another carpet-coordinated employee who says "Leaving! Porto Fourteen!" Alex races me to the gate, where we stand panting in a line that takes forever to board.

We're flying in Europe, a continent of smokers who've recently been banned from lighting up on planes. Everyone around us has the DTs; they're desperately uploading caffeine and wishing they could just step out on the wing for a puff. The guy on our aisle is shaking his foot and studying the Icarus Air evacuation cartoon . . . In my opinion they should let people light up and drink from takeoff to landing. All this pent-up fear and deprivation would certainly mess up an orderly ditching at sea.

Give up trying to understand other people, I remind myself. Why, I wonder, has this revelation taken so long?

At thirty-nine thousand feet I look around at my fellow man with a new lightness, the enormous burden of comprehension abandoned at Duty Free. They're all digging into a mysterious seafood starter. Icarus is an airline that serves food for revenge. Fortunately I have the picnic skills to meet this challenge.

"Alex, let's have our banquet before the headwinds hit."

I detect a little hostility from the guy on the aisle, sawing uselessly on his seeded roll as Alex lays out our smoked salmon, pumpernickel, Brie, and Chablis. Unless it's an involuntary reaction to the cheese, with its whiff of socks left out in the rain.

"Would you like some smoked salmon?" she asks him.

"*Signome?*"

"No. Salmon," says Alex, squeezing the lemon.

"Alex, *signome* is Greek for 'excuse me.'"

"Oh."

"*Thelete ligo*—would you like some . . . ?" I try. But the word for salmon escapes me. I point at it.

She looks back. "Pointing is Greek?"

"*Oxi, efharisto.*" No, thanks. "*Eime hortophagos.*"

"He's a vegetarian," I explain to Alex. "And the Brie is ripe enough to moo, so let's skip that."

"We ought to offer him something," she says, displaying her notorious generosity.

"He can have my entire Icarus lunch." I say in an attempt to imitate her—though you could hardly call this a test.

"*Oxi, efharisto*—no thanks," he smiles discerningly.

I pour him a cup of Chablis.

When dessert comes around it's Turkish delight, in celebration of the three-thousand-year blood feud between Greeks and Turks.

"God, that looks terrible," she says.

"Not as terrible as it tastes."

She brings out our crème brûlée. During which I share my revelation, inspiration deleted.

"You mean to say you've been trying to understand *everyone*?"

"Well, not Charles Manson or the Spice Girls . . . but as a rule, yes."

"What a wild idea." Alex puts down her spoon. "How's it turning out?"

"I've just given it up."

She raises her cup of Chablis. "How do you say 'bravo' in Greek?"

"I think it *is* Greek." And we click.

A few hours later we cross the Corinth channel and drop into the haze of Athens. The landing gear bangs into place. Moments later a stewardess comes over the speaker. "We'll be coming through the aisles to collect unwanted items. Please fasten your cups and throw away your seat belts."

Sometimes I wish I could follow directions.

2

We get in with barely an hour to catch the ferry. I quickly search the cab rank for a zippy-looking driver who isn't eating breakfast behind the wheel and whose headlights are intact.

"Where you go?" says the winning cabbie.

"Piraeus—THE PORT. The ferry to Rhodos, quickly please, and please start the meter."

He turns to us, shocked. "No fix price?"

"No thank you . . . Vassilis," I say, squinting to read his mug shot. We ricochet into traffic without incident, but it's a long ride.

(I love bargaining in Egypt. All the shopkeepers are Zero Mostel. Buying anything from an Indian is exhilarating—you just need stamina and a bottomless capacity for tea. Then there's Nepal, the Buddha's eye over the doorway. The price . . . well, what is *anything* worth? You stand there together, drenched in mystery. But in Greece it's no fun. Maybe they're still smarting from the Trojan horse deal.)

"Rhodos, eh. You see Anatolia from there." Vassilis has some opinions about the latest Turkish provocations. Alex sees an opportunity to sleep. Whereas I'm saying the mantra and watching for death. The road to Piraeus has an unmarked middle lane where everybody drives.

Eventually we turn a corner and beneath the suburban haze the dock tumbles out at the bottom of the hill. Where's Fellini's folding chair, the camera towers, the boom mikes? Fruit sellers, hat sellers, canary sellers, nut vendors, street jugglers, dogs chasing cats, panicky chickens, hippies looking for the sixties, happy drunks sitting on half-submerged pilings, flocks of nuns, soldiers squatting in their boots, smoking and shooting dice, enormous families crying out to someone who waves from an upper deck.

Vassilis is cruising, looking for our pier. "The ferry to Rhodos?" he asks as he sideswipes an old man pushing a cart of apricots.

"You ignorant son of a—" word I don't know—says the vendor as he stoops to retrieve some rolling fruit. *"Eki."* He points to a line of trucks disappearing into a cavern on the dock opposite.

We jolt to a halt. Vassilis jumps from the car like a calf-roping cowboy. Alex opens her eyes.

"Will he carry our bags?" But she's still dreaming.

Haggling with Vassilis over the tip, I lose Alex behind some walking beach chairs.

"Alex. Wait!"

People with TVs, beach umbrellas, inflatable boats, whole hams are streaming around us. I finally catch up to her.

"Where are these people going?" she asks.

"To Mykonos, Naxos . . . this ferry stops at all the islands along the way."

"But if they need all that stuff . . . ," she says, eyeing our relatively modest load.

"They don't. But they read Homer, and according to *The Odyssey* the islands are rocky wastelands."

"You mean the Homer who's been dead a thousand years?"

"He's still in print, though." I say this with a touch of envy that Alex gracefully ignores.

We wait for a family of six to clear the gangway, each of them carrying a tire.

"Good idea," says Alex. "Something to cling to when we go down."

From Rhodes we catch a small caique to our destination. The island of Pharos is a cluster of arid volcanic rocks off the Turkish coast, with about two thousand inhabitants not counting cats and goats. I discovered it four years ago in the Classical manner (viz. *The Odyssey* above) when the boat I'd chartered with friends pitched up there by mistake. It was me on the dog watch, steering by a star, and it set. Just a slight navigational error; slight! We didn't end up in another language.

It doesn't matter that I'll never live it down; I've found my native land. The days are mild, the water warm, the sky an unfiltered blue. Pharians are by nature generous and embracing. Any visitor who makes the slightest attempt to speak their impossible language is practically adopted. Life here is intoxicating in its simplicity. No airport, it's too remote to attract many tour boats, and you'd have to be lost to just drop by. Though its face changes in August. Then the old men desert the *tavernas*—their backgammon boxes mold under the bar; farmers stop coming to town for an *ouzaki;* no goat herds trot through the village churning the streets to dust clouds; the fishermen stow their nets and turn their caiques into beach ferries. But this is May. Take a deep breath.

The boat docks just after midnight. Stavros, bent like the new moon, older than Charon, is there to meet us. In these narrow lanes his wooden pushcart is the only means of transporting our stuff, the donkeys having bedded down at sunset. He's happy to see us, his only customers tonight.

"Harika na se dho," I tell him, a phrase learned over the winter. Until then what I'd thought meant "Happy to see you" was actually "I'm so thrilled to see you I could jump into bed with you right now." Which may explain my popularity on Pharos.

Stavros hugs me and smiles at Alex. He's not too old to notice the waist-length chestnut hair, dark eyes under darker lashes, the sculpted angles and curves of a workout maven. He steps back, surveys our pile of bags, shakes his head—a Turkish rug dealer agreeing to a ridiculous price.

"It's no more than last year," I tell him.

"But me, I'm a year older." His crow-bright laughter echoes across the shuttered port.

A boy appears from the moonshadow of the street lamp and picks up a suitcase.

"Costas, my nephew." He's twelve or thirteen, lean and wiry with dark hair and darker eyes, stooping to be invisible. I'm looking at Stavros, how many years before, waiting for his life to begin. Will he leave as Stavros never did, as eager to be gone from here as we are to arrive?

"Welcome," he whispers, eyes down.

We set off under a black sky pricked with stars. The streets are narrow, lit by a half-moon falling on high whitewashed walls. As we climb out of the port to Kastro they taper to twisting passages no wider than Stavros's cart. We fall in behind, silent, listening to the dogs calling, the night birds, the tinny carillon of goat bells in the valley. I'm thrilled by the stillness, the sharp nightlines, the soft jasmine air. Below us the sea suddenly appears, a skein of rough silk.

"Look," says Alex, her voice husky with amazement. Far below now, our ferry is rounding the tip of the harbor, its wake a fan of diminishing pleats scattering the moonlight.

3

Stavos leaves us in Kastro, a tiny village whose ancient white villas spill like marshmallows across a mountainside woven with wildflowers. Daisies, pink laurel, and Queen Anne's lace float above the thick low patches of thistle and thyme that drive goats wild with happiness. In the late-spring sun almond trees sing with blossoms that will shiver and fly on an evening breeze.

The house I've rented belongs to Gina, an architect from Athens. Three years ago, on my first *intentional* trip to Pharos, it was just Gina and me on deck during a storm that started soon after we left Piraeus. It picked off all the passengers who'd been downing warm beer and cold cheese pies since we'd sailed. With the sea spray in our faces and the wind snatching our words, conversation was mangled. I couldn't see her clearly. But there are people you meet who feel more like found, and that day on the deck I had that feeling.

"You will stay with me while you're looking," she'd said in the un-cluttered way Greeks have of conversing. I'd come to the island without a reservation, the lure of travel being, after all, the unknown, the unseen, the untasted (though here I'm a bit squeamish)—definitely the unreserved. I knew I'd find a room. The instant you disembark on any island you're

surrounded by a posse of tiny crones in head scarves. "*Simmer*? . . . rooms? . . . chambers?" they chant while they look for clues to your mother tongue. But Gina didn't find this acceptable. "If you are writing you need a house. Rooms are too noisy . . . the neighbors, the toilet, the cats. I will find you something not expensive." Meanwhile I would stay with her.

During long dinners in her overgrown garden we roamed vast territories of families, philosophies, dreams. Fortified by retsina; intoxicated, at least I was, by night-blooming jasmine. Our histories were nothing alike and we didn't agree on much. But we both saw life as a fantastical comedy with astonishing plots and miraculous characters, and we ransacked each other's brains with carnivorous delight.

I'd go out after breakfast to look for a house. My friend insisted on coming along.

"I'm an architect, these old places interest me. Also your accent is expensive."

My expectations were modest—something clean, light, no plastic covers. Gina's were not. "Are you so fond of spiders? . . . that reading lamp's useless . . . too close to the ouzo bar . . . I don't trust her husband . . . it stinks of cats." And by the end of the week, "Really Sarah, I don't understand what you're doing. My boys are in Athens, their room is empty. There's a desk in front of the window, a terrace for your yoga . . ."

If you let it, logic will wear you down.

I settled into a writing routine for the first time in my life. I'd always written—school paper, camp paper, the end-of-term skit that got us all suspended. Pharos offered me silence and a window overlooking the sea. I started a novel. When I left six weeks later, I promised myself I'd keep coming back until I'd finished it.

As I lead Alex through Gina's rooms and gardens and along the terraces, I see that nothing's changed . . . everything's just where I left it: the drunken granite staircase, smoke-stained olivewood ceilings, the gnarled jasmine arbor, blue-veined marble sink, the smooth black stones of the courtyard. I belong to a thousand-year tapestry of invaders who've left nothing behind but their vibrations.

"Really old, isn't it?" says Alex, as she runs her fingers over the iron handle of the bread oven.

"Yes!" I cry, spinning around. It's the same delirium that I feel on the beach when I watch a wave erasing my footprints.

4

"The port town of Pharos, on Pharos island, is littered with ouzo bars," says my guidebook. (Kathmandu, same series, is "littered with stupas"; is Rhodes littered with butterflies?) We walk down from Kastro the next morning to rent motorbikes and introduce Alex to my favorite places. Nikos's café, in the curve of the small fishing harbor, caters to the fishermen who tie up their caiques across the road. Ulysses would feel right at home. Veined lumpy plaster walls, impasto of smoke stains, family photos fierce and faded, crusty amphorae leaning in the corners.

Nikos's relatives are pictured fishing or eating, stuck up with early Scotch tape. Over the windows are gilt-framed, garishly tinted portraits of the last king and queen of Greece (lately of Primrose Hill, North London) not eating or fishing but definitely looking last. There's a calendar from a sports club in Astoria, last flipped ten years ago in May 1988. There are small square tables with plastic ashtrays from Metaxa, simple rush-matted slat-backed chairs—you can just make out an *N* that Nikos once painted on the top rung—and some wine-stained backgammon boxes. Along the far wall in a pale blue wooden cupboard with a dimpled glass front are little piles of cigarette packs and chocolate bars, wrappers faded beyond recognition. Above the cupboard are two long shelves, the top one lined with thick squat glasses opaque from eons of saltwater washes. The one below sags dramatically with ouzo bottles, a few brown torsos of whiskey and brandy, and a dusty collection of homemade wines that haven't been moved in the four years I've been coming here. And before that? When any of them are finally opened, maybe at the christening of Nikos's first grandchild, let's hope the island's doctor is (1) not visiting his uncle in Santorini, and (2) not drinking at the same party.

At a right angle to these shelves, which run the length of the wall, is a retired fishing bench balanced on top of a small fridge. Generations of paint jobs bleed through its splintered sides. If this were Hydra, or any of the Greek islands littered with artists, this bench would figure on a thousand canvases. At Nikos's it's simply the kitchen; on it sits a metal tray with two small gas burners and two brass brikis for making coffee, a chipped earthenware pot of sugar, another of tin spoons, a stenciled hexagonal coffee tin, and a pile of matchboxes.

Nikos is sitting beside it studying his lottery form when we walk in. "Come in! Come in! How are you?" He jumps up and holds out his hands. "When did you come?"

"This morning."

Alex gasps.

("You have to lie," I explain later. "People are really offended if you don't see them instantly. There's no allowance for unpacking.")

"When do you go?" Always the follow-up, which used to offend *me*. Hold on, I've just arrived! But that's not it; these are the children of Herodotus.

"Niko, this is my friend Alexandra."

"Welcome." He bows his head, but to one side so he can continue checking her out. "You are a writer too?"

"No, just a reader. Very pleased to meet you."

"Me too," says Nikos. "What do you like?"

"Orange juice, please."

"Is he Nikos or Niko?" Alex whispers as he gets up.

"Both. You drop the '*s*' when you're talking to him."

"Why?"

"And you, Sarah *mou*?" Nikos turns back. "*Café sketto?*—black, no sugar."

"*Nai*—yes," I agree, pleased he remembers.

"There is no 'why' when it comes to Greek," I say as he departs.

The orange juice is nectar here, but I order coffee to watch the performance. Short limbs thick and hairy, charcoal hair clinging to the rim of his round head—Nikos is kin to a hobbit. But in the kitchen he's a dancer. He strikes the match with his huge thumbnail; the head flies, a little spark is produced. (Greek matches never flame—not enough stuff on the tip; whoever translated "safety match" must have been picturing dynamite.) Two spoons of coffee powder sail toward the briki like basketballs from the free-throw line. Then a waterfall from a tin pitcher. The thumb and forefinger of the left hand gently rock the briki while those on the right, arched over a tiny wooden spoon, slowly stir the brew. The back is tilted, all the weight on the toes, chin cocked to test the aroma. (Trikonasana, the Tree Pose, would be a snap for Nikos.) He pours out the brew slowly, to catch the sediment. Then he puts the solitary cup on a tray and leads the way to a table.

Here, under a bamboo awning wound with grapevines and hung with neon tubes, is the heart of Pharos. Old men come early to drink coffee and read the papers, returning in the late afternoon to play backgammon, drink ouzo, and talk politics. Fishermen mending their nets along the dock come in all day. On Sundays after church they bring their sons and nephews. Tourists don't usually walk to this end of town, so there aren't many women at Nikos's. A lull as we appear, then a faint rustle as the regulars adjust to mixed company. The ones who recognize me nod and break into scattertooth smiles.

Nikos sets down our order, then sets himself down. Anchorman for the island news, he's anxious to fill us in: who married, died, fooled around, had the wrong operation—he leans forward, fixes us with a bright squint, and in a loud raspy whisper serves up the raw and the half-baked.

The hot issues this summer are the proposed road to the beach and a third telephone line. The beach road is a pretty straightforward issue. For several thousand years Plati Alou, the island's one sizable sandy beach, has been reachable only by sea.

"And by goat—not a load-bearing animal," Nikos adds. ("Load-bearing"? Is he channeling Buckminster Fuller?) From June to September the fishermen have the dead-easy job of ferrying tourists from the town harbor to the beach.

"So the fishermen don't want the road?" Alex asks.

"*Malista*," he says. "Of course not. They catch lots of money in July and August."

"But how can they stop it?" With guilty delight I'm picturing myself on a motorbike, coasting down to Plati Alou.

"They're talking about it now," says Nikos, "the natural beauty of Pharos." He nods toward a school of fishermen a few tables away, all drinking ouzo and spitting their pistachio shells onto the *platia*. Their cousins the taxi drivers see things differently. They are, to a man, free marketeers—rhymes with *buccaneer*, their line of work before the wheel. "Fixed price" is the price they fix after checking out your shoes and your watch.

"The fishermen are calling the taxi drivers revolutionaries," Nikos laughs.

"Revolutionaries!" I say. "Who built the first roads anyway?"

"The Romans," says Alex.

"*Oxi*—no—we did," says Nikos. "That's how they ran over us."

I'm ill equipped to mediate; my Roman emperors start with Armani. But the future of Pharos is dear to my occupying heart.

"Niko, are you talking about a highway that's likely to wipe out chickens and kids?"

"*Oxi, oxi*, there's no money for that. A dirt road wide enough for two cars."

"Would anyone have to move?"

"Some tomato fields."

A town planner's dream. But the fishermen aren't Greek for nothing.

"We invented bureaucracy," says Nikos. "They're petitioning Athens for an environmental study, a geological survey, and in case they lose, a limit on the number of taxis. Gina, where you're staying, works for the planning commission, so she will do the study. And . . ." he adds, after a pause you might call dramatic, "all her cousins are fishermen."

"But what about Rich Tino?" I remind him—her uncle who drives a '78 Chevy Impala taxi.

"He's not leaving her anything," says Nikos, who is somehow privy to Tino's last wishes.

The new telephone line is less divisive, since there's only one family against it; but there aren't any small families here. The only telephone up in Kastro lives in the sitting room of *Kyria* Kassoula, the postman's mother. It's a sort of shrine, sitting on its own pedestal table on a lace mat embroidered by the postman's grandmother. Last year a telephone directory arrived to keep it company. That sits on a footstool next to the electric counting box that clicks away as you shout, adding up the price of the call. On top of the directory sits a sassy orange tabby. Her gossip must be the talk of the alleys.

If you're staying in Kastro, this is the number you leave—for emergencies. It takes some time for *Kyria* Kassoula's unhurried sons to locate you, so calling in could wipe out your Social Security. Then there's the problem that the slightest act of God, like a tuna bumping the underwater cable, or an octopus with an itch, will result in disconnection, or an interruption of hours while the money box ticks merrily away.

Kyria Kassoula's sitting room has a sofa, and about a dozen wooden chairs. If you make or receive a call very early or very late you have the room to yourself. In order not to inconvenience *Kyria* Kassoula, you never do this. Instead you usually play to a full house. This is because the operator in Rhodes books the calls in order, but she rings back using chaos theory.

"He wanted to tell you himself, but we can't find him."

"Bring me two dozen suppositories and those pads."

"Everybody does that. Make her take you back!"

A dozen people sit in hushed communion while the caller shouts down the unamplified line. Anything that merits the drama of a phone call gets its first and freshest reading in *Kyria* Kassoula's sitting room.

There's a second line down in the port at the post office. It's on the wall next to the very busy stamp counter, and of course it's only available during post office hours. To say these hours vary is to describe the desert as dry. It's more private than *Kyria* Kassoula's, since no one can really hear what you're saying. On the other hand, neither can you.

"Where would they put the new line?" I ask.

"They're thinking about the old army garage," Nikos says, getting up—suddenly aware of his other customers.

"It's a pity," I tell Alex.

"It is?"

"The army garage is deserted. Nobody's been in there since VE-Day."

"So it'll be private," she says, studying my worried look, her chin propped on her fist. "You know, like in the rest of the world."

"I know this sounds romantic, but I like it the way it is."

She puts down her glass. "You think Pharos should be kept quaint and backward so all us city slickers can have somewhere to escape."

"It's not that. It's just that progress isn't always progress. I'd rather have earwitness accounts. Now we're going to get rumors instead of reality."

"That *is* romantic. In a place like this where everybody's related? I'd say this island is a rumor surrounded by water."

Nikos rushes by with a tray of coffee. "One more thing," he says, turning in midair (another tricky yoga move). "The mayor's old Volvo coupé is missing. If you see it, tell me first."

5

A reckless wren is building her nest in the television aerial on our neighbor's roof. I'm on the terrace watching with interest. It's not that there aren't trees around here—bugs for breakfast, branches for shade. She's still at it when Alex appears. (Alex arises with the island cats, about two hours after me—on account of their nightlife.)

"Why would a bird do that?" Alex asks.

"Hoping to give birth to a TV anchor."

"Of course, thanks . . . *efkareestee.*"

"*Efharisto.* When you think about it, reincarnation can explain a lot of odd behavior."

"Please Sarah, I haven't had coffee."

"There's some in the thermos."

"I never noticed that aerial before. What's on Greek television?"

"Snow."

"Just because you hate TV . . ."

"I'm serious. The reception's really terrible. Last year the mayor asked me over to explain what was happening on *ER.*"

"God! They ask the only American who doesn't know who George Clooney's dating."

"The whole family was sitting there riveted to the set and all you could make out was shapes walking around in a blizzard. It could have been shot in Anchorage. Which just proves that television . . ."

"Stop! Please. Thank God we're not still living together."

"Really? . . . I bet you miss my coffee."

"Not *that* much," says Alex, starting down the precipitous stairs to the kitchen. "But . . ." I wait, I must admit, expectantly. "Won't that bird get electrocuted when they turn on the TV?"

"Uh . . . not unless her other foot's on the street. She'd have to be grounded."

Alex stops midstep, her eyes glazing over. Oh wow, she's been picturing dead birds crashing to the pavement whenever she's watching TV. And how about the phone! *All* the time she's talking . . . splat! splat! splat! What a fabulous piece of ammunition. If only I can remember it the next time I'm exercising my own ignorance.

I discovered the wren's building project just after dawn, when Iannis Milos, the mailman, delivered a telegram from Julian. Birds moving in is an auspicious sign, so it shouldn't have surprised me.

"They ate n0 jvailable step?* nX easibl prodution atde ntil mArch. d0n' thurry. 0mm!!" I read it aloud to Alex at second breakfast. Since I'm toasting pita, I use a Middle Eastern accent. "I am loving these telegrams—so many grown-ups cutting and pasting."

"But what does it mean?"

"Well, we are not knowing exactly."

She grabs it from me and frowns through the text. "Telegrams are for conveying urgent information."

"*Urgent* is really a Western idea," I say, dropping my accent.

"But isn't Greece the cradle of Western civilization."

"It's more like the hammock."

Alex looks up and sniffs. "Whatever you're burning is done."

"You can't change a culture just by importing modern technologies," I say while scraping off the black edges and buttering the bit that's left. "Hmm . . . That's actually good material for a book." I put another pita into the toaster.

"Good material for a book is vellum. That's the stuff they use to make covers for books that are actually finished."

"Ha ha." If I rose to every occasion she mentions my work-in-progress I'd have massive calf muscles.

"Don't you think you should try calling Julian? It must be pretty important."

"I'm not really sure when it came."

"You said this morning. Now that one's burning!"

"That's when Iannis brought it." I blow out the flaming crumbs. "But look, it's already turning yellow, and it's crispy on the edges. Iannis said something about the postmaster losing his scissors."

"But there's got to be a date on it." Her voice is rising as she scans it. This is a person who's comfortable using *deadline* in a sentence.

"Nope. Must have been pasted on the end of the previous telegram. They come in like one giant snake, you know."

She turns it over and back again. "And no signature!"

"Well, there was one of course." I add a little honey to the pita, which disguises the charcoal flavor. "Now it'll be the greeting on the one after mine. 'Yours so-and-so. We arrive the tenth . . .'"

"Hopeless."

"No it's not. Have a look—it ends with *om*, the root of all mantras."

"*You're* hopeless. Don't eat that, it's carcinogenic. How do you know it's from Julian?"

"That's his post code at the top. And I think he's trying to tell me our show's been postponed. 'Don thurry omm.' What else can it mean?"

"Oh, right. Now you're channeling the oracle at Delphi."

Julian's follow-up letter arrives the very next morning—probably in real time. There's a hit show at the theater we'd booked for our fall production of *Noël/Cole;* our get-out clause gives them a get-out clause, and they've exercised theirs. It's too late now to find another theater in time for September, so we'll have to put off our next show until February, when the duds of winter shiver and die.

"Ten more weeks! Ten more weeks!" we chant like two giddy summer campers.

"Who can we invite?" says Alex as she squeezes orange juice. A tower of scooped out shells is rising on the counter.

"Nobody. *What'uv I— what'uv I— what'uv I done to deserve this . . .* " I decorate my breasts with rinds and dance around the kitchen. "D'you think this is how Madonna got started?"

"Nobody? Aren't you working on generosity?" she says as she empties the pitcher of orange juice into her glass.

"I'd rather work on my article for *Yoga Journal.* Now I'll have plenty of time to finish it."

"Article? What article? What about your novel?"

"I'm talking about the short term."

"Whereas the novel's for life."

I stop dancing. "Why's everyone in such a hurry for me to finish it? Do you think I'm deeply unconsciously worried?"

"Are you?" She goes back to squeezing, feigning indifference.

"I'm deeply consciously *un*worried. Alex, what are you doing?"

"Good. I'm making cairns. Remember the postcards Julian sent back from Nepal? Those little markers along the road?" She steps back to admire her work. "Maybe you should ask Julian to come? He's got the time off now and you could, you know, come to a happy ending."

"We already had one of those. Now he's dating the costume designer from last season. You remember those dreadful frocks in *Sail Away*. We fought with her right up till opening night."

"Good God! What does he see in her?"

"Practically everything. Her idea of a skirt is a tutu with a hem. She used to be a dancer at Sadler's Wells. All her tops are tanky."

"Does she have a name?"

"She does," I admit. "But I've given up malicious gossip, so I don't want to talk about her."

"You don't *have* to be malicious."

"She's a horrible costume designer; what else is there to say?"

"OK, so no Julian. You'll write. Fine. What's the article about?"

"Choosing a mantra for meditation." I dance to the garbage can and dump in the rest of Madonna's costume.

"Choosing? I thought they give them to you."

"Well, yes, if you have a guru. But some people don't, so they get 'em from books, movies . . . cocktail parties."

"You mean there are people out there chanting *Scotch 'n soda, scotch 'n soda*?"

"In New York. In London it's probably *Gin 'n tonic, gin 'n tonic*."

"Weird," says Alex, adding two more rinds to her tipsy creation.

"There's more to the article than that, actually." I put some bread on to fry. I have her attention, but only because the kitchen could burn down.

"My idea is that people could use different mantras for different times of day. Like Indian ragas. Or for different situations. Waiting for their luggage, the subway . . ."

"I-R-T, I-R-T."

"That's the general idea." I'm not worried; Alex isn't my target readership.

"No more butter, use olive oil. And turn down the flame. I just hope you'll have some funny bits. *Yoga Journal* can get pretty heavy."

The room fills with smoke.

"I'll add some cartoons," I say, opening all the windows and the door to the courtyard. "Let's eat outside. Your cairns are beginning to steam."

"M-T-A, M-T-A . . ." She follows me out with a tray.

I'm in a nice writing groove when Tula, Gina's housekeeper, comes to tend the garden. She's always panting by the time she reaches the terrace because she holds her breath on the stairs. ("Breathe," I told her last year. She looked at me as if I were crazy. I admit she was breathing at the time.)

The pause while she fills with air gives me a chance to shift into communication.

"*Kalimera*, Tula—good morning. Are you well?"

"*Kalimera, Saraki.*" A suffering smile. "*Etsi ketsi.*" Greek for *comme ci, comme ça*, which is top-flight health for Tula.

"Is Gina coming next month?"

"*Oxi.*" She starts digging around the jasmine. Only Tula can make digging in dirt a noisy activity.

"What about July?"

"Working in *Athena*."

"Then the house won't be full?"

She stops digging and turns to me. "Full?" She rolls her hand across her considerable belly.

Occupied is what I'm after; *pregnant* is what I'm saying. I try again. "No one else here?"

She thrusts her chin skyward, the Greek "no."

"Alex!" I shout down to the courtyard. "We can stay through July!"

About the garden: Pharos is a bare volcanic rock and dirt is precious, as is space in this hilltop village. Water is rarest of all. So the garden is an assortment of amphorae and clay pots stuffed with hydrangeas and gardenias and long troughs planted with bougainvillea and jasmine. The vines run up the walls right to the roof terrace. Little basil plants are spaced like turrets along the terrace walls. In a corner of the courtyard an olive tree gives shade from the afternoon sun. The old marble sink next to it is Diana the tortoise's bathtub.

Tula fills a huge old spouted clay pot littered with bleached crustaceans (the Louvre has one just like it) from a well to water the plants and wash the tiles. This happens three times a week at ten AM. Since I'm up at six, she doesn't interfere with coffee and meditation. But writing's impossible while she splashes through the courtyard humming to herself.

"Have you told her to come *after* you've gone to the beach?" Alex asks.

"A million times."

"And?"

"She nods and comes at ten."

"All maids are tyrants."

Being Greek they're also philosophers. Tula has just watered the espadrilles I left on the terrace when there's a rap like justice at the front door. I open to an enormous puffing tomato-faced guide who got his fashion cue from a touring company of *Die Fledermaus*. A breathless cluster of sundazed tourists is strung out behind him.

"*Bitte.*" We're friends right away. "Where is Church *auf die* Virgin?"

I point silently to the huge stone building they've just passed.

"*Ah! Danke.*"

Are they putting us on with that "ah"? I back into Tula as I close the door.

"What did he want?" Rattling her chins.

"The church."

She shakes her head and laughs: "*Kosmos trellos*"—The world is crazy. There we have it, from Tula.

6

The weather is wreaking havoc with my routine. We all know writers have routines (some writers even *write* about them), but I'm especially sensitive to this issue. Thanks to Marjorie, my sister-in-law who sends me articles recounting the iron discipline and Spartan lifestyles of every struggling Pulitzer prizefighter. Stories from the *San Francisco Chronicle*, the *Waterloo Reaper*, the *Wilton Wallflower, She, Oui:* Everyone is fascinated by the woman who forgot to eat and lost forty pounds finishing her self-help treatise, and the crack dealer in Sing Sing who writes three thousand words a day between lockup and lights-out. Nothing escapes Marjorie. I actually suspect her of having a clipping service for this purpose. How could she read all this and still run a day-care center? "FYI," she notes cheerfully in the margins.

"She's just trying to create some common ground; something you can talk about at family gatherings," says Alex. I doubt it. More like pure envy of the creative (unstructured) life. If Marjorie starts showing up in my meditations . . . but I digress.

In Pharos, where silence caresses you and ice trays are still being test-marketed, my routine is dead-easy: rise with the wrens, coffee, yoga, and meditation until Tula arrives to break the spell. Then write until lunch and sail to a beach. But the write until lunch part is coming unstuck.

Since our arrival almost three weeks ago the sun has burned off any clouds by nine, the wind has vanished, and from the top of this mountain I watch a silent parade of small fishing boats drawing oily streaks on the distant water. The islanders call this weather *bonatza,* and I defy anyone but Marcel Proust, who *never* went out, and Marjorie's other marvels to stay inside.

"So move your desk outside," says Alex at second breakfast.

"I can't write in the sun."

"Then I guess you're a ghostwriter." She looks thrilled with herself.

"Ahhhhh. I divorce you I divorce you I divorce you."

"Once is enough. I ran into Georgos the beach chair guy at the Meltemi bar last night. He asked us to go fishing."

"Again? How many times is that?"

"It's kind of embarrassing to keep saying no."

"Really? He doesn't seem embarrassed to keep asking."

"Can't you ever rest your brain?"

"Are you interested in Georgos?"

"Not at all. I said we'd meet him at one."

Georgos spends his summer mornings setting up beach chairs at Acro Yiali. Needless to say he's the first generation of his pre-Hellenic family to combine this activity with fishing. Birds on a wire, sunbathers in neat rows, what is this instinct for lateral gathering? I like to picture Georgos in heaven, running into his grandfather and describing his work. I want to see the old man's face when Georgos tells him, "They *pay* to sit there."

(Are fish stories allowed in heaven? No, the question is, is heaven a fish story?)

At one o'clock we're stepping onto his immaculate blue yellow red green caique. Various friends are gathered on the beach to wish us well.

"Watch out for Georgos's fuel gauge."

"*Dhen birazi*, don't worry, the lighthouse comes on at eight thirty."

"Have you got some Turkish money?"

And just as we cast off in a din of coughing diesel, "Don't forget to write, *Saraki*!" comes from Theo, the thirty-something doctor, who's always inviting me on *his* boat. (How a guy as gentle and great looking as Theo can still be single is a mystery right up there with the Shroud of Turin.) I've wanted to accept several times, but Tula has me brainwashed. "Say yes, Sarah *mou* . . ." Her cautious eyes roll heavenward and she slips an imaginary ring around her finger.

"That's ridiculous," said Alex when I mentioned it. "Just keep it light."

"It doesn't work. I can't explain it. Whenever I try that, I end up sounding like Eleanor Roosevelt."

"That explains it."

Georgos takes us along the coast past the tiny fishing village of Agios Vasilis at the end of the footpath. Our diesel engine sets a soft drumbeat. A few hungry gulls dance above our wake, occasionally diving to feed on flashing small fry that leap in the spray of our prow. A fastidious sea monster has neatly bitten out huge hunks of rock along the island's south rim, leaving perfect semicircles of sandy beach. I'm about to suggest that we fish from one of them when Georgos abruptly cuts the engine and drops his anchor.

"Here is good place; fish here yesterday." He's looking triumphantly at Alex, as though he's already landed the big one.

"Can't we fish from the beach. Or the rocks beside it?" Alex says, poaching my thought.

"But the fish I think are *here*." He begins to unreel his net.

I was wrong—Georgos really means to fish. I forgive myself, though; it's a fluke. When a single Greek male looks at a single American female what he actually sees is a little blue rectangular book with the US eagle stamped on the cover. This disease, riding along on the Y-chromosome, seems immune to the true-life stories of uncles in Astoria and cousins in Chicago. Unless they all lie like weathermen to torment their relatives back home.

"That's a gross exaggeration, and from you, a civil rights nut!" Alex said when I tried to enlighten her this morning at breakfast.

"A civil rights *nut?*" That isn't just French roast pounding in my ears.

"Sorry; *nut* was the wrong word. I just don't see how a person who marched on Washington can say a whole country is looking for a passport to America."

"Just the men. And there was probably a lull when they could send you to Vietnam. But I can tell you that every guy I've gone out with here has proposed."

"That's because you're irresistible!"

I fold my arms.

"You don't think Julian was the world's last man, do you?" She looks serious.

"Certainly not."

"Then why don't you let me form my own opinion?" She smiles.

What can you say to that?

Now we're in the middle of the bay and I'm elated to be fishing—mainly for the literary experience. I must hold a record for coming to the islands so often and never casting a line. As for Alex, she grew up on a coastline, with three brothers.

"Hat, please."

She digs into our beach bag and hands me my Abercrombie duck bill.

"Fat." Out comes a tube of Kiss My Face cover-up. We cast. Georgos says that *sargoss* and *melanouri*—both delicious—are running, and they like bread better than anything else. That disposes of my biggest objection—cutting bait. We start rolling dough balls. Alex's are marbles covered in sunscreen while mine, as I mull over mantras for staring out to sea, are little prayer wheels.

The sun plays on a lightly rippling sea, its rays shooting clear to the sandy bottom.

"*Ella*—come, look!" Georgos shouts as he pulls in a big *sargoss*.

"*Ella* too," cries Alex a few minutes later. Suddenly we aren't alone. Three small caiques just visible on the horizon as we anchored have begun a slow coughing march in our direction. The chains of silver fish scales flashing as Georgos pulled in our catch have caught the fishermen's squinting eyes.

When you're out on a vast sea and another boat approaches, why does it always look like it's going to run into you? But they stay far enough away not to queer our fishing with the shadows of their hulls. They're well within earshot, though, on this flat glossy surface.

"Georgaki, what have you caught!" one cries, not looking at the fish. Alex and I are dangling our lines over the freeboard, in our bikinis naturally, but looking businesslike, I think, in the hats.

"*Sargoss*," he replies merrily.

"Don't you want some help?" But this is no place to land a passport, and after a few remarks that I don't understand they cast their own nets.

After an hour or so I've had all the literary experience I want. Smashing the head of a sparkling creature writhing on a hook, gills surging for air, isn't my sport. Even with my eyes closed the smack of death breaks in my head. One of the caiques near us reels in a broad net boiling with small fry. It's flipped onto the deck and the fish shaken out. No need to strike them; they suffocate there in the sun.

"I'm going to swim ashore. Wanna come?"

"No, I'll stay here," Alex says. And after my long look, "I'm OK."

I tie up my book and towel in a plastic bag and swim one-armed to the beach.

7

Om namah shivaya or *Ham sa*? I'm trying out fishing mantras the next morning against a background choir of wrens when there's a knock on the door. I lean out over the terrace and see the top of the doctor.

"Good morning, Theo." On this warm morning the first two buttons of his white shirt are open at his throat, and his cuffs are undone and rolled back. Silky black hair is escaping; it must cover his entire body.

"Good morning, *Saraki*. Am I so early?"

"No no, I've been up for hours." True today, but sometimes not. I tell myself I'm sparing the intruder embarrassment, but really it's because I'm terrified of sleeping through life.

"You make the best coffee." He puts his satchel inside the door.

This is true. I suspect this has led Theo to the false impression that I can cook. I suspect this because he often happens to be passing by around dinnertime.

"Georgaki tells me you catch many *sargoss*. Do you make some?"

"No." I could destroy all his fantasies with a single serving. "But I *have* made coffee."

"Yes, thank you. I have many patients this morning so I am brief if you don't mind."

"I don't," comes out much too fast. I turn to lead us back up to the terrace but he sits at the kitchen table. I sit down opposite him.

"You know I am director of the play."

"What play, Theo?"

"You know the Pharos Players, *Saraki*." He looks bewildered, and hurt.

"Sorry, but . . ." I make a sorry face.

"We have a play in July. A very good play. Everybody comes."

"But I've never been here in July."

"Ah, *sosto*, right." He refills his own cup.

I sit up straighter and look expectant. Theo isn't known for brevity, and already his promise is in grave danger.

"I hear you stay more this year, yes?"

"Through July," I say briskly, to set an example.

"You see the hospital is now ready, the building I mean."

"Yes."

"And now I must put everything together. All the machines are waiting in boxes so many years. I have no time for the play."

"No."

He puts down his cup and looks intently into my lidded morning eyes.

"I am thinking you will do it."

His rich baritone sounds grave and deliberate, like the queen dispensing territory—though I'm guessing here—*I give you India and Belgravia.*

I have many good reasons for saying no.

"OK, yes."

"Wonderful!" And he reaches over and kisses me. "Excuse me please."

I think he's referring to the kiss. But he jumps up and strides to the door, leaving me no time to react. I sit for a few minutes listening to the birds and wondering I how I feel about the kiss and what part it's played in my decision.

"It'll be fun!" Alex is no help as I sit regretting it at second breakfast. "Everybody will love you or hate you, and you'll meet the five people you don't already know. And I'll help you. Don't worry." She goes back to her cheese omelette.

"But I've never directed a play."

She looks up, fork arrested. "That's never stopped you doing anything before," she says. It's the sort of historical accuracy that makes newer friendships so attractive.

8

On Wednesdays the shops in the port close in the afternoon, in sympathy I guess with French butchers—unless, but I don't think, it's the other way around. So I go in early, when the sun on my bare arms is just strong enough to warm the breeze I create as I kick back into neutral and coast down to town. I've just parked Ernie Banks, my motorbike, in the shady forecourt of the post office when Stephanos, the chief of police, approaches. No raincoat, but I recognize the nonchalant gait from *Columbo*. My front wheel is leaning against the No Parking sign, not a reason for Stephanos—arrogant, self-conscious, wide enough to cast a shadow at noon—to notice me.

("A No Parking sign?" Alex asked on our first day in town. "There aren't more than fifty cars on the whole island."

"I think they're for the goats."

"Goats can read red?"

"On white.")

Stephanos steps around Ernie Banks and stops inside my airspace. I reel slightly from the sweet aftershave on his neck rings. "Shakespeare, Sarah, he is favorite writer of me. I know all."

"Do you, Stephano?" I return his conspiratorial smile. "I'm going to start casting very soon. Look for a poster with all the information." And instantly wonder if there's a postering regulation.

"No way," says Alex at second breakfast. "Look at Popi."

"Popi?"

"The hairdresser. She has signs everywhere, including *inside* the port police office."

"Pharos has a hairdresser?"

"I'll bet there's a poster in the jail," says Alex.

"Yeah, we won't worry about that."

Stephanos has taken root. "Is there piece for me? 'Hello Dolly, well hi ho Dolly.'" Rocking in his boots, he sings for the hills. "Last year I am star!"

I see us in a grainy fifties film. Stephanos sits behind a metal desk under a bare bulb, his fat shadow falling across the desk. A menacing buzz shoots up my spine and I step back. "A piece, a part . . . , yes, could be. But you have to audition."

He cocks his head closer; I'm breathing sweet tires.

"Aw . . . dhishhh . . . ?"

"Read out loud for me."

His smile freezes. I pat myself until I find my pocket dictionary.

"*Akro'asi,*" I read out.

"Yes, yes," he cries, "interrogation!" and smiles Columbo's winning, I'm-sure-you're-innocent smile. The author of my phrase book appears to have overlooked a second meaning.

I point to the post office, which is about to close.

"Excuse me, Stephano. Must go."

He salutes me and steps aside.

"You like Missippis Williams?" the postmaster wants to know.

Literature? And everybody thinks he just reads their mail.

"One of my favorites, Gerasime," I reply. "Got any letters for me?"

"No today, but *dhen birazi*, I bring to you."

"*Kalimera. Ti kanis?*" Kalliope calls out from the stamp counter. The man on the phone nearby hisses at her.

How are you? "Two hundred drachmas" is all she's ever said to me.

"*Kala*, Kalliope," I rush over to whisper.

"My uncle has a shop in Astoria. They make *Goodfellas* near his café. Use his tables."

"I have fresh chicken today," says the butcher in my ear.

"*Kalimera*, Prifti." I step back to give his bloody apron room to flap.

He hands Kalliope a large package; the tape is smeared with red fingerprints. A nice opening shot for *Silence of the Lambs*.

Gerasimos the postmaster steps between them. "Where does it go?" he asks Priftis.

"Astoria," Priftis replies. So, props for *Goodfellas Part Two*. "*Cherry Farm* is one beautiful play, *Saraki*. Is my perfect mustache?"

"You've read Chekhov, Prifti?"

"Many."

"My cousin has acting in Athens," Gerasimos puts a huge hand on my shoulder. "I see his playing many times. I can do it!"

"That's great, Gerasime. Everybody please come to the *akro'asi* Wednesday."

Or we could cast the whole thing here in the post office.

I enter the bakery cautiously.

"*Yasoo*, Sarah. *Ti kanis?* How are you?" says Maria. It's her usual greeting. But is the tone different?

"Fine, and you?"

"Fine too. What do you like?"

"One sprouted-wheat bread and two *kourambyedhes*."

Maria wears a bikini at the beach. She baked the first sprouted-wheat bread on Pharos. I consider her a feminist. Her shortbread-sugar cookies belong on an altar. She wraps the *kourambyedhes* with the bread and hands them over. There's no mention of my new calling. But then feminists often get the news a little late.

Maria's teenage son Foti comes in—a chubby (no blame!), outgoing mechanical wizard. Repairer of toasters, radios, VCRs; hero of the August aliens and surely the richest kid on the island. Foti, I'm reflecting on the beach that afternoon—cast him as anything just to have him around. What was I, I wonder, before I was a director.

9

"Let's eat."

I look up from my article to find Alex in mascara, a sure sign of hunger.

"Where?"

Her shrug, attached to her eyebrows, is followed by a distant gaze that I probably mirror as we run through the options.

"What do you feel like?" I ask.

"Spring lamb?" she says hopefully.

"Would you settle for the grandmother?" We fall into ravenous reverie.

"Pathetic," she eventually mumbles.

"I warned you in London."

"But why? What about the famous Mediterranean diet? And isn't *recipe* a Greek word?"

"Ancient Greek."

"Which is when the tavernas cooked their vegetables?"

"Actually, they boil them at dawn."

"Like heretics," she notes.

"Right, but that's when the kitchen's cool."

Alex shakes her head. "Let's go and come back in winter."

"What a good idea."

When I come down in my dinner jeans, she's flipping through one of Gina's recipe books.

"These do exist. Written in our lifetime."

"I did try to give Dmitri's wife a couple of suggestions last year."

"And?"

"I even brought her celery. Also Ari's wife at Angira, and the cook at Kima. They want to learn new recipes like cats want to learn to swim."

"But this book!" She taps it ferociously—a defense lawyer summing up.

"Gina must use it to press flowers."

"I'm still hungry. How about Tomasi's?"

"His eggplant's oily."

"Argos."

"Everything's oily."

"Platanos, then."

"Not in a south wind."

"Café Kriti."

"Are you kidding? Not even the cats . . ."

"How about the fish place near the post office?"

"Angira? Pretty good. But it's always full of Italians."

"*Andiamo.*"

The sky is still lit blue and orange, so we coast down to Pharos with our motorbike engines and lights off. There are no cruise boats out in the harbor, only a flat glassy sea with dozens of small fishing boats trawling. We stop on a ledge to listen to the dusk; doves and finches and the first cicadas against a faint windsong of goat bells. In the stillness and from this height we can hear waves tossing the stones in an unseen cove below.

Suddenly the bells rise to a din as the hill above us comes alive with goats leaping over rocks and bushes and rushing toward us. The goatherd is shouting and whistling, his dog yelping and diving at legs, but it's too late to change their course. We're engulfed in a cloud of smelly ragged romping *katziki*. Their sharp hooves clatter and skid over the stones as they dart around us full speed, like cow ponies in a cactus field. I don't realize I'm holding my breath till they're well past and I take in a quick breath of warm musty feta. Alex is brushing the dust off her pants and shirt, and smiling.

"Weren't you scared?"

"God yes," she says, "till I pictured myself coming to with my head in the lap of that shepherd."

"That's Theologos, and he's a goatherd, but I see what you mean." Because he's turned around and is cheerfully waving his blue cap above ropy dark-roast curls. Long flat muscles on a finely carved frame. Leading man.

"Maybe we should be doing *Hair*," says Alex, riding parallel. "I wonder if he can sing . . ."

"Mmm—too bad he can't come to rehearsals."

"That's always the trouble with goatherds."

Angira is crowded, which means that Ari, who is a captain as well as the patron, has a fresh catch.

"Order it, whatever it is," I tell Alex. "I'm going to try to call Lucky Steve while it's still his birthday."

(Steven is my brother, known for his singing voice and his way with fate. "Inexplicable good luck," my sister-in-law always says, with a sort of grudging pride.

"All luck is inexplicable, Marjorie." I can repeat myself too. "That's what makes it luck."

"Mmm." She replies, not in recording mode. But who is? The number of people who are grateful to be corrected is roughly the same wherever you go: nil. What a comfort my Heathrow revelation is going to be on my next trip home.)

Lucky Steve benefits from the epithet stigma, just as Homer keeps calling his hero "brave Ulysses" even after he's ducked out of some hot battles. And Poor Harold, our second cousin who was born myopic, is still called that even though he won the state lottery years ago and moved to a beach palace in Laguna Del Mar. In Steve's case, he uncovered a twenty-dollar bill on his first Easter egg hunt. And that was it; blessed for life. I mention this because it's Steven's possible good luck that makes me even try to call him before the underwater choir has bedded down. But it's windy tonight, so the odds of getting through are really terrible.

When I return the salad is just arriving, along with a brand of retsina that could start your motorbike.

"So soon? . . . He wasn't there."

"He was there. Just his inexplicable good luck. Maybe all the mermaids are watching *ER*."

Six tanned yachties at the next table turn toward us: three of each, identically dressed in navy polo shirts and white trousers, surrounded by platters of *meze,* drinking Ari's only decent wine. The wind's come up, and they've heard English. Yachties abroad are known to be thirsty for new blood, having shed most of one another's over endless cramped days at sea. I angle my chair and lower my voice. "He's actually got a song in the top twenty. He's ecstatic."

"My God, after how many years?"

I smile . . . guardedly. This collision of time and art is a touchy subject. "Guess what it's called."

"Never Say Die."

"Ha ha. No."

"As Time Goes By."

"He's not a plagiarist."

"No, right. He'd have had a hit years ago. I give up."

"Coming Around to You."

"A love song?"

"I think it's a lost-love song. You'll recall that Steven has twenty–twenty hindsight." We sit back and sip retsina, silently reviewing his heartbreaks.

"Speaking of hindsight"—Alex arrests her glass in midair—"why don't you reconsider inviting Julian? He could be a big help with the show. I'll bet he'd leave Miss Tutu if you asked him."

"Too soon. Tutu soon. We only broke up last month."

"But I never really got why." She cups her face in her hands.

I dismiss the invitation. It's not something I want to discuss, especially with an ex-lover. Alex knows this, of course. We must have talked for thousands of hours. But our own romance broke up swiftly and softly and left no splinters.

Now, as then, silence is my favorite option. This is easier to pull off when you're out in public. And sure enough, before too much tension builds, Ari's son arrives with a basket of bread and silverware and a stack of napkins. These take flight the moment he lifts out the silver. Then the oilcloth starts flapping. The plastic ashtray shoots halfway to the yachties' table. Pretty soon we're all playing Beat the Clock, trying to hold down the napkins and the tablecloth with tin silver and cotton bread. Ari himself hustles over with a huge elastic band and surrounds the edge of the table. Then he tucks in a few gritty napkins that he's caught under his shoe. Onto this beautiful setting, moments later, comes a platter of *melanouri* and fried potatoes. *"Kali orexsi." Bon appétit.*

The brush with death-by-goat-trampling has fired my appetite. Also the fish is sweet and perfectly cooked. I lapse into a feeding trance.

"My money won't hold out for ten more weeks," Alex says, breaking the spell.

"Mmm." It's hard to listen when your stomach's singing. Also I dislike tricky subjects when I'm eating fish.

"I don't suppose you could pay me to be your stage manager?"

I shake my head. "I'm out of work until next year. Besides, they don't even sell tickets here."

"Can you think of anyone who'd hire me?"

I switch from fish to potatoes. They taste like insulation—a guess, admittedly. "Maybe you could work for Petros, my friend with the tourist agency."

"Yes! He must need extra help in June and July."

"Pass me the lemon sauce, please."

"They call this sauce?"

"It might help the potatoes. But you'd have to know something about the history of Pharos."

"It's just lemon and olive oil. It's a very small island."

"More."

"That's more than Maggie Smith knew about Jameson House." Our favorite play several years ago: flapping wide-eyed untidy Maggie as a National Trust guide posted to the dullest castle in Sussex. Every weary busload was treated to a more and more fantastical history until you wondered why the BBC wasn't right there shooting a series.

"I guess there are some books you can read. But we'll have to ask him soon; he always saves a job for a summer romance."

Alex saws at a potato for a while. She finally drenches it in sauce and puts it in her mouth. There follows a long macrobiotic chew for the wrong reasons, and when it ends she looks at me, exhausted.

"Are you sure we can't find better food on this island?"

I shake my head. "The thing is to eat before you come."

"*Yasoo, Saraki!*" Iannis appears just as we're mopping up with Ari's sponge bread. He teaches waterskiing at Archos Beach and is surreptitiously known as John the Baptist. A sinewy blond sea god with chestnut skin and eyes bluer than my passport. He learned his English from Greek World War II movies—nevertheless, one listens carefully to everything he says.

"I think to see Vovo of the mayor today. Maybe he gives money for this!"

"Great. Ianni, this is my friend Alexandra. Alex, this is Iannis. He's a fisherman, and in the summer he teaches waterskiing."

"*Kalispera.*" He takes her hand.

"Yes, kali spare . . ." Alex shifts to soak up Iannis.

"A part. Last part." He indicates the back end with his graceful chestnut hand. "I'm out far from Archos, close to Tragi. Inside bushes I see car. So much."

"On Tragi?" I peer into his rockpool eyes.

"Yes."

"No, Ianni, it can't be."

"Why no?"

"On Tragi *Island*?"

He nods vigorously; the glittering tresses are distracting.

"How did it get there? Did someone drive it over the water?"

A troubling thought creeps into his face. I can see from the lines that he's had them before.

"But you saw something," Alex finally emerges.

And the Baptist notices her. "He looked like Vovo."

She nods enthusiastically, ignoring the gender issue. "You have a boat, don't you?" she says, putting one and one together.

More flailing of tresses.

"Well, let's sail over tomorrow after lunch and check it out."

"*Entaxi,*"—OK—he says, and leaves slowly, thinking.

I look at Alex, who is carefully extracting fish bones from her teeth as she watches him go. "Maybe we should talk about Greek men."

"What? Why? Let's talk about the play."

"*Kalispera,* Sarah." Vienoula, the ticket seller for Kokonis Ferries, has never spoken to me outside her office. A bad thing, considering the ferry's the only way on or off the island.

("She likes chocolates," Gina once suggested. "Or perfume. Channel Five, I think." But I'm no good at bribing people. I guess those Eastern baksheesh incarnations are way in the past.)

"*Kalispera,* Vienoula."

"*Ti kanis?*"

She's using the familiar "you." Maybe it's a case of mistaken identity. I push the curls away from my face. "I'm fine, thank you."

"You make the play?"

Not a mistake.

"Yes, Dr. Theo asked me. This is my friend Alexandra."

"Please to meet you." She smiles . . . and sits.

"May I?" Alex pours some wine in the glass Iannis just emptied.

Funny I'd never registered Vienoula's obsidian eyes and that perfect Minoan nose. Maybe I don't notice people who don't notice me?

"Thank you. I like Shakspoor. Many times I read."

"Shakspoor, ahh," I say, having no wish to correct her.

"Maybe I can be something?"

"Do you have time . . . with your work . . . ?"

"*Signome?*"

Dumb question. *Ferry schedule* is an oxymoron here. Vienoula must have more free time than the telegraph man.

"Good. We have the *akro'asi* next week."

"Oh! *Signome.* There is ferryboat!"

"And if she's terrible?" Alex demands in her wake.

"That wouldn't be good. She sells all the ferry tickets. Great nose, huh? And those eyes."

"Eyes? You want a good show, don't you?"

"Of course. And I want to be able to leave when it's over."

Alex pours more retsina. "Maybe we should talk about Greek women?" The yachties turn around.

"Keep your voice down. If she's really bad I'll send her some Chanel Number Five from London."

Ari brings a plate of watermelon, dessert on the house. Prepare to blow up like a beach ball.

"Alex, I've just realized something."

"Your mother's right about melon."

"My coffee supply won't hold out."

"Oh! You'll have to go back. And leave me here with . . . look who's coming."

Because Iannis is returning at speed.

10

"You're not jealous of John the Baptist, are you?" Alex is up earlier than usual, waterproof mascara applied.

"Of course not." I put down my book. "But you have to be careful."

"He doesn't look dangerous to me." She adds hot water to her coffee.

"He's not, unless you're swimming near his speedboat. How can you do that to my coffee? But there's a custom here that you can't ignore."

"Which is?"

"If you go out with someone, everyone assumes you're together."

"C'mon, Sarah. Then you go out with someone else."

"Only if he's carrying a spear. Why don't you make some tea. There's just no casual romance in a place like this."

"Romance! We're looking for a Volvo. Weak coffee is still coffee. There's no rule against . . ."

"Don't change the subject."

"But it's your favorite." She comes over to hug me. "You know how rarely I get serious about anyone."

"But *they* don't know that."

"This is Middle Ages stuff." She shakes her head.

"Around here middle age starts at ten."

"So I'm supposed to be a monk for the next two months?"

I take a sip of coffee. "You'd look better as a nun, in my opinion. Could you get all that hair under a wimple?"

"I hope you mean Julie Andrews."

"I'm ready to change the subject. Any coffee left?" I extend my cup. "Why 'John the Baptist'?"

"Better give me that last *kourambyes*. It's all unrefined sugar. *Baptist* as in total immersion. He teaches waterskiing at Archos Beach. But he's never heard of dry-land instruction and he's incapable of gradual acceleration."

"Is he?" she says brightly. But I've been awake long enough to dodge a double entendre. "Let's share it." She takes what looks to me like the bigger half.

"After he takes off all you ever see is a rope skipping over the water and a little whirlpool of foam with someone kicking in it."

"No one ever gets up?"

"Well, there was one guy. But he came from Malibu."

"And he makes a living doing that!"

"In the summer."

"It must be his eyes."

"Yeah. So just to recap, don't give him any signals he can misinterpret."

"*Entaxi.*" She leaves without glancing at the fragment of mirror next to the door. And I've somehow failed to mention the powdered sugar on her chin.

11

The next morning I'm on the terrace practicing the tai chi move "Walking with the Moon on Your Head" when a tinny carillon reaches me. The last plumes of seven AM mass bells have just dissolved above the valley floor when this clamor begins. It can't all be coming from Tula.

I put the moon down and look into the narrow streets below. It's a Philip Glass opera staged by Peter Brook. Twisting black ant lines of housekeepers young old and ancient are streaming mutely through the village, determined as the tide coursing through sandy channels to the sea. Big blue gas cylinders bang against their chests or dangle from their arms. No voices in this piece, only timpani. Whereas "Good morning, slept well? How are your children?" is normally the minimum greeting among this group. I'm transfixed.

I hear Tula's key at the outside gate—she can only be sleepwalking—then her panting in the courtyard as she heads for the kitchen door. She manages not to trip on Diana, who has ambled across the courtyard from her bed in the jasmine. The commotion must have awakened her. (Who knew such tiny ears could be so sensitive?) Tula's mottled red face is cramped with anxiety and her brown-gold hair, unexpectedly freed from its net, is a runaway haystack. There's a shattering sound as her shoe finds the wine bottle left just inside the door.

"What's up?" I call.

"Gas boat from Piraeus . . . next in September!" expelled between gasps because she's already in the kitchen struggling with the warped doors under the sink where the cylinder lives.

I recall hearing about this ritual—a sort of Cycladic gold rush. There's a shortage of gas canisters on the island, so it's not breathlessness that silences the housekeepers, but fear of spreading the word. Never mind the deafening testimony of all those cylinders being hustled over the stones and the whiff of sleep rising over the village from the ones that leak. Tula reappears with our rusty blue missile and careens out the front door like an impatient artilleryman.

I can't practice tai chi against this commotion, so I set up the computer and go back to the mantra article. Not that tai chi takes more concentration, but it does require moderate internal serenity, whereas writing just requires tuning out.

("Born to scribble," snarled a friend with writer's block. "I'll bet that was you sending dispatches from the Trojan horse.")

I'm weaving an intricate thought when there's a rap at the door. It's barely eight AM. I hit "save" and will myself into society. Looking down to the street I see Dr. Theo's luxurious black hair; unlike Tula's, it's under control.

"*Kalimera.*" He looks up smiling. "The gas boat; I don't want you to miss it."

Miss *It*?

"Thanks. Tula's already been there. Sorry I can't make you a coffee." But I can't just send him away. "Come in. Please leave your shoes here," I remind him. "We live barefoot."

"You pick the play?" he asks while I make orange juice.

"Not yet, but soon."

"We do *Hello Dolly* last year. It's a big hit."

"So Stephanos tells me."

"He is OK, I am amazing."

"Amazed. Has he ever given you a parking ticket?"

"What?" Theo's smile has frozen into a confused grin.

"I'm kidding, Theo."

"Oh. The singing everybody likes. A musical is best I think." Then for the sake of modesty and because he's courting, he concentrates on his orange juice.

Alex wanders in in her nightshirt. Her lightstruck lidded eyes expand to wide angle as she takes in Theo in his socks, with an orange juice in his hand. He turns just his head and beams at her.

"*Kalimera*, Alex."

"*Kalimera*," she whispers as she looks over at me and takes a step backward.

"How did you sleep through it?" I ask.

"Through *what*?"

"The gas rush."

Theo rewards me with a big laugh that somehow sounds intimate.

Alex is watching us like a tennis match. "I dreamed I was back in London."

"Let's go to the *platia* for a coffee," he says. "Plato's taverna always has an extra gas tank."

She nods and retreats. Theo the director seems oblivious to drama, whereas Theo the doctor doesn't recognize shock.

Every foreigner in the village is having breakfast at Platanos. In the fresh pale sunlight there's a religious atmosphere as they bend over their coffees, praying, no doubt, to be invisible. (These people normally don't see one another before nine PM and never without makeup. But they need to know who's there, so lots of furtive peeking.) It's so crowded we have to join someone else's table, and Theo goes in search of a third chair.

"Did he spend the . . . ?" Alex aborts the question as our table mates, Hans and Sylvia, who live in the next street, turn to follow the conversation. So do the French couple I vaguely know at the next table. Why is language never a barrier to dishing the dirt? My eyes bore into Alex, and Hans and Sylvia go back to their omelettes as Theo reappears with three chairs, his mother, and her sister, and wedges them all between the two tables.

Mikhailis, one of Plato's sons, brings a tray of coffee. I'd order an omelette but there's nowhere to put it. Theo mistakenly picks up Sylvia's coffee and starts drinking as his mother turns to Alex. "I know you from before," she says brightly, "with your little boat. My son is too happy you direct his play."

Alex is tall and underfed, with a Venetian nose, bittersweet hair, and a mermaid's glistening charm. It's a perfectly natural mistake for an aspiring mother-in-law.

"Mama, *this* is Sarah"—Theo's voice rises as he puts down Sylvia's cup and winds his free arm around the back of my chair. Mama downshifts smoothly and offers me a smile. An actress, I can't help noticing.

A farmer who's delivering tomatoes to Plato limps to the table. "*Signome, Kyrie* Theo." He takes off his shoe and sock, and sticks his blistered sole on Theo's lap. We're all too jammed in to recoil. I make a snap decision never to marry a doctor. Plato rushes over flapping his arms. The farmer grabs his shoe and hops away. Plato alertly pockets the sock.

"Did he stay . . . ?" Alex begins again, taking advantage of the distraction.

I interrupt her. "An omelette please, Plato." I'll balance the plate on my lap.

"*Cara!*" Arabella walks over to us, swinging her chair. She's a bottle-tan red-haired Neapolitan art restorer slash houseguest who spends every summer with a different guy. The Pharians have taken to assigning them years, like vintages. ("Is he single?" I asked her last year about Luigi '97. "All Italian men are single," she replied.)

She lifts her chair over Mama's head and squeezes in between Alex and me. Her chair seat bangs Alex's elbow. Alex yelps. Arabella's repelled by the sound and turns her back, brushing her polished tresses across Alex's wincing face.

"A little bird tells me you direct the play. I am perfect for everything."

Alex pretends to choke on her coffee; Arabella throws her a stiletto smile. I turn to the "little bird" for help, but he has a tongue depressor in his hand and is peering down Hans's throat.

"You are an actress?" Mama is excited.

"*Si,*" says Arabella, who has five days till confession.

"Yes," says Alex, which is true, if not lately.

"Very difficult to see," Theo says, turning away from the throat. Arabella, not following along, throws *him* a stiletto.

My omelette arrives. The sight of food clears Theo's mind. He closes the patient's mouth, reaches into his coat pocket, and puts his business card into Hans's huge putty hand. Like many Greek business cards, it's got a thick black border. If Theo stops saving people and starts burying them, the template's already there.

"Please come later to my office."

Hans and Sylvia helpfully depart. Alex has spotted Petros looking for a table and waves him over. Mikhailis, thinking she's waving at him, arrives and is bombarded with orders.

"A big German cruise boat's coming in today," says Petros. "The taxi drivers have decided to strike to show how important they are."

"*Trellos,*" Theo's mother observes. Crazy.

"*Trellos,*" nods her sister.

"*Trellos,*" Theo murmurs.

Origin of the Greek chorus.

"But it won't work, of course," Petros says, "and the fishermen will love all the extra business, taking people up and down the—"

"No taxi! I have a leg wax at eleven!" Arabella wails.

Every female on the *platia* looks down at her legs.

"Leg wax!" Alex's fork is frozen in midair. "Where? Who?"

"Popi the hairdresser. She does manicures too." Arabella's a walking edition of *Women's Wear Daily*.

"I'll take you down in my jeep," says Petros.

"You will?" says Arabella. "*Grazie mille*. I'll just change."

"Into a . . . ?" says Alex. But Arabella has fled.

Petros sits in her chair.

"Aren't you going out with Tino's daughter?" I ask him.

"She's studying in Athens." There's a pause. Theo's mother and aunt await breaking news.

"Oh," he says casually, waving in the direction of Arabella's retreat, "I'm not interested in . . ."

"Insurance?" says Theo, who's also been paying attention. And they have a big stupid laugh together.

"Ask him," says Alex sotto voce. "About a job."

"Petros, you've met Alex."

His head swivels. It's a talent reserved for cats of prey.

"Of course," he says. "Hi."

She sends him a smile that would melt polar ice.

"She's looking for a summer job," I continue. "We were thinking she'd be good at . . ."

"Guiding. Yes!"

"*Nai, nai,*" the chorus follows along.

"That's great!" says Alex.

The heat is now rising in cellophane waves from the stones of the *platia* and curling over the heads of the coffee worshipers. No one is leaving and I can see this turning into a day at Platanos, whereas my article lures me to my shady veranda.

"Mind if I leave you to talk it over? I'm writing an article that's overdue. Nice to meet you." I smile to the ladies as I get up.

"*Adio, adio,*" they sing.

Theo rises politely. Alex looks from him to me.

He didn't, I tell her silently.

12

I've got to choose the play and not just to appease Theo; only six weeks till opening night.

The sea's the place to think, as everyone knows who didn't drown in the last life. I pack a picnic right after breakfast and go down to *Soapdish* (*Dishy* for short), my three-meter inflatable Zodiac. She's all I need. Or want. See the people with real boats staring longingly out to sea, like Meryl Streep in *The French Lieutenant's Woman*. See them applying sunblock as they scrape the algae off their hulls; see them applying more as they move on to endless anti-fouling and greasy diesel adjustments. Whereas within minutes of reaching the pier where *Dishy* is tied up, I'm casting off for a solitary beach.

It's blowing three Beaufort, with a few scattered mare's tails in the phony blue sky; perfect weather for a sail. Since I haven't got one I ease up on the throttle, strip to my bikini, and cruise quietly along the coast dodging barely covered rocks and the surface buoys of fishing nets. My destination is Sandsoon, a small cove of clear water ringed with tall wind-worked rocks and sheltered from the Meltemi. It's one of the few sandy beaches on the island and the only one where I can sit in the shallows and read. When I arrive, the small stupa I've erected for tying up is occupied by a seagull. He screeches and flaps as I cut the engine, throw out the anchor, leap into the water, and run up the beach with the painter. He retreats to a higher perch, baleful eyes following me as I splash back to the boat to secure the anchor and unload my gear. There's a brief truce while he waits to be invited to the picnic. "Buzz off," I say, flapping my wings.

"Breeek," he replies, then departs in an effortless arc.

I make camp, collecting rocks to hold down towel, clothes, papers, and books. For a person with no flair for homemaking, I do a great job. After a long swim I wade to my chair, taking care not to drip on the books. I've narrowed it down to *The Tempest, The Seagull, Our Town,* and *Itchin' to Get Hitched.* They're all highly dramatic, they'd be exciting to work on day after day, and except for *The Tempest,* they're fairly simple to stage. Plus I've been in all of them—at school or camp—which I figure is the minimum criterion for a directorial debut.

Several hours later I look up, ears stuffed with dialogue but hearing something else. The afternoon ferry has just left the harbor and its wake is creating huge rollers all along the coast. *Dishy* pitches and writhes, and the sea washes the edge of my towel. I sprint to the stupa, take a couple more turns with the painter, move my stuff to higher ground. In a few minutes the drama is over and the sea is wearing its baby-faced mask.

My brain is spinning; time to stop. I pick a spot high on the beach where waves won't interrupt me, and I sit down to meditate. In this place, a few breaths is all it takes. From deep in the silence I see Prospero leaning against a rock, reading a water-stained book.

"The Tempest." A beat. Alex turns just her head. "That's Shakespeare!"

"Right."

"Are you crazy?"

That's not the gung-ho response I'm looking for. Plus, in my tentative state, it sounds rhetorical.

"You're aware he's the hottest author in the history of the world."

Alex shifts her reading position from prone on the elbows (I don't know how anyone can lie like that) to half lotus. She closes her book slowly for emphasis. "I don't think it's a good idea," she says softly.

"Why not? There's a very good translation. They can read it in Greek first and they'll know what they're saying."

"Did this come to you in meditation, by any chance?"

"What?" I say—which is *yes* in the passive defensive.

"Your spiritual body must be flying in from London. I mean, if you want to be difficult, why not do Euripides or Aristophanes?"

"They're probably done all the time."

"And Shakespeare isn't."

"Right."

"Well, maybe if it's a comedy . . ."

"Alex, you've never seen *The Tempest*? Read *The Tempest*?"

"So am I missing a vital chromosome?"

"No. But you're missing one of the greatest things ever written. It's funny, it's profound, it's the last word on everything Shakespeare ever thought about. Love, politics, art. He was probably the best observer of human nature till, I don't know, Henry James, Gary Larson . . ."

"You mean Larson the cartoonist? Is it that funny?"

"Well, it's a little drier. Sixteenth-century humor, you know."

"I *don't* know. So nobody dies?" Alex sits up. "Nobody gets killed?"

"Not unless they fall off the stage and break their necks."

"Huh. Well *you're* the producer, *Saraki*," she shrugs, and smiles. "It *might* work."

"Mmm." I can feel doubt creeping into my steady state. "I think I'll go up to the terrace and do some yoga."

"I'm off," she calls up sometime later.

I'm three minutes into headstand, gazing upside down out to sea. "Where to?" I shout through my cupped fingers.

"Talking to Petros about the job. Do we need anything in town?"

"I don't think so. Wait . . . Check the kalamata supply!" (I suffer from *horis-elies-phobia*—the fear of running out of olives.)

"You bought a kilo yesterday. Unless you're planning to burn an olive pie . . ."

"*Adio!*"

Is *The Tempest* the right choice? I should discuss this with Theo, who might be considered to have his finger on the pulse of Pharos. Well, we know he has. I decide to walk down the mountain and ask him.

"*Thavmasia!* Bravo! A great idea. We never do Shakespeare." Theo has just delivered a baby who wouldn't wait for the ferry to Athens. He's looking, as they say in spiritual circles, expanded.

"You never do Shakespeare. That's what Alex thought. I mean, that Shakespeare may be new territory for some people. Difficult territory . . . ?"

"No, no. Why difficult? Tragedy, comedy . . . Greeks understand everything. We study in school. They must only read in Greek first."

"That's what I thought. And I know a good translation. I'll have Julian mail me a copy. I'll need an assistant, though. Someone who's fluent in English."

"My nephew Omiros, my brother's son."

"Good. OK. If you're sure about Shakespeare." (What would Harold Bloom think of this conversation?) I suddenly notice he's wearing his vanilla linen suit.

"You delivered the baby in that?"

"The father finds me at church. It's my name day today and I sing the service."

"Ah. *Hronia polla*, Theo!" Many happy years. I lean forward and kiss him, too quickly to wrinkle his jacket, or raise his hopes.

"*Efharisto*. But this baby . . ." He grins and spreads his arms.

"Doesn't care about clothes yet?"

"No." He laughs in a very appealing way. "They name him Theologos."

"Wonderful." Something hits my pause button. I'll have to think about that later.

"You must come, and Alex, to my house tonight. I cook for the Theos and all my friends. You meet Omiros."

Walking up the mountain at sunset, replaying the events of the day, I contemplate the Greek tradition of celebrating your name day with lots of people. What an unselfish, thoroughly un-Western idea. Imagine an Ed from Omaha sharing his big day with all the other Omaha Eds. Or me, a bundle of birthday ego for weeks in advance, celebrating with a quorum of San Francisco Sarahs.

Then there's Theo, attracted to me. No problem yet, but this is an island, requires a plan. How did I feel in his office? Charmed . . . by his sweetness, his humor, his naturalness. Very compelling in his linen suit. But I want him to stay dressed . . . for now anyway.

13

Alex is reading on the terrace when I come in. Diana is asleep beside her in the fluttering shade of a wayward branch of bougainvillea.

"Theo's cooking dinner?" She tips over onto one elbow. "That's interesting; a Greek man who isn't a cook cooking?"

"It's probably code for 'My mother's cooking.' Real Greek cooking can be fabulous, by the way."

"You're sure we're both invited? I have the impression he's aiming for you."

"Both of us. Anyway I'm not a target."

"You're not. OK. But you're still interested in men, aren't you?"

"*Malista!*"

"English please."

"Of course! Absolutely! They're fifty percent of my hunting grounds. Or forty-nine. When did you start wearing glasses?"

"Hmm . . . that's good. When I couldn't read the phone book. She wouldn't make chicken, would she?"

"No. God, I hope not. I think she's more the stuffed-lamb type."

"I really need a vacation from chicken. It doesn't bother you that Theo speaks only in the present tense?"

"How did you get there from chicken?"

"I don't know."

"Well, for some reason it doesn't. His present tense is very good. He thinks *The Tempest* is a great idea, by the way."

"He's smitten," she says to my back as I go down to the fridge for my lemon-mint water concoction.

"Here." I return with a glass for Alex and perch on the stone bench opposite her. I leave a lemon slice beside Diana for when she wakes up. "You know, there's an ancient Greek theory called *Nepti*. It's based on the concept of living in the present."

"Wow. Your goal in life."

"Exactly."

"And so Theo's a kind of natural yogi."

"That's an amazingly profound insight, Alex. Have you been repeating *Scotch 'n soda*?"

"So what's wrong with him? It can't be his beautiful body or those deep black eyes."

"Nothing's wrong, really . . . Maybe he's too . . . earnest."

"Poor Theo. But Julian's not earnest."

"Julian is the past."

"Ooooh. Past is even worse." She sounds grave, but it's clearly an acting job.

"Not always. Look what great pals *we've* become," I say.

"True. Is there more?" She holds up her glass. "This almost counts as cooking."

I return with refills. "That's not the phone book you're reading."

"Petros gave me the job. This is the only thing I could find in English about the island."

"That's great, Alex."

"Actually it's pretty interesting. Did you know this place was a refuge for Saracen converts to Christianity?"

"I didn't."

"And that Jesus's grandmother Anne settled here briefly after the crucifixion."

"What? I doubt that. And *settled here briefly* is an oxymoron."

"That's so helpful, *Saraki.*" She returns to the line her finger's on. "There were pirates operating from Kastro during the Second Crusade. They charged a ransom for safe passage."

"Who wrote that?"

" 'Kalokero . . .' an impossible name." She closes the book. " 'A retired monk,' it says on the back."

"I wonder how you retire from being a monk."

"I can think of lots of ways." Alex grins.

" I'll bet he moonlights for some Greek Orthodox placemat company. All the monasteries have tourist cafés now. Remember that mat at the lobster pound in Maine?"

"Wasn't it a sketch of the coast with all the little harbors and lighthouses?"

"Right. 'Do not navigate by this placemat,' it said."

"But you kept it."

"As a *souvenir*, Alex! This is serious. You can't tell people a bunch of lies."

"I'm quoting a monk!"

"Is monk a magic word? Hitler was a Bible student, as I recall. I think you should check it out with some of the guides."

"Can't. They're all jealous . . . they think I'm stealing their tips."

"So take a few tours in disguise—that's what Maggie Smith would do."

"That's a great idea."

"Except they're probably quoting placemats too. Let's get ready. I think this evening's kind of dressy."

Theo's veranda is crowded when we arrive: cats pacing the steps, lying on the wicker chairs, draped along the railing—formally dressed, chatting, waiting for the first course.

"You're sure Theo treats people?" Alex says.

"They're probably all called Theo," I explain as we pick our way over flicking tails to the front door.

Two dazzling caryatids are posted either side. Theo's roof appears to be resting on teased capitals of buttery spun-sugar atop generous columns of flowering drapery cinched at the waist; the bases are white patent stilettos.

"You are Americans," says one, reading our invisible labels.

"We are. I'm Sarah." I take her hand.

"Alexandra," says Alex, not touching.

"Sophia," "Elena," say the marbles. Sophia is staring into my eyes, a fixed Cararra smile.

"There's Theo," says Alex loudly, to break the spell. And she steps between them.

"You look for an actress?" The pillar doesn't release me.

"Ah. Yes . . . yes, I do." But they're all moving parts, I don't say.

"I am actress."

"That's good. May I come inside?"

"Malista!"

Theo is snaking toward us, a tray of something held aloft. "*Ella,* come, welcome." A Lacoste shirt, chinos, loafers; off-duty Santa Monica surgeon. Wouldn't *that* make the family happy.

"*Hronia polla,* Theo."

Sophia releases her grip and I give him a hug.

"Thank you, Sarah," he smiles, and waves his tray at the crowded room. "Everyone is waiting to see you. *Parakalo,* please!" All faces turn toward us. "My friends Sarah and Alexandra."

"*Kaloste, yiasas, harika . . . ,*" they smile and murmur.

Dinner party or casting call? A dark thought broken by a kiss—Iannis the Baptist soaked in ouzo, aiming for Alex no doubt.

"We think we find Vovo!"

"Yes! We find it!" His friend, in freshly washed overalls and bare chest, is nodding vigorously, spreading the smell of Clorox. But curly brown hair on all the exposed parts has an erotic effect that cuts through the bleach.

"That's great, Ianni. Right here on Pharos?"

He frowns as he jumps on a train of thought.

"*Signome.*" A short heavyset girl with mustache steps between us, squeezes through the flowered columns and hurls a pot of water onto the terrace. Shrieks and hisses: cats flee. She retreats beaming . . . and drags my clean fisherman with her.

Into the gap ooze two eager fellows with champagne in both hands.

"*Theo, exadelphos tou Theou,*" says the one in a UCLA sweatshirt.

"Theo's cousin Theo," I tell Alex.

"*Kai ego eime Theo,*" says his friend, handing us drinks.

"Him too," I tell her.

"Are they putting us on?"

"I don't think so."

"Everybody with the same name," she whispers. "My God—it's your dream party."

"*Efharisto,* Theos," I address them all. It *is* an exhilarating experience.

"*Ego eime ekeinos pou efiaxe to mihanaki sou,*" says UCLA Theo.

"May I translate?" Petros angles in, trailed by a young Liv Ullman look-alike.

"You're a Petros. Are you allowed here?"

"What's in a name?" he says theatrically.

"Oh no, not you!"

"No, no, I'm kidding, too busy. I'm just a family friend. Like you." He grins at me. And refills our glasses. "The one from Youkla says he fixed your motorbike last summer."

"Thanks, Petros. My motorbike . . . Ahh, I do remember . . . He was in overalls . . . The garage was pretty dark. Please explain to him. "

"No dark, dirty—I was oil," says grease monkey Theo, his black eyes glittering.

"Youkla, Petros? Where is that?" But this Theo is anxiously whispering in his ear.

Petros grins at me. "He says he can sing."

"Not now," I practically shout.

"You direct for the play?" asks the Theo next to him.

"Auditions Wednesday . . . *akro'asi Tetarti.*"

"Sarah *mou*! *Harika*—pleased to see you. You buy many sponge from my caique." Another guy arrives bearing bubbly. It's the sponge diver from Kalymnos disguised as a fine-boned fair-haired Bacchus. His battered caique is my favorite gift shop; nothing's lighter to pack than a sponge.

"Theo, *signome,* I didn't recognize . . ."

"No worry, no worry. I like to be actor." So, a sponge diver on the side.

"Sarah, Alex"—indicating Miss Ullman—"this is Monika from Malmö. She's a painter."

"Monika, hello." I take her hand. The grip is strong. Painters can't be actors, can they? "Where's Malmö?"

"It's a small town on the Swedish coast," she says. "Very small. You can run around it in a day."

"And she does." Petros the wolf lightly taps her thigh. So Arabella must have made it safely to her leg wax.

"Are you painting on Pharos?" Alex scents competition in the girl-guide category.

"Yes, but it's difficult. I'm not used to such clear light, such perfect shadows. And even the beauty of the place makes it hard; everything is so . . . picturesque."

"What a problem!" Petros is being an idiot.

"No, it really is. There's no contrast, no tension."

He looks stranded. A smart blonde is terra incognita. But not for all of us. "I've turned my writing table away from the window," I tell her. "Otherwise I'd be staring out to sea. And they don't give Pulitzers for daydreaming."

Alex throws me a quizzical look. Even I wonder why I said it.

"Come my friends, let's eat!" calls the host. A feast is laid on the kitchen table, enlarged for the event by stacks of orange crates: all the *mezedes* never seen in tavernas, plus grilled vegetables, roasts, fish stews, potato casseroles, and breaded small fry. The caryatids are handing out plates. Sophia, unless it's Elena, gives me a quick kiss with my knife and fork. "You have beautiful hair," she whispers. Theo and his mother, behind the table, are bringing famine relief. "A little less, a small amount," some of us plead uselessly.

Alex and I find some floor space behind a large ficus where we might be safe from petitioners and kissing caryatids for a few courses. The room grows reverently quiet. Not total silence, though—the cats have returned to the terrace. They talk among themselves as we eat.

"Why don't you ask Petros if there's anything else you can read?" I ask Alex as I'm sifting the raisins from a luscious rice pudding. She takes a spoonful and sprinkles them over her *galactoburiko*.

"Mmm . . . good idea. If we can find him."

"He's over there between the caryatids and the baklava." I happen to know because a corner of my brain has been following his date around the room.

"Is he?"

We set off through the Theos, all too busy eating to notice the director passing among them. (There's no Greek word for "dieting." Or maybe there is, but it lost its cachet with the fall of Sparta. Theo's banquet table, for instance, looks like it's been cleared by a Kansas tornado.)

Petros is finishing Monika's walnut cake while sponge-diver Theo is spearing a miniature baklava off the other side of her plate.

"Hi," Monika says brightly. "I hear you are a theater producer. My friends and I come to London a couple of times a year. For the theater and clothes."

"Look me up next time; I can usually get house seats." It just pops out; something I never volunteer.

"I will," she says, cocking her head to one side and sending a buzz through my lightly fermenting brain.

A couple of hours later we exit through the Calibans Prosperos Mirandas dukes, assorted knaves, and walk-ons. Good night good-bye, but not for long. We'll be seeing them all *Tetarti*.

The veranda is littered with stuffed cats. Not a fin or a bone in sight; just a few bread crumbs in whiskers. We tiptoe through them.

"We never found out where Iannis saw the Volvo," Alex says as we start our motorbikes. It's the sort of one-pointedness the Buddha would admire.

14

"Telephone for you," Tula calls to me as she rushes up the staircase the next afternoon. She hands me a note with the letters JUNIAL penciled in block letters. Close enough to deduce that Julian is desperate to talk to me. (We've agreed to resort to the phone in extremis only.)

I stop by the bakery for some cookies to sustain me en route to *Kyria* Kassoula's telephone parlor. Theo the baker has seen me coming down the alley and has a lemon cake wrapped by the time I arrive. You never know, nor does he, when he'll feel like baking these exquisitely tart loaves, so I always buy one and then pull together a dinner party. All that butter keeps them moist, and nobody on the island has a social calendar that extends beyond Theo's cakes.

It's oddly quiet as I approach *Kyria* Kassoula's house. I step in holding my breath. Vassilis, the mayor, is on the phone; he has his hand cupped over the mouthpiece as he booms down the line; something about the insurance on his missing car. Vassilis has an early Volvo coupé, once purple, now with a sandblast finish, and many rusty features. Goats would move in if he left it in a field for a couple of days. Why would anyone steal it?

The people waiting their turns in chairs around the parlor are ignoring him. This is completely irregular. *Kyria* Kassoula comes out of her kitchen, embraces me with a loud sigh, and motions to a bed in the corner. Her husband lies there, a spindly fisherman whom I've only ever seen squatting on the dock, mending his nets. Without his blue cap his black fearful eyes are enormous, while his Dalí-esque mustache makes a comic mask of his tiny face. "Dying," she announces, looking straight at him. I step back reflexively, as if dying were contagious. She puts out a hand to steady me.

"Of what?" I ask softly.

She shrugs. I turn to the assembled neighbors, thinking someone will volunteer, but they're all gazing at him with equally lifeless expressions.

"Has Theo seen him?"

"Last night."

"What did he say?"

"Christodolous's heart is not good. He was carrying many suitcases . . . taxi strike . . . Germans on the cruise boat . . . and suddenly he . . ." Her shoulders and knees crumple in mock collapse.

"Can that be fatal?" I wonder aloud.

"*Adio!*" Vassilis hangs up the phone, but nobody moves or even asks him for the latest on this marvelous crime. Exit Vassilis.

Kyria Kassoula sighs over her husband and crosses herself. So does everyone else. So do I, though maybe in the wrong direction.

"I want to talk to Theo. Please call the post office."

I get right through to Kalliope, though I'm sharing the line with some singing fish. She abandons the stamp counter to fetch him.

"Theo, can you hear me? It's Sarah! Listen, I'm here at *Kyria* Kassoula's and she thinks her husband's dying. From carrying some German suitcases. That's crazy isn't it? These fishermen are made of steel cables!"

"I don't know for sure. He tears some muscles in his chest, probably breaks some ribs, and he is not strong to walk."

"For God's sake, that's not fatal. You've got to get him to a hospital. If he just lies here bleeding in his chest he could drown!"

"The nearest hospital is Limnos," he shouts over the chorus. "And maybe the boat trip kills him."

"How about the army helicopter?"

My audience, at least, comes to life. An old priest looks heavenward, presumably to the helicopter, while the women begin crossing themselves vigorously.

"Sarah! The helicopter is for veeps! Christodolous is just a fish . . ." His voice falters.

"Theo, this man's family has lived here for centuries; he *is* a VIP. The mayor just left here. Find him or Stephanos."

"It's not that easy."

"Maybe not, but you can't just leave him here. What if he dies? The fishermen will blame the taxi drivers for going on strike." Exotic music clutters the line as Theo considers.

"There goes your road," I yell casually.

"All right. Yes!"

"Great! That's great, Theo! And send a taxi up here! I'll get some people to carry him out to the road!"

I hang up and go over to the bed.

"You're going to the hospital! You'll be all right!" I shout as if I'm still on the phone. Christodolous smiles up at me.

By the time the taxi arrives we're on the set of a big-budget film. At the end of the road, where it meets the footpath to the monastery, Christodolous is lying across three wooden chairs. A covering shot would be last rites. There's one priest at his head, another at his feet, most of the village and their children (home from school for lunch) milling around the altar, a herd of British tourists who've just emerged blinking from the monastery trying to reload their cameras, and at the edge of the frame, Pendis the garbage collector with his broom and his chain of defecating donkeys.

Theo gets out of the taxi and waves his arms to part the extras. Several attempts are made to fold Christodolous's body into the backseat; they nearly kill him. The accompanying sound track is a hearty soup of advice, automatic film winders, and authentic incantations. Only the star is silent, black eyes flickering with pain. He's finally laid out with the back door tied open to accommodate his bony legs; I picture them plucking the eucalyptus trees all along the road. Every Greek crosses himself as the taxi departs, and again as it just misses a tree while making a U-turn before fleeing down the mountain.

Petros, a harpy in denim, has followed the taxi in his jeep. The blond painter is riding with him; her hair flies out behind her, revealing a fabulous profile. As Petros stops, she leaps over its half door into the crowd. Petros offers *Kyria* Kassoula a lift down to Pharos but she declines, no doubt picturing herself in a helicopter. Too excited to disperse, everyone's milling on the set where the sun pours down on three blessed wooden chairs. "*Etsi-ketsi, etsi-ketsi,*" they chant (the demotic equivalent of "Bananagravel, bananagravel"); history is already taking its distorted shape. No one has drifted to Plato's taverna yet, but that's where I'd set up my next shot, with enough film to last the afternoon.

Alex is suddenly at my side.

"What are *you* doing here?" I ask her.

"The whole island's here. You haven't noticed? And what's up with Junial? Such a great name for him."

"Oops, I forgot."

"I guess you organized this, huh?"

"Well, I had to. They were all sitting around like it was a wake."

"I just wonder how you square this with your non-doer-ship philosophy. It seems like you saved his life."

"What an interesting time you've picked to discuss this."

"Well, I just thought while it's fresh in my mind. I can never think of examples when we're all sitting around trying to fathom your yoga."

Over her shoulder I see *Kyria* Kassoula and hordes of her immediate family advancing.

"Listen, I promise to remember this the next time the subject comes up. If we don't leave now, I'll be trapped for hours."

"OK. But what about Julian?"

"I'll call him from the post office. Has Petros left yet?"

"With all this action?"

"Find him, will you? Promise him a tip on the missing Volvo. I'll start down on foot."

"*Entaxi*."

The jeep catches up with me at sunset corner. Monika is riding next to Petros and jumps out to let me swing in. Alex, riding in the backseat, sweeps up some drawing pads to make room for me.

"What were you drawing up there?" I ask as I land.

"That scene on the *platia* was a painter's bonanza," Monika says over her shoulder. Her voice is low, slightly husky, the accent adding a melodic inflection. You'd have to be tone-deaf to escape its charm.

"Sarah arranged the whole thing," says Alex. "They were all just waiting for the funeral."

"Another bonanza." Monika laughs. At herself, I note approvingly. I'm about to flip up a drawing pad when Petros brings us to a rodeo stop in Pharos's main square.

"*Adio*, unless you want to come up to the helicopter pad with us," he says.

"No thanks," Alex and I reply.

We split up in town.

"I'll find you at Angira," I tell Alex. "I've got to call Julian now or the post office'll close. Ahhh!"

"What is it! Foot cramp?"

"No, no. Nothing. The post office is going to close whether I call him or not."

She turns away. Ex-lovers are immune to your low-grade infections. I curdle from *or*s that set up false oppositions. Professor Davis ruined *or*s forever, not to mention (ah, but I *am* mentioning) *hopefully*s. Davis was the writing guru at graduate school and my friends and I enrolled in his Elegant English Sentences class hopefully. He turned all us tie-dyed Ulysses worshipers into elegant intolerant pedants.

I get right through to Julian—is he inexplicably lucky?—and the line's clear. Julian's decided that whatever play I direct should be something we can produce in London so we'll be ahead of the game when I get back. *Ahead of the game* is one of Julian's greasy leftovers from business school.

"Forget it," I tell him. "*The Tempest* is always playing somewhere in the Home Counties.

"How are things between you and the costume designer?" I continue. "I'm sorry, I've forgotten her name."

"So have I," says Julian, laughing. "I miss you, Sarah." Which is when a big fish overpowers the undersea cable. I don't try to redial. I'd have to choose between being honest and saying I miss you too.

15

Alex has found a table downwind from Angira's octopus grill.

"We'll have to move," I say.

"Naturally." ("Why do I bother to choose?" is what she said in our salad days. Who'd ever go back to romance?)

"You remembered not to order the goat stew," I say when we've re-settled.

"I remembered once I saw it in the pot. Anyway I've decided to stick to fish until we leave; they don't have digestive tracts."

"I'm not sure I follow that."

"That's OK, it makes perfect sense to me. What did Julian want?"

I fill my beachware with Ari's retsina, reputed to cure intelligence. "Picture this." I pause to sip for dramatic impact. "Harold Prince is rehearsing *Death of a Salesman* and Alan Bates is playing Willy. He's having trouble with a light moment and he comes down to the footlights to talk it over.

" 'Are you sure this works?' he says to Hal. 'I don't think it's funny.'

"Hal's been touring it in Greece. He waves him off. 'Trust me Alan; it got laughs in Limnos.' "

It doesn't take Alex a second. "He wants a West End transfer?" she whoops.

"That's it. I mean, if they're howling in Hydra . . ."

"If it knocks 'em dead in Delphi . . ."

And so on until the fish comes.

"This isn't bad," she says, her fork dangling *tsipoura*. "Does Ari fish all winter?"

I hold up a hand for silence. (I don't actually know anyone who's choked to death on fish bones but that doesn't prove they aren't fatal.) When there's nothing on our plates but skeletons and fish heads, we move on to the relative safety of zucchini fritters.

"Yes, he fishes all winter," I tell her. "Ari is short for Aristotle, by the way. We've had breakfast with Plato and dinner with Aristotle. I'm definitely feeling smarter."

"Good. So please tell me how you square taking over at *Kyria* Kaseri's with your non-doer-ship yoga."

"Kaseri's a cheese. *Kyria Kassoula*."

"A casserole then."

"Non-doer-ship doesn't mean you're passive. You take action if you think you can help. You just don't get caught up in the result."

"Why not?" She pops a fritter into her mouth.

"Because cause and effect aren't what they seem. Think of that kid in Manhattan who hit the lamppost with his baseball bat and thought he'd caused the blackout. We do that all the time. Look . . . you fall in love, it's totally unplanned. Then you take this unplanned event and you try to reshape it, change it, control it. I don't mean you. And with all your efforts you screw it up."

"Usually." She's smiling.

"OK. So the ego wants to take credit, right? That's its nature."

"Uh-huh."

"So it takes credit for being this terrific person who someone's crazy about. But screwing it up? That's the other guy's fault." The fritters are dwindling. I take one, soak up the oil with my napkin, and chew.

"Unless you take responsibility for everything," she says.

"Now *there's* an ego trip! Think of one situation where time, or the weather, or something else you couldn't possibly predict doesn't affect the outcome."

"Sure they do."

"So." I hold up the boat I've made with Ari's sponge bread. "It's my boat and I have to sail it. I'm heading somewhere. But I try to remember I'm not the wind, I'm not the sea. I'm just the sailor. That's all it means."

Alex looks off to sea. We listen to the no wind blowing.

She turns back. "Got it," she says.

"Uh-oh."

"What?"

"I just noticed how impressed my ego is with that explanation."

"Eat your boat."

Ari's nephew brings a fresh supply of the house retsina. Alex picks up the tin pitcher and pours.

"It looks like paint stripper, it smells like paint stripper . . ."

"It's an acquired taste," I say.

"Over lifetimes."

"As a matter of fact," I continue, since nothing we're eating can get any colder, "I think liking retsina at all is proof of reincarnation. If you weren't born Greek, that is."

"Help! And I-R-T, I-R-T. What's that for?"

"A mantra is a sort of verbal link to your higher consciousness."

"Very handy," says Alex.

"Everybody's got one, Alexi *mou*. It just gets drowned out by the noise of life."

A tiny caique, radio blasting, cruises up to the pier. It's sailed in on a trickle of moonlight. The black sea splashes against creaky pilings. The fisherman throws his painter to a child walking by and hails Ari as he cuts his engine. The *patron* hustles over. I think he's going to tell the guy to turn off his radio. Everyone around us is watching—straining to recover the quiet of the night. After some animated discussion the fisherman ducks into his little lighted cabin. He comes out with a basket of fish. Ari takes it and turns toward the kitchen.

"*Yasoo,*" a man on the pier calls to the fisherman. He jumps ashore. They start talking, hands flying. The music seems to get louder. People turn back to eat, raising their voices. The fisherman turns back and leans down to his rope. Since I'm closest, I get up to help him cast off. Instead he takes another turn around the piling.

"You're not going?" I yell over the music.

"NO!"

I stand up and gesture toward his cabin. He looks at me ferociously. It could be the noise or the audience, or maybe my question.

"Would you please turn off your radio?"

"What?" he thunders and starts to walk away.

I step onto his boat and reach into the cabin. He leaps back and grabs my arm. The plank beneath me splits and I fall backward into the sea.

"I thought you were offering him a part," Alex says as I shiver in a towel in Ari's kitchen. I'm not cold, just furious. You never win an argument by falling in the sea.

"I was turning down his radio."

"Too bad you couldn't just turn up your higher consciousness."

Ari's wife has come out from behind her oily vegetables and stands over us shaking her head. "*Trelli*, Sarah *mou.*" She's holding a wooden spatula aloft. I think she's going to swat me.

"Give me." She plucks at my blouse and pants. "I put at the oven."

I hesitate. Do I want to spend the evening in wet clothes or smell like souvlaki?

"Off," says Alex. Souvlaki then.

16

I'm riding down to Theo's office the next morning to set up auditions when Iannis the mailman, coming up the mountain on his motorbike, passes very close. *"Yasoo!"* he shouts without cutting his engine. He reaches into his beautiful old leather sack and drops a packet of mail into my basket. I recall lovingly my days with the pony express.

"*Efharisto,* Ianni."

We roar off in opposite directions. This doesn't happen in London or New York. It merits an orange juice. What if there's something interesting in the mail? Luckily, Nikos's café lies conveniently between almost everything and everything else.

I imagine myself beating the dust off my chaps as I order my orange juice.

My gaze falls on the postmark on the watermarked packet—it's a week old. Iannis has been carrying this around for days, knowing he'd see me sometime. The pony express image comes into clearer focus: guys sitting around a butt-burned table in a saloon, playing poker and drinking beer, while their mounts doze at the rail in the dusty road outside.

The contents inside are dry: a letter from my sister Susan, bank statements, bills, a seed catalog, the booking form for the Glyndebourne

Opera Festival. My neighbor has trouble identifying first-class mail (I should have known from the weeds in his garden), so he forwards everything. Not quite: not the flyers for street fairs and and mushroom walks in Sussex. If you're out of London even for a week, you come home to a Matterhorn of junk mail that's been stuffed through the letterbox. You can't get in the front door. On the bright side, neither can thieves, and British thieves wouldn't *think* of using the back door.

"Dear Sare" (that's Susan, long on words, short on syllables). "You make your island sound so charming. Why don't you find a little villa for Den and me and the kids to rent this July?"

Why? Because I'd chop down the family tree first. But I'm working on compassion this summer. "Susan dear, I'd love you to come. I have to tell you, though, that besides the huge cost of getting here (no airport, so no charter flights), there are no decent hotels and places to rent are very expensive. No hot dogs, no tacos, no fast food of any kind except yogurt, and goat, if you can catch it, and then it's very stringy. Remember David Elliott from pottery class? He runs a Tuscan time-share. It must be great because he gets booked up early. Give it a try. Here's my international calling card number . . ."

I shuffle through the dazzling invitations to debtor's prison. Several gold cards, two platinum, and something brand-new, a Visa Titanium, which will come in handy when you've got a little hole in your rocket ship.

There's the usual schedule conflict between the seed catalog and the Glyndebourne opera season. If I let my zucchinis grow over the weekend they're performing *Figaro*, I'll have bleachers in my garden when I get back. You'd think the music-loving farmers of Sussex would have managed to fix that by now. Except they'd have to be raising golden calves to pay for the seats.

Nothing in the package makes me homesick. Though a note from my editor at *Yoga Journal* encouraging me to "post it soon, because we know what third-world mail is like," takes me right back to the Kit Carson handover.

(I confess third-world mail delivery goes nicely with my writing habits, and blizzard TV exactly fits my viewing tastes.)

John the Baptist comes over as I'm about to pay and slaps some money in the waiter's hand. Does he know about the play?

"Nothing," he says as I protest.

"*Efharisto*, Ianni. How are you?"

"Good." He nods his beautiful hair enthusiastically. There's a pause. I'm fresh out of waterskiing anecdotes.

"Where's Alex? I like to buy her a drink."

"She's not here. I think she's still up in Kastro."

"Oh." His face wrinkles along the lines previously described and he looks truly sad—Alex will be happy to hear.

"Shall I give her a message?"

"*Oxi, dhen birazi,*" he says and saunters away through the maze of tables. The few females turn to follow his retreat. Just as the males are turning the other way: Petros's girlfriend is walking deliberately toward me.

"Hi, Sarah."

"*Kalimera.*"

"I've lost Petros." She's carrying a big drawing pad and an easel. A small canvas chair is rigged to her backpack.

"Not for long, I'll bet."

There are an assortment of greens around her elbow and a pinkish smear over one eye. Her ragged cutoffs are a de Kooning palette.

The pale blue tank top's clean, though, and the weight of all that stuff in her arms shows off the muscles.

"I've been sketching the fishermen across the road; asleep mostly. I thought Petros said he'd meet me here. It doesn't matter."

"May I have a look?" Did I say that? *Merde* . . . what if they're awful?

"Sure, if you want to."

Nikos comes right over.

"Beautiful," he says, looking at the first sketch. "*Ti thelis na peis?*"

She looks at me.

"Monika, this is Nikos—Niko, Monika. He's asking what you'd like to drink."

"Oh, is it OK? Am I keeping you?"

"Not yet . . . I'm meeting Dr. Theo at his office in a few minutes."

"Great. Iced coffee, please."

"Nescafé frappé?" Nikos asks me.

"Yes. I'll have one too, please."

"*Harika*," says Nikos, to Monika, exactly as he says it to ugly guys with no teeth. With a few sure lines she's caught the fishermen; their fatigue, the relief of sleep, the light tangled in the cocoons of net, their old broken boots. I turn the page and find a bright pastel of three chairs in the town square, Christodolous lying across them. There are faces in the crowd I recognize; heat, excitement, mystery.

"Wow."

"*Thavmasia!*" Nikos looks down, then leaves our drinks.

"They're really good," I say, with unguarded surprise.

"Thanks." She gracefully ignores it. "Can you explain something to me?"

"I'll try."

"When is Nikos Niko?"

"When you're talking to him. It's the form of address. And Takis is Taki, and Georgos is Georgo. But not always. Nothing in Greek is always."

"Nothing?" She smiles.

"Every common verb is irregular."

"Then I'll stick to nouns. Like frappé. This is delicious. Is it really just Nescafé and milk?"

"Yes. But Niko is a magician. I think he's just impersonating a guy with a bar."

She puts down her glass and looks at me seriously.

"You're writing something aren't you?"

"A magazine article. It's about mantras."

"Mantras? For a magazine? Aren't they supposed to be secret?"

"Only if you're exploiting them."

"I don't understand." (Monika can't know this is my favorite expression on earth. Because I haven't known five people in my entire life who can say that—just that.)

"Well, yogis have been using mantras for thousands of years. So have Buddhists, for that matter. They're a great tool for dropping into meditation, and they're all well known. The secret stuff was just a trendy guru trying to make something new and mysterious of something very old."

"And charging for it."

"Right. Kind of like selling you your own breath."

"Hmmm. What's yours?"

"I can't tell you."

She laughs. So do I.

"Not just like that. Mantras are simple, but they need a little explanation." I feel something warm pouring into my skin. My hand wants to reach out to her arm. Instead I turn over another page of her sketchbook.

"*Ella!*" Petros is steering a clutch of clients. "Folks, this is a typical ouzo bar." He surrounds our table. "May we join you?"

"Hi, Petros, sure," says Monika.

"*Ciao!*" I leap up. "I've got an appointment."

Monika throws me a look that I contemplate en route to Theo's office. *Co-conspirator* is the best my ruffled brain can deliver .

The door to Theo's examining room is closed so I sit in his outer office on a gray metal folding chair. They're probably the only ones on Pharos, unless the police station has them under Popi's ad for shampoos. I don't exactly sit; perch is more accurate, because I hate these Venus flytraps, liable to fold you up and suck you into oblivion.

The room is decorated with bright anatomical posters: an inside look at the digestive track in Day-Glo yellows and greens; a cross section of the spinal column that looks like a chain of broken shells; a pen-and-ink Escher-like doodle of the inner ear. Right next to Theo's hand-painted No Smoking sign is a huge poster of an open heart, with neon blue arrows piercing it to label the working parts.

I'm studying this—who knows when *aorta* will come up in conversation—when Theo strides out of his office with a beautiful young widow (she's dressed for grieving, anyway). Seeing me, they stop in mid-sentence, possibly discussing a sexually transmitted disease or an untimely pregnancy. I assume my lost-in-thought expression—the one lovers find so annoying.

"Ah, Sarah," Theo says, "how are you?" He doesn't mean it professionally, and before I can reply he turns and walks her out the door. I have a moment to consider what a catch he must be in this tiny sea.

He leads me into a small office next to his examining room.

"Can I make you a Nescafé?"

"No thanks, I've just come from Nikos."

"Orange juice?"

"*Oxi,* Theo, *efharisto.*"

"*Neraki,*" he announces, determined to give me something. He removes a glass from a neatly arranged cabinet and takes a bottle of water from a small fridge. Then he clears off the desk and stacks the files on the windowsill. I might as well be doing yoga on a riverbank for the sense of limitless buoyancy I'm feeling today. The water tastes delicious.

"Are you sure it won't be an interruption, using this room?" I ask.

"No, no. I give you a key you use when you want."

"Good. Then I won't have to disturb you at night."

"At night?" He sounds worried.

"Well, that's when most working people are free."

"Working people?" Why this echo? Or is *working people* a nonsensical redundancy on Pharos. "I mean since people work during the day, they can only come after dinner."

"Yes . . . of course." He surfaces slowly. "You are not using *xeni*—foreigners?"

"Oh no; I want this to be a Greek production."

"Yes. It's just that maybe you have trouble finding the locals to perform, especially the women."

"Trouble? I need a disguise to buy vegetables! And forget the post office! How did you manage all this?"

"*All the world is a stage.* Shakespeare, no?" He smiles. It's a terrific smile.

"Bravo, Doc. We have one problem. There's only one female part. And I've got housekeepers and ticket sellers, bakers . . . I'm thinking of having a chorus for the imaginary banquet and the wedding scene, to give all these ladies something to do."

"Very smart, *Saraki*—"

A fisherman bursts through the door with a writhing howling child in his arms. Blood is streaming over their clothes and the man's voice booms over his cries. With the noise and the collision of energies it takes several moments to discover that the boy's left hand is a ripped cushion of fishhooks. When Theo attempts to take him in his own arms the fisherman holds on, trying desperately to explain.

"*Siga, siga,*" Theo pleads until he manages to pry the boy from his father's slick embrace. He kicks shut his office door and the two of us are suspended in this space. As I turn to leave a sharp cry breaks over us; flinching, I turn back. The father is flat against the wall, sweating like a freshly sliced eggplant. At first he doesn't see me, then he does, and my unfamiliar face adds to his confusion.

I try smiling, which prompts him to offer me a cigarette from his bloody shirt pocket. The electric heart is just over his head, next to Theo's decree.

"I don't smoke, thank you." I sit down, ashamed that I was about to leave him alone.

"Never he comes . . . today no school . . . please Papa . . . when his mother sees, AHH! . . . Georgaki! . . . busy we roll the net . . . hand in the water . . . today hot . . . many hooks for *colyus* . . . *O Theos mu* . . . Georgaki!" He's shaking the wall so hard the poster could come crashing on his head. I walk over and put my hand on his shoulder.

"He'll be OK." His eyes focus, and his body stiffens as his energy shifts into his mind. And speaking proto-Greek, I more or less say that the doctor knows what to do . . . you know how loud kids scream . . . how fast they heal . . . it'll be a great story to tell his friends . . . In the middle of my ramble he lights up and slips into a chair. I notice he looks down suspiciously when it shifts under his weight. We listen to the whimpers through the wall.

"You are from Germany?"

"America . . . But I live in England."

"Ah . . . *Amerikanidha*." (He has pleasant memories of JFK. Or his English teacher; he obviously paid attention. Or maybe he wears jeans.) "My uncle has one shop in Astoria."

This must be a greeting in phrase books.

We jump up as the door opens and Georgaki appears. Grinning, though his cheeks are muddy with tears. Theo is bent over, holding his right hand; his tenderness hits me like a wave. Georgaki's wounded hand is bandaged and hoisted in a muslin sling. The boy rolls toward us like a drunk.

"Don't pick him up!" Theo says, as his father bends to do that. "Just keep hold of his good hand; he's a little tired from all this."

Tired? Drugged to Olympus.

"Keep his arm like that for tonight. Put him in a chair with his feet up when you get home and cover him. He'll go right to sleep."

"*Pedhi mou!*—My child!" he cries, kissing the boy. "His hand?" He touches his arm with his fingertips and tries to see through the bandage.

"It's OK. But you must bring him back tomorrow for a clean bandage; and every day for five days."

Georgaki's green eyes sparkle. In five days he'll be a junkie.

"Papa," he sings, gazing in the direction of his father. And I see that he's beautiful; his face just turned from cherubic to mischievous, blond hair curling down his narrow back, arms and legs long and slight but defined, delicate neck and shoulders the light brown of June. A high glistening voice. I have my Ariel.

When I come back from Theo's office I find a praying mantis stretched out on the terrace, mumbling over some pages. Diana is sleeping on an open book at her feet.

"Thought you were going Volvo hunting with Iannis."

"Petros came by with these. My first job. The ship docks tomorrow morning."

"You're going to put them to sleep with that delivery."

"Fine. They'd *have* to be dreaming to believe this stuff. Cisterns lined with pirates' gold, caves painted by a Turkish harem. One house has a bread oven where they locked up the pope when he dropped by to convert some Orthodox knights!"

"Turkish harems with crayons?"

"Maggie Smith's got nothing on Petros."

"Well, I suggest you stick to his script. I mean, if you want the job."

She turns from the neck only. "I want the money. Maybe I should just sell my body." She rotates her neck to look it over.

I do the same. Sometimes a cliché can be thought provoking.

"What d'you think you'd get for it?"

"You're not taking me seriously."

"You're right, sorry. I'll try to think of a price. But the *Tempest* auditions are in three days. Will you look over this list with me?"

I've been gathering names; a heady exercise in character assassination and superficial revelations on the nature of beauty.

"Wouldn't Manolis be a perfect Antonio—handsome, scheming, a murderer down deep?"

"Who's Manolis?" Alex sits up.

"The taxi driver with the pointed beard. His meter's been broken since the seventies. Nikos says Manolis bought a racehorse last year. He must drive tourists around in circles. And then there's Spiros, his brother with the red Fiesta taxi. He growls like a bo'sun."

"It's just like New York," says Alex. "All the cabdrivers are actors."

"May we press on?"

"Who's the one who smashed his meter when a guy complained about the fare?"

"That's Stratos Gavritis. Hadn't thought of him, but he's a natural Caliban. His hair's always dirty, he's even got scaly skin. I wonder if he can memorize lines?"

"Doesn't Caliban have some accomplices?"

"Yeah, but that's no problem, just think of all those Theos," I say. "Prospero and Ariel are the tricky characters to cast. I'd like that boy with the fishhooks in his hand."

"With or without?"

"Wait till you see him. He's angelic, and his voice hasn't broken yet."

"Will his mother let him stay up late?"

"Hmm . . . that may be a problem."

"You could always cast her as Miranda."

I must look pensive.

"Just kidding!"

After an hour or so I have a pretty good idea who's for certain and who should audition. Alex isn't happy.

"Some people have to be in it," I explain.

"You mean the chief of police."

"Stephanos of course. Also Priftis, Iannis Milos, his wife Maria, Stella, and Kostis." These are the butcher, the postman and his wife, Tula's unmarried daughter, and the public notary.

"Not Priftis! He keeps food in his beard."

"But if he washed it . . . He does have a kind of wise Prospero-esque look."

"The butcher *has* to be in the play?"

"If we don't want last year's chickens."

"And Stella—with those enormous teeth and dyed red hair?"

"Would you rather have spiders in the bathroom? Tula thinks her daughter's Aphrodite. Besides, Stella will just be in the chorus. You know Miranda's the only female part."

"And I used to think that was a drawback." Alex shakes her disillusioned head.

"Politics is new for you," I console her. "I guess you've never run for office."

She gives me a long, almost serious look. "Is there something I should know about your past?"

"Class president of the fifth grade."

"Excuse *me* . . . But Maria Milos? Doesn't she carry a Chihuahua?"

"Can't have her husband without her."

"Let's do Gilbert and Sullivan."

17

That evening in the village, we poster for the audition. Interest is intense and so's the work. Walking with the Moon on Your Head is easier than balancing on a broken chair sticking dull thumbtacks into lampposts.

I'm surrounded by Pharians and their kids dripping ice cream and declaiming Homer. I shout above the soliloquies, "Come to the audition on Wednesday. My mind is open." Sadly I have no idea what *my mind is open* may mean in Greek.

"We forgot John the Baptist." I'm removing the bones from my mullet; probably the skeleton reminds me. We're eating at Selini, where the fish is fresh and the french fries are cooked in today's oil. Another unique feature is the terrace that extends so far over the beach that when any ship passes by, waves break over your feet, sometimes your knees. Which is why the locals call it *To Kima*, the Wave. Obviously the dress code is shorts.

"Iannis—how could we!" Alex wails.

"I'm sure it's for a good reason—no talent, for instance, no mind . . ." I carefully remove a fatal bone. "Don't worry, I'll find him a part."

"But it can't just be a walk-on; I want him around for rehearsals."

I'm trying to think, but Selini's retsina cuts the blood supply to the brain.

"We could try him as Ferdinand, the king's son—hardly any lines but he's on stage a lot."

"Great."

I lift the skeleton off my plate and fling it into the sea.

"Oh no, forget that. It's Ferdinand who says *These sweet thoughts do even refresh my labours.*"

"I'll teach it to him," she volunteers. "It'll take weeks."

I don't protest. A few weeks with Iannis and the spell cast by those golden tresses is bound to wear off.

A tourist shrieks. We all pick up our feet as a ferry rounds the headland.

"Is that where the line comes from?" Alex asks as the terrace sloshes and drains.

My glass is arrested in midair. I'm about to say *No, it's from Music Man* when I recall that I've given up sarcasm for compassion.

"Yes," I say.

"That's poetry."

"Especially *The Tempest*. It's his last play; the language is so beautiful you could sing it." I sit back and look into the night. Two tiny caiques have appeared noiselessly, as if by magic, on the horizon. Fishermen standing in the stern are throwing their nets onto the phosphorescent surface of the sea. "Elizabethan England was pretty corrupt in Shakespeare's time, and Arcadia was his vision of a new world. He believed in love and redemption. Miranda and Ferdinand's speeches are really love songs. If I'm going to sit through rehearsals I want to care about what I'm hearing."

"Even if the butcher is butchering it?"

"But he won't be; you'll be coaching him . . . them."

"I will?" Alex looks surprised.

"Didn't I mention that?"

"You mean didn't you *ask* me that."

"That *is* what I mean."

"*Kima!*" shouts the waiter—a nice bit of timing. Except this one washes away a small calico cat that's been dining on fish heads. A woman at a table near the edge dives into the sea. She surfaces near the cat and grabs it by the neck. They both go under. Her free arm flails the water, she surfaces again, kicks her way back, and tosses the calico onto the terrace. It slides along like a mop. Two young men jump up from her table and haul the woman out. It's happened so fast nobody else has moved. She pushes her long hair out of her face and stands there dripping in transparent clothes. Somehow nothing looks as wet as a fully dressed wet person.

I recognize Evdhomada, the petite shy music teacher from the high school, someone you'd never have picked for amphibious rescues. Her matrimonial stock has just taken a quantum leap. Now everyone comes to life. A little girl picks up the cat, which should be wrung out, and starts blotting it with paper napkins. One of the heroine's friends hands her his jacket. Sounds of approval and some applause from a long table of tourists. For a moment I think she's going to bow and drench her companions. The *patron* walks over with a plastic tablecloth, though it's not clear what he expects her to do with it.

"Do you still have that swimming towel in Ernie Banks's basket?" says Alex. "The pelican in the sailor cap sipping a martini?"

"Yep. It's so ugly I can't lose it."

"Here's your chance," says Alex.

I fetch it and Evdhomada gratefully wraps herself up. "Keep it," I say. "And please come to the *akro'asi* on Wednesday."

Things settle down, which is good because we're eating fish. This is when you discover how many ideas come into your head in a single minute, all screaming to be let out. For instance, I've now solved the mystery of why Selini is the only taverna on Pharos not littered with cats. And I realize I did forget to ask Alex if she'd coach the cast. Her diction's perfect, she's studied at the Actors Studio, and then she was Nurse Ellen on a daytime soap. She covers her eyes when you take out a splinter and faints at the sight of blood, but people still stop her on the street to ask for medical advice.

The waiter comes over with a dish of lemon sauce, though we already have one. "Ah!" he says with mock surprise, and doesn't go away. Instead he inclines toward me in a rather intimate way—I catch a whiff of ouzo.

"O what a fool and pleasant slave I am."

I recoil. He's encouraged.

"And I can sing; I give you 'Hey Notty Notty'?"

"No thanks, Stratos, not here. But you may give it to me at the audition on Wednesday."

"Are you crazy?" says Alex when he retreats without his lemon sauce.

"It's Stratos the taxi driver."

"Luckily we have motorbikes."

"But why is he moonlighting here? D'you think the fishermen managed to get the road canceled?"

"Cabdriver . . . waiter . . . pleasant slave." She gestures to heaven.

"Well, that's why we're having auditions. Everyone gets to try out and nobody poisons our well."

"What well?"

"Cara!" Arabella and her host—Aldo '98 we call him, not to his face—are weaving toward us like mice through a maze. "I've seen your beautiful poster! We will sit with you?"

"We're just leaving," says Alex, over a plateful of food.

I get up and kiss Arabella on both cheeks. Her hopes visibly soar. "I'm so sorry you can't join us, but Alex and I are having a meeting."

"You don't live together?" Rudeness tempered with genuine confusion.

Alex looks up with a loaded fork. "There's an empty table just there." The fork points directly into the Aegean.

"Which part will I be?"

Can I please be reborn with Arabella's obliviousness.

"There's a reading Wednesday to decide who—"

"Cara, I'm going to take that table," says Aldo.

"A reading . . ." she repeats. I note that thinking doesn't mar superficial good looks.

"Yes. See you Wednesday, Arabella." She backs away, smiling into the air.

"I don't think we're safe in public until the show's cast," I tell Alex softly.

"Really?" she says. "You think we'll be safe after that?"

18

I'm getting up earlier and earlier. These are long June days. The moon rises late from the sea, a fiery penny that quickly turns to silver as its climbs steeply into a black star-net night. I leave my window open and fall asleep in the moon's path. From the same unshuttered window the sun spills onto my sheets not many hours later.

I wake up and lie in bed repeating mantras. Easier to do in the stillness of an island morning than the din of a city street. But city streets are where people need them most. So I'm looking for ancient phrases, sounds that still vibrate in modern brains and can trick them into silence. Mantras that can transform a subway ride, for instance, or a long wait in a hospital corridor. Practical mantras, if you happen to consider higher states of consciousness practical. Which I do. But I was amazed when the people at *Yoga Journal* agreed to fund me. Unfortunately they have a fixed publication date—a date no mantra can alter.

I'm trying out *Om mane padme hum* (The jewel is in the lotus) for gate changes at O'Hare Airport, because it's the longest mantra I know. Suddenly I hear Iannis Milos calling from the street. The jewel is in the lotus. The letters are in his bag. Maybe this is the one when you're waiting for your Greek mailman, or anyone, to deliver.

"*Yasoo,* Sarah." I look down into the street. Iannis is swinging off his motorbike with a letter in his hand.

"Why doesn't he leave it at the door?" Alex is following me down the stairs. "Like they do in the rest of the world."

"He's probably got some sizzling gossip." I turn to her. "Or hopes he's bringing me some."

"He could just hold it up to a candle to sneak a peek."

"And miss my reaction? *Drama*'s a Greek word, remember. Did you do that when we lived together?"

"I'm going back to bed."

Guilty, Your Honor.

I open the courtyard door. "*Kalimera,* Ianni. Would you like a coffee?"

"Greek coffee, please—*metrio*"—with a little sugar. He drops his sack inside the door and walks past me into the courtyard. I picture the inscription chiseled in the granite lintel of Manhattan's central post office—NEITHER SNOW, NOR RAIN, NOR HEAT, NOR GLOOM OF NIGHT STOPS THESE COURIERS . . . Here on Pharos the lintel's smaller, but there's plenty of room for "Erratikos."

"We saw Stratos Gavritis last night working at Selini. Have the fishermen stopped the road?" I'm boiling water in a covered pot—my culinary secret.

"*Oxi, oxi.* Stratos is the owner's son-in-law. His taxi broke down."

"But wasn't that in May?"

"I think yes."

"And it's not fixed?" I stir in the sugar and coffee powder.

"Is only *last month,* Sarah."

Om mane padme hum—when will he get to the point.

"They say you are boss for the play. You know I am actor?"

I hand him the tiny cup of lava. "I do now, and you'll be in it."

"Yes?" His weary face erupts in delight. We're a living coffee commercial. He drains the cup, ignores the ominous dregs, and departs before I open the letter.

"His face literally broke into a smile, just like the cliché," I tell Alex at second breakfast. "You could hear those wrinkles cracking up."

"Umm." She's unimpressed as she drizzles honey into a bowl of yogurt. "Which part are you thinking of?"

"I don't know . . . a walk-on . . . a few lines."

"I guess he could deliver a letter." She stops for a spoonful. "Did they have mail deliveries in Shakespeare's time?"

"Several a day."

"Then it couldn't be Iannis."

"No. But he did deliver today and there's a letter from Copper. He wants to come for two weeks. Alone."

"Really?"

A mutual friend, painter-turned-set-designer, terrified of flying. Living in England, he can drive to his gigs. Vacations offshore are rare. Alone is even rarer. Copper never ends a relationship before starting another one, with messy overlaps requiring lies, stratagems. If we were doing *Othello* we'd have our Iago.

"He says alone." I wave the evidence. "It's God's blessing on the project. He can do the sets, the costumes, maybe even the lights."

"I thought your God was neutral?"

"She is."

"Well, how about her blessing on Copper? I'm sure he thinks he's coming to swim and pick up girls."

"There'll be plenty of time for that."

"Oh no. Don't start pretending you can tell time." She adds more honey. "You've got to warn him. And give him room to say no."

"OK. Remember to put honey on the shopping list. I'll write and invite him this afternoon." Plotting gives me an appetite; I start making an omelette.

"Wonder what happened to Ann-Marie," says Alex, "she with the gorgeous black eyes and the shoplifting record. Use a smaller pan. He seemed very keen on her, spent Christmas with her dysfunctional family, I recall. You need a little more milk. Not that I liked her much. Her name was only one of many hyphenated qualities: friendly-superior, sloppy-critical, sullen-gregarious."

"Timid-feisty," I add. "Pastel-primary."

"You're thinking of his work again. That's too much heat, it'll curdle."

"Would you like to make this?"

"Why? You're doing fine."

I add a little feta without incident.

"Copper on his own. Imagine. I'll have some of that," Alex says.

"At least I could ask him to bring some gels; there's nothing like 'surprise pink' around here. And a few pieces of gauzy material for Ariel's wings . . . and Prospero's robe." I cut the omelette in half and give her the bigger piece. I'm never very hungry after the mess I make.

"Mmm . . . it's good. Pepper please."

"There's pepper on it."

She grinds away.

"You could introduce him to that Icelandic landscape artist."

"Who?"

"You know—that paint-stained Valkyrie Petros is towing around."

"You mean Monika? She doesn't look like a tow job to me. And she's Swedish, by the way."

"Aha! You *do* like her," she says, pointing the final forkful at me.

"I what?"

"You remember her name."

"That's hardly a . . ."

"Helloooo . . . it's *me*, *Saraki*! But don't worry, I can't imagine that Copper will come. Wait till he finds out they fly Fokkers to Amorgos."

"What time's your tour?" I get up.

"Eleven. You're changing the subject."

"Actually I'm changing the object. I've got to finish this article. See you at Theo's."

"Uh-uh," she replies. "Monika Monika Monika."

19

We arrive at Theo's office for the audition to find the doctor arranging cheese pies and *taramosalata* on a table under the open-heart poster. "Welcome, welcome. I'm glad you're here."

"Episis"—ditto. "Have I got the wrong night?"

He looks puzzled, a very attractive expression, something to do with huge black eyes and the two deep lines in his otherwise untracked brow.

"We're having auditions tonight," Alex says, overtaking me.

"I know!" he exclaims, spreading his arms over the table. "Mama tells me to bring these from the party."

I'm about to say this isn't a social event when I remember I'm in Greece.

"Thanks, Theo. Have you got any more chairs?"—the ones I hate.

Before we're entirely set up the hopefuls begin to arrive. A lot of them—excited, nervous, hungry. Each one tries to strangle me while dropping an impassioned plea in my ear. Except for Stephanos, who drops a chocolate bar in my pocket. (Clearly he knows the criminal heart.) Theo produces a case of Sprite and starts pouring. What we've got here is a rerun of his name-day party. The food, the guests, even Theo's caryatid sisters, motionless at either end of the buffet. The only no-show is my translator.

"Theo, have you seen Omiros?"

"He drives Tino's cab. Don't worry, after Tino he comes. I help you before."

"But what if Tino's in the play? Who's going to drive his cab?"

"Oh, you can't have Tino; he never loses the business."

"Then why is he here?" Do you have to be Greek to follow this?

"Look around, *Saraki*. He will hate it to be left out."

"Alex, let's hand out the parts."

The excitement increases. It's a challenge to gossip drink eat and read at the same time.

"Good evening everyone. I'm very happy to see you all. I'm going to call you into the other room to read, one at a time. There are lots of you so please be patient."

All smiles—different from casting calls in the West End. (My last was for a sheriff for *Oklahoma*. I opened the waiting room door to the smoking remains of the OK Corral: a dozen identical biceptual blonds pacing and glowering at one another. Bring on the cheese pies and Sprite.)

"This looks more like a lineup than a casting call. Don't you want me in there with you?" Alex says. "The caryatids can handle the party."

"Of course I do. You're an accessory."

The butcher, the hairdresser, the ferry ticket seller, several cab drivers, Tula's daughter, the gorgeous sponge diver, the public notary, the chief of police: one by one my heart sinks. In the beginning I look to Theo for guidance: the Pharos Players . . . was he kidding? But no, he seems enthralled. Whereas Alex can see that my spirit's drifting back to London. And that I'm chewing on my nail.

"Sponge diver Theo might be okay as the king's jester," she says brightly.

"*Sosto*—true," says Theo.

"*Sosto,*" I say. "If he can stop laughing at his own lines."

"I'll get Priftis," says Alex.

The butcher has taken off his bloody apron, which does nothing to disguise his profession. It's not so much the blood under his nails as he rattles the script, as the bits of . . . what . . . entrails? in his lively beard. Which makes it hard to concentrate on his performance. But slowly his rich unbridled voice and infectious energy clear my brain and grip my imagination.

"*We are such stuff as dreams are made on,*" Priftis announces with a butcher's unflinching certainty. "*And our little life is rounded with a sleep.*"

I can't help picturing his massive cleaver separating a goat from its head.

"Thank you, Priftis, you're our Prospero." I jump up and grab his hand. "Please send in the chief of police."

When Stephanos, the first prince of Naples to simultaneously pick his teeth and dig in his ear, finishes his soliloquy, we wonder why Prospero decides to spare his life.

"Thank you, Stephano. I'm afraid you aren't right for the part."

He glares at me from a rolling prairie of chins.

"The part isn't right for *you*, actually. But I'll find one that is. I do have one question. Would you have time to rehearse?"

"*Malista.*"

"Well, that's good. I'll let you know."

He winks at me and exits. Which reminds me of the candy bar; I need sugar at this point.

"Why did you ask him that?" says Theo.

"Because he's the chief of police."

Nothing.

"Doesn't that keep him busy?"

"Doing what?"

"Doing what . . . ," I echo.

"But Priftis was terrific," says Alex, and she looks at Theo. "Can we do a one-man show?"

"Go see who else is left out there, will you?"

She bows and leaves. I look down at my notes.

Kostis: Caliban or Alonso the king. whispers—looks murderous—gold teeth—spray them?

Popi: nice nail color. grins right through tragic speech . . . but we need wigs.

Vienoula: where did she find that hat? stammers. stage fright now . . . onstage?

Bus driver: wart is distracting.

Manolis: taxi driver. Antonio, duke of Milan. intense, distracted, vain. reminds me of an actor.

Theo sponge diver: absurd facial gestures, beautiful hair, smells good. (Here I begin to doodle.) the king's jester?

Priftis: Prospero

Stephanos: help! digging in his ear. has something in his teeth? (Good likeness of his chins . . .) maybe Sebastian, the king's brother.

Alex reenters with her finger in her ear. "How about *The Pirates of Penzance?*"

Omiros rushes past her. "Sorry Sarah, but you haven't seen Tino yet!

"God, I forgot. Please send him in."

Tino takes off his cap and plants his feet in front of the medicine cabinet and stretches out a knarled waxy arm holding the script. The office is small; if he steps forward he'll smack me.

"Sorry; I left my glasses in the taxi."

"That's OK. But don't move!" My first stage direction.

Alex has given him the wrong page. He begins to read Caliban. His voice is oily, edgy, ironic. His body sways like a Gila monster, he projects high and low. Like an actor! I venture a look at Alex, no longer picking her ear. Then at Theo, who looks worried. (Is Uncle Tino a heart patient?) Tino concludes with a sneer. We applaud.

"Adio." He grins and slithers out.

To hell with doctor–patient confidentiality. "What's the matter with him, Theo?"

"Nothing."

I look puzzled.

"He's got a taxi. He never leaves it."

"I forgot! This is impossible!" I want to cry.

"Isn't there a mantra for this sort of situation?" says Alex, putting her arm around my drooping shoulders.

"A what?" says Theo.

I think. "There is. 'It's all one.' "

"Means?" she asks.

"It's Shakespeare's version of *dhen birazi.*" I take a deep breath.

Omiros brings in Georgaki, the fisherman's boy—a dead ringer for a messenger of God. He hugs Theo—his pusher, I recall.

"Well, I better go, if you don't mind." Theo gets up. "I have much work to do." He pats my hand. Can't he see I'm in critical condition?

"Sure, Theo, we're fine."

Omiros produces a guitar and Ariel begins to sing.

"Where the bee socks there socks eye . . . On a cow ship's bell I lie . . ."

"Hold it, whoa." Laughing . . . "That's not quite it. Here are the lyrics." A sense of humor is all you really need for this job.

20

"A villain who picks his ear? And a princess who giggles *and* lisps! Didn't you ever notice that?" Alex and I are sitting under a plane tree at La Venezia. It's a romantic beachside taverna with dreadful Italian food. The trunk is painted with polka dots and Christmas lights are strung between the branches. No one would ever look for me here.

Alex puts down her menu. "Did you tell them it's a comedy by any chance?"

"Of course not. They're just nervous."

"Offstage fright."

"I guess so."

"And what about Maria, the postman's wife? They don't have Chihuahuas on desert islands."

"I'm sure we can get her a sitter."

"And for the dog?"

"*Yasoo,* Sarah," says our waiter Peros, plainly amazed to see me. "*Yiati eise edho?*"

"What does that mean?" Alex asks.

"Why are you here?"

"Ahh . . . what a nice omen."

"Good to see you. Pero." He works days at the boatyard and has never seen me in clean clothes. He puts an unripe tomato salad on the table along with a basket of cement bread.

"*Efharisto.*"

"What makes this place Italian? Is the chef from Italy?"

"The chef, Alex? The name." I close my eyes for inspiration. "We'll have lasagna, please."

"I'm ravenous," she says. She stabs at a tomato and nods sadly. "How do they do this—here in the land of tomatoes?"

"It's a mystery. As is Manolis's German accent. But Tino makes a great Caliban, doesn't he? His voice is perfect and he looks positively slimy." I pour olive oil on my plate and try to revive a piece of bread.

"Isn't he the one who can't be in it? Rich Tino, who never leaves his taxi?"

"That's right." I stare at my soggy bread.

"Ariel's great," she offers.

"The Pharos Players . . . How did Theo ever pull this off?"

We pause to consider.

"Lots of patience." Alex cracks herself up.

"That's *the* worst pun I . . ."

"Sorry, couldn't help it." She wipes her mascara.

"I think I'll tell Theo I'm resigning."

She blots. "Why don't *you* set up the hospital and let *him* direct the play."

"That's a great idea!"

We drink thoughtfully. The retsina in the tin pitcher is mercifully cold. I'm trying to remember what disease tin causes . . . is it memory loss?

"Priftis makes a pretty good Prospero. Can he double as Caliban?"

"Impossible, Alex. They've got several major scenes together."

"You could always rewrite the play," she says cheerfully.

I stop drinking and look severe.

"Just kidding. That was a brilliant idea for Stella and the caryatids," Alex continues, to distract me from the hospital plan, "but can we put them offstage?"

"Put the chorus outside the church? But they could sit on a bench in the nave. Vienoula can prompt from there too."

"Great idea!"

Peros rushes over. "Problem, *Saraki*?"

"*Oxi*. The lasagna?"

"*Amesos*." (In India they say, "Just now coming." Greeks say *Amesos*. They both mean "No one knows when.")

"Manolis makes a pretty convincing duke of Milan with that squint and that great head of hair. I wonder if he blow-dries it." She holds up two tomato slices. "I could use these as earrings."

"Except they'll rot."

Peros sets down the lasagna. I wave dismissively over Alex's salad but he's reluctant to take it away.

"You don't want?"

"*Oxi*."

He looks bewildered as he retreats. An actor?

I dissect the plate before me. Something white is peeking out under lots of gelatinous red and brown. (It's hard to be discouraged on Pharos, but things *are* piling up.) "We still don't know if Manolis can memorize lines. He never charges the same fare for two identical trips." I move some sauce around. "It's the duke who has all the expository monologues in the first act and who sums up the play at the end."

"*Our revels now are ended?* I thought that was Prospero. You're playing with your food."

"That *is* Prospero. It's considered Shakespeare's retirement speech. Everything *before* that. And I think you're right about Manolis's hair. Maybe he's another one of Popi's special clients."

"His retirement speech?" Alex stabs at a noodle. "How old was he?"

"Thirty-something." I push something green around my plate. "I do believe this is canned basil. Can we never come here again?"

"We're hiding, remember?"

"Right. And we're starving." I drink deeply. "A condition we may take to bed."

Alex holds up a dripping wad of spinach. "Seaweed? Where are we?"

"Venezia."

"Oh no, that's a sacrilege. We've got to rename this place."

"Mmm . . ." I'm wrestling with a mushroom.

"Was he sick?" Alex looks worried.

"Shakespeare? Oh, no; he inherited his father's land and settled down as a gentleman farmer."

"He settled down?" (Ordinarily we'd be using some of this time to chew, but under the circumstances . . .) "Do you think he got writer's block?"

Now she's looking at me with equal parts amusement and sympathy. Could this be a late salvo from the Monika skirmish?

"No," I say evenly. "I don't think a person who writes forty plays and hundreds of poems before he's thirty-five can be considered blocked."

"No, he certainly can't." She smiles.

Late salvo.

Peros passes by with plates for another table.

"Look," he says. The full moon has risen over the mountain sheltering the left side of the bay and thrown a copper ribbon from the horizon to the small dock below us. It falls in reckless calligraphy between the warped boards that reach over the water and wind above the sand, until it breaks up on the splintered steps to the taverna.

Moonstruck and pasta-worn, we chew on.

"Vendetta!" I break the spell.

"What?"

"The name for this place. *Ecce!*" I hold up my glass.

"Ah! *Perfetto.*" We click.

21

If I sit in the middle of Sandsoon Beach on the shelf just above the waterline I see nothing but blue when I open my eyes. The ideal place for meditation—antidote for a casting call.

Perfect stillness, no sensation of breath, floating. Stephanos picking his ear. Stillness, ripples of light on a blue field. Maria Milos's Chihuahua peeing on Theo's kilim. No thought, no body, no sound. Vienoula screaming as her chair collapses. I bring back the mantra to obliterate her scream. *"Guru om, guru om."* Joy streams through the top of my head, I lift off, disappear. A vision: Elena and Sophia are standing in a doorway between my eyebrows, mixing a cheese-pie filling with their bare feet. Theo walks up to me, a loving gaze, with two kittens asleep in the crook of his arm.

I'm determined to spread myself thin. If this is the age of supermoms, a sax-playing president, and the Academy of Ballet and Refrigeration (or was that a *New Yorker* cartoon?), there's no reason I can't direct write meditate sail and master the omelette. As long as I don't throw in romance. This would be a bad time to get involved. And I have as much control over that as I have over the wind.

A clatter and hiss of waves brings me back. My legs are awash. The ferry, now out of sight, must have rounded the entrance to the harbor.

But two hours have passed since the Carrara sisters vision, and I'm rekindled. And back on the job. Why wasn't the music teacher from Kima at the audition? Was it the ugly towel I gave her? And where was Arabella with her hairless legs?

"What could have happened to our waxing queen?" It's cloudy so we're having lunch up on the terrace.

"We can guess . . . though I'd have expected her to make *that* little change of plans last night. Not that it matters."

"It might. We still don't have a Miranda. Arabella's got presence, and she's funny, though she doesn't know it. She would definitely add something."

"I don't want to go there," says Alex, pouring the retsina that can remove nail polish. "I really wonder how we can drink this," she adds between sips.

"*Aleex!*"

She goes to the terrace wall, turns back.

"It's John the Baptist. Have we got another yogurt?"

"Sure." I rise slowly. I didn't think I was antisocial until Alex came along.

"Let's tell him he's Ferdinand. He does look like a prince."

"Come in, Ianni," I call, leaning out. "I'd really like to go over this cast list with you," I tell her.

"Don't worry, he won't stay long."

"I find Vovo!" Iannis rushes up the stairs with his shoes in one hand. He's so excited he pours out all our honey on his yogurt, and there was a lot.

"That's great, Ianni!" we cry. *Vovo* makes it sound like a pet.

"It's very . . . *epikinthinos!*"

The yogurt disappears in a flash. Discovery seems to be a real aperitif. But I notice that he's a delicate eater, which boosts his stock unexpectedly. If Alex starts bringing him home at least we can still have dinner parties.

"Dangerous? Why?"

"In the tomato field of Theo Kaveris."

We haven't learned anything, as our expressions express.

"*Exadelphos tou Stephanou.*"

"The nephew of the police chief," I tell Alex. "That *is* interesting."

"Have you told anyone?" asks Alex, who once had a small part in *L.A. Law.*

"You. I wanted to tell you first."

She beams at him. Is being first something romantic?

"Come and see," he says.

I guess it is. They get up.

"The cast list . . ."

"I won't be long."

"No. Just a second. We have to think about this." Which is a figure of speech; *I* have to think about this. They sit and finish off the retsina.

"After you show Alex, are you going to report it?"

"*Malista!*"

"To Stephanos?"

"*Oxi.* To the mayor. Vovo is him."

"Good."

"After, Stephanos."

"Ianni, listen. I think you should let the mayor report it to him."

"*I* find it!"

I seem to be asking Jason to keep the Golden Fleece to himself.

I look from Alex to Iannis. "I just think Stephanos might feel . . . bad . . . for his nephew, and you might be . . ."

"*Oxi, oxi. Dhen birazi.*"

"But I do *birazi*. Alex, you see my point."

"It's all Greek to me." She grins. "But I think your sense of drama is overwhelming you. It's not New York, after all—these people all know each other. Stephanos is bound to hear who found the car."

"*Dhen birazi, dhen birazi.*" Iannis has found his mantra.

"I won't be long," says Alex, repeating one of hers.

"Uh-huh." I cork the retsina bottle and wonder for a moment why I'm so compulsive that I even close empty things. "If you happen to see Evdhomada . . ."

"Who?"

"The wet music teacher from Selini, or Arabella-*legsa*. Please ask them to come over."

It's all one is running through my head as I work on the article. How did Shakespeare know that? Maybe I should drop this obscure piece and go for gold with "The Bard Meets Maharishi" or "What Can William Tell Us?" But there are probably a dozen PhDs out there who owe their assistant professorships to this revelation. I'm thinking along these lines when Theo calls up to me. My horoscope would show it's a day of entrances and interruptions.

From the terrace I watch four people, puppets from this view—bobbing heads, loose limbs, shortened torsos—filing through the doorway. I go back and cover the computer in case Tula comes in and feels like cleaning up.

Theo has brought Costas, the island's best carpenter, Foti, the baker's son, and a beautiful unknown. "Tina will love your coffee." He introduces the henna-haired slinky-built forty-something woman in DKNY sweats. Our Miranda? Where did she get her Princess Di haircut? "She's a designer from Athens. Her house is just behind the *platia*. Every year she makes the costumes."

Not Miranda.

"Theo tells me you're a producer from London," says tiny Tina, taking off her Hermès backpack. "I go every winter to see the shows."

"You're not from the States? You speak perfect American," I say as I put on the kettle and break out the French roast. Pretty as Tina is, Theo only has eyes for my measuring spoon.

"I lived in Daytona Beach for many years. But since my divorce, I'm back in Athens."

"Costas is building your set," Theo announces triumphantly.

"Really? Are you sure you can do this?" I know at least four people waiting for their windows and doors and a lot more who would shoot him if they weren't related.

"For you, Sarah, anything," says Costas. Talk about a mantra.

"That's great, Costi! Your work is beautiful. But can you do it on time? We can't wait; it's not like a house. We fix a date . . . we put up posters . . ."

"Yes yes, *dhen birazi,*" says Costas.

"And Foti is your getter."

"Gofer." I smile.

"Yes," says Theo. "He can fix everything."

"Theo, this is terrific, really." I start brewing. What a guy, if you're in the market.

We move over to the table. I bring cups and a plate of *kourambyedhes* fresh from Foti's mom's bakery. The guys dig in. Not Tina, who probably celebrates her birthday with a candle on a meringue.

Costas—thirtyish, ropey forearms, blond leonine head, bleached blue eyes—is a girl's fantasy carpenter; especially if you picture him working on your house for life. Which you should.

"Costi, have you ever built a set before?"

"No, only flat . . ." He indicates with his hand.

"Platform, that's right. Theo, you told me."

"But no problem," Costas says, smiling. "You draw for me."

"Ahh . . . OK." I hadn't thought of that. When is Copper arriving?

"This is great coffee," says Tina, drinking it black, *malista.* "I've never tasted anything this good on Pharos."

"I bring it from London," I say abruptly. I'm nervous sitting here sipping with Costas when people all over the island are camping in their building sites.

"I have to go." Theo gets up. Is he reading my mind? "But you stay. I want to check up on Christodolous." He isn't.

"Sarah, she saved him," says Costas, taking another cookie.

"Did you? Oh please tell me," says Size 4.

When the cookies run out and Tina has emptied the pot, I figure I can suggest other ways to spend what's left of the day. "Where can I get a basket for my motorbike?"

"I've seen some behind Dmitri's vegetable shop," says Foti.

"Great." I rise. "I've got to go to town anyway."

"There's one in my chicken yard," says Costas, also rising. "I'll get it."

"No thanks, Costi."

"*Ti*—what?" asks the carpenter. Have those buzz saws made him deaf?

"No thanks." I raise the volume.

"Why not, *Saraki?*"

"Ah . . ." Shall I be candid? It's the quickest. "From your chicken yard?" Pinching my nose and wrinkling my face.

"*Kalimera!*" cries Arabella from the door. Must be five planets in entrances. We all twist to look. "Oh, *cara*, I'm so sorry I couldn't come last night. "The heel broke off my shoe."

"That's a shame." Tina, being Greek, recognizes tragedy. "And there's no shoemaker on the island."

"Something broke? I fix." Costas's aquamarine eyes have locked on Arabella's short shorts. Those windows and doors are winging into the next century.

"Oh *thank* you. Theo isn't it?"

"No, that's a Costas," I say.

"Costas . . ." She's almost overcome. "Thank you, Costas. Shall I go get it?"

I get up. "I really have to go to town." The Ugly American, what the hell.

"But Alex said you want me. There are some parts left?"

"Come to my shop with the shoe," says Costas. "Sarah, you too, with the basket, I put on for you."

"Arabella, you'd better get it right now. Costas is very busy." No lightning strikes. Well, he should be busy; maybe God allows for that. "We can talk about the play tomorrow." I start down the stairs. In another minute Theo's going to return and *adio del'oggi*.

22

A fog drifts in at sunrise, shrouding the fields and hillside houses below us, the circling sea, even the distant coast of Turkey. I'm alone in the world except for the monk whose window in the monastery atop Kastro is always lit. I imagine he's been sitting at his desk since the fourteenth century and nothing has changed but his light source. No family ties, no telegrams, no flourless chocolate cake to distract him. He'll have read thousands of books by now. Unless Tula cleans there.

The salt air is trapped and settles over me; the perfect atmosphere to contemplate mantras. But I have a date with Tina to discuss costumes. The lack of a phone makes me deceptively reliable.

I fall in behind the garbage donkeys tapping their way up the lane without their master. Is Pendis lost in the fog? Turned into a donkey himself?

Eventually we pass the basket weaver's door, and I see Pendis having a coffee with old Antipas, the basket weaver. Antipas has turned into a bundle of reeds, but Pendis is still in human form.

"*Kalimera, kyrios.*"

"*Kalimera, Sarahki,*" they reply. "*Thelis café?*"

"I'm so sorry I can't," I say sincerely. Drinking and talking with an old basket weaver and his lifelong friend, the donkey-driving garbage collector, is after all why I'm here.

But now my mind is running ahead to its next appointment. Tina greets me at her door wearing a gossamer djellaba the colors of sunset.

"Wouldn't Miranda—Prospero's daughter—look great in that?"

"That's just what I thought," says Tina. "I've been re-reading *The Tempest.* Too bad she's the only female part; my costume department has so much great stuff for women. Can't we change the plot? Maybe the ship that gets wrecked on Arcadia is coming from Delphi and is full of priestesses?"

"Sure. And Prospero retires to a monastery and Caliban is left to destroy Western civilization."

"OK," she shrugs, "that *is* a small problem. But if Prospero redeems everybody, why is it still a man's world?"

"Shakespeare was still a guy, wasn't he?"

"*Sosto.* I've made fresh orange juice since I can't compete with your coffee."

"That's fine. I've had enough caffeine."

We walk through her blossom-laden courtyard into a grotto living space sparsely furnished with antiques and littered with ancient sculpture and amphorae, each in its own niche beneath a skylight.

"I collect Hellenic and Etruscan. These simple island houses are the perfect setting, don't you think?"

"I do. Maybe because they belong here."

"Exactly." We sit on a carved fruitwood Venetian bench beneath an orange bougainvillea that's growing through a skylight.

"But I didn't realize these things could still be bought by private collectors."

"Well, they've become very expensive, of course, but there's still so much being excavated. I travel to Turkey quite often; the Greek ruins are just incredible. I suppose you've seen them."

"I haven't. I was planning a trip with Alex this summer but then the play came up. In fact something always comes up."

"You really must see Aphrodisias and Miletus and the villages along the coast."

"Next year, *insh'allah*."—God willing.

"*Insh'allah*? They've existed for three thousand years." She laughs.

"I meant me."

"Ah . . . well then." She lifts her orange juice. "*Stin yiasou*—to your health."

"And to yours. Thanks so much for helping out."

"Shall we go to my desk? I've got some photos to show you."

Tina's a pro; she's had her office ship her an edition of *The Tempest* illustrated with sets and costumes from several London productions. We dive into period and characters. I've decided to set the story in Crete. Most present-day Pharians are descended from nineteenth-century Cretans, and the women still have trunks of clothes from those times. As for the Italians shipwrecked on Arcadia, we'll need a few ruffled shirts. They wore black trousers then, black trousers now. Most of the men here still have mustaches.

Tina likes the idea. "Just tell them to let their hair grow. If it weren't for my Athenian friends in their Calvin Klein T-shirts and Nikes, this place could fit snugly in a time capsule. Except for the catsup."

Her *friends*? Has she forgotten her own closet? But why antagonize a collaborator.

"Shoes?" I ask. "That's always the dead giveaway in these amateur productions."

"I'll see what's in the wardrobe from *Il Trovatore*."

She quickly sketches the few things she won't be able to find.

"I'll get a couple of local women to make these as soon as you send me your actors."

"Terrific. Thanks, Tina." Never judge a person by her designer labels.

"No problem. This'll be a lot easier than *Hello, Dolly!*"

"Was Stephanos in that?"

"Oh yes. And he was terrible, but he was the only one who never forgot his lines."

"Then I'll make him the prompter. Jerry Herman's one thing . . . I just can't massacre Shakespeare."

"But Stephanos . . . you love coming here. It wouldn't be good to alienate the police chief."

"How about prompter with a walk-on. And a great costume."

"I doubt that'll work. But you're thinking like a Greek."

The small triangles of light falling on her amphorae have shifted ninety degrees before we're interrupted. A slight older woman with white hair pulled back and deep dancing eyes comes in—softly, I note—with a platter of zucchini, baby artichokes, and deep-fried kalamari.

"I hope you'll stay for lunch; my cook's prepared something very simple. Lukia, this is *Kyria* Sarah."

"*Harika,*" we overlap.

She leaves without knocking anything over, and I realize Tula has me trained for destruction. We eat in silence. Lukia's food is sublime. I begin to feel the mystery of Tina's tiny figure overrunning the other mysteries in my mind.

"The kalamari were light and not the least bit greasy; and the artichokes must have been grilled in truffle oil."

"Do I want to hear this?" says Alex. "Couldn't you have slipped a few in your purse?"

"What purse?"

"I don't want to hear this."

"Yes you do. It proves there's such a thing as Greek cuisine. And not just the zucchini fritters, Alex, even the *pitas* melted . . . she must make her own filo."

"Stop torturing me. I'm gaining weight and I wasn't there."

"You'll come to the next meeting. Let's look over this cast list."

We spread out our audition notes.

"Yours are better than mine. These doodles aren't that helpful. Though this drawing of Stephano's chins . . ." I hold it up for her.

Alex takes my page and puts it next to hers. "OK, I've counted nine main characters. Prospero the exiled duke of Milan; his daughter Miranda; his sidekick Ariel; his servant Caliban. They're all on the island. Then the guys from the shipwreck. There's Prospero's brother Antonio, Alonso the king of Naples, his son Ferdinand, his butler, and his jester . . . small parts, and . . . who is Sebastian?"

"The king's brother."

"So two brothers and no sisters. And seven other guys." Alex looks up. "D'you suppose Shakespeare was gay?"

"They're on a ship, Alex. It's a guy thing. OK, so we need some villains. Antonio and Sebastian plot to kill the king. Caliban tries to seduce Miranda and kill Prospero."

"It *is* a guy thing. Actually it sounds like the *Godfather.* Too bad we can't get Marlon Brando for Prospero."

"Or Houdini. Prospero's not just a duke, he's a magician. The whole play depends on his magical powers. It all takes place in a single day, you know."

"Later," Alex waves her pencil. "Priftis the butcher is Prospero, right? And Ariel is the fisherman's son."

"Right. Georgaki, without the hooks. I don't know about Caliban. Maybe we should steal Tino's cab . . ."

"Speaking of cabs, I think Manolis should play Antonio," Alex scribbles. "He's our best bad guy." She looks up from her list. "Best bad guy. That should be an Oscar category. Who else?"

"Sebastian, the king's brother. Let's give that to Stephanos."

"OK," Alex writes it down. "But he won't like not being king."

"Who does?" I grin at her.

But that pencil's like a prop. It's turned her into a serious person. "And who plays the king?"

"That's a problem. Gerasimos the postmaster—he who reads Mississippi Williams. He looks right. He's tall, and he's got a strong voice. But it's a pretty big role."

"So what's the problem?"

"Gerasimo has a terrible memory. According to Nikos, they changed him from mailman to postmaster because he couldn't remember where anyone lived."

"You're kidding."

"Tula says he forgets to pick up his kids at school. The king has lots of lines."

"Stephanos remembers everything; maybe he could prompt him."

"Gerasimos hates him. Stephanos once sold him a lame donkey and wouldn't take her back. Gerasimos tied her outside Stephanos's house when she was in season."

"You really should forget this play and write one yourself."

"You're still sore about Lukia's kalamari."

"No I'm not," she says. "Let's have some retsina. It clears the mind."

"Of thought," I note.

She goes down the stairs and returns with wine and olives. It's dusk. We watch the caiques tied to their mother ships being towed out to the fishing grounds, a pair of lanterns hanging above their sterns to attract small fry. Just enough light on the sea to catch the reflection of their giddy hulls.

"These guys paint their boats so brightly," says Alex. "Why do they wear such gloomy clothes?"

"Modesty?" I venture.

"And their boats?"

"Pride?"

"Hmm. I think the retsina's working."

The big boats slip their lines and drop off the horizon as the light falls fast. No sound of the engines from this distance, nor any from the stars as they appear all at once, so close to the sea the nets could catch them.

"I'll give Gerasimos something to memorize, see if he can do it."

"Mary had a little lamb . . ."

"That's a good idea." I laugh. "His father was a shepherd."

"Yeah, but what was the king's father?"

"A king, I think."

"Ah . . . *Once more into the breach, dear friends.*"

"So let's stick to lambs." I say.

"Lambs. Mmm," she dreams. "Where shall we eat?"

"I told Petros and Monika we'd meet them at Octophdhi."

"Wasn't I sick there the last time?"

"Tino's wife is cooking there now."

"She is? Why? Wait! You're going to tell me the old cook died."

"Once more into the breach . . ."

23

"I love these fish places," says Monika. She's wearing a halo, the sun having bleached her blond hair river gold. Below that is a black-and-white Joffrey Ballet T-shirt tucked into black hipsters; the dancers are pas-de-deuxing over Monika's small unsupported breasts.

"*Ik ock*," says Petros the Conqueror. "That's Swedish for 'me too.'"

"But you must have the same thing in Sweden," says Alex, who's chosen the poor-fisherman-dangling-threads look tonight.

"Lots of places that serve fish, but they don't have this atmosphere. Even the outside cafés there are all . . ." Monika makes a sour face that does nothing to dim the voltage. ". . . modern."

"Dmitri thinks *this* is modern," says Petros, raising his arm off the back of her chair, "covering the lights with fishnets."

"Mykonos fifteen years ago," I recall.

"Do you think Pharos will be spoiled?" Monika addresses this directly to me. My ego does a little somersault; my heartbeat picks up. I know not to look at Alex.

"No," Petros answers for me, "no airport, no discos."

"No movie theaters," says Alex. Monika is still looking at me.

"No music," I say. A deep breath restores my balance.

"Music? You like music? We have." Dmitri has appeared with his order pad. "Tomas has coffee, then he plays."

"Great!" we say.

We're in luck. Tomas the shipwright is a terrific fiddler, and his younger brother Takis plays wizard bouzouki.

"*Thavmasia,* Dmitri *mou,* let me get the first round." Petros must be head over heels.

"You eat something?" asks Dmitri.

"Oh yes." He spreads his arms. "*Octopodhi* everyone?"

"Not for me, thanks," I say. "I'll have *tsipoura.*"

"And I'd like kalamari," says Alex.

"Me too," says Monika in English.

Petros contracts slightly. "But the specialty is *octopodhi*..." He looks from face to determined face. "Well, I'll have it. And a pitcher of your house white."

Except Dmitri's house white will take baked-on bugs off your windshield.

"Dmitri," I say, arresting him, "let's have a bottle of the Malamatina retsina too."

"Good evening, Doctor." Dmitri turns to Theo, who has appeared suddenly, like a cruise missile.

"I've just come from the hospital," he tells me. "Is it OK?" Indicating our table.

"Of course," I say. The others are already making space.

He moves in between Alex and me. When he takes off his jacket his tight black T-shirt reveals taut biceps. I've never seen Theo in short sleeves and now I'm wondering what the rest of his body looks like.

"How are you, Sarah?" His voice is soft and intimate.

"Fine," I say brightly, hoping to define the mood.

"You finish the casting?"

"Almost. We've still don't have a Caliban, or a Miranda."

"Why don't you play her yourself?"

"Myself?" I laugh. Which catches everyone's attention.

"Seriously," he says, his eyes now plainly adoring.

"Because Miranda is about seventeen, Theo."

"*Yasoo*, Sarah!" The postman slaps a letter on the table.

"What's up, Ianni?" Though erratic, Iannis's deliveries are usually made in daylight.

"Sorry, *Saraki*," says Iannis, smiling. "I lose a few days."

"Who's it from?" asks Alex.

"Copper." I squint. The postmark is fuzzy.

Iannis hovers. "I am in your play, yes?"

I look up at him. "Yes, Ianni." I tear open the envelope. "He's not coming . . . new gig . . . new girl . . . blah blah blah."

"Bad news?" Iannis seems to be joining us.

"Not really," I tell him. But it is.

"Good thing you've got Tina." Alex is on the same track. "I'll bet he heard about the little planes."

Iannis's wife Maria, who's come as a jelly doughnut—a short white polyester dress with big red circles on the hips—is pulling her Chihuahua along the ground. I see Dmitri, in the distance, planning an alternative route to our table.

"You are the boatswain, Ianni; a very big part in the beginning of the play. The ship's in a terrible storm. You curse at the king's men and order them below. Then you can go and have dinner." I smile up at him. "We don't see you again till the very last scene."

"*Ella*." Maria is pulling him by the arm. The dog has a trouser leg.

"*Ena leptaki* . . . boat sway . . . ?" he asks.

"Ianni!" she shouts.

"*Malacca!*" He slaps at the dog, which dodges easily. "*Efharisto, Saraki!*" Exeunt.

Dmitri brings a collection of *mezedes* with the retsina and we dig in.

"What's a *leptaki*?" Monika wants to know.

"A fraction of a second," says Petros, tapping the back of her hand. She looks at him quizzically.

"An interesting word for Iannis to use," I say, "a man with no sense of time . . ." I inspect the envelope more closely: "God, it's more than a week old."

"Ahem . . . ," says Alex, "you'd be the very *last* person to accuse . . ."

"OK, OK . . ." I wave her off the case.

"A week old? Isn't he the postman?" Monika asks. She's new here, and from the north.

"He is," I say.

"You've heard of the Peter Principle?" says Alex.

Monika shakes her head.

"The what principle?" Petros says.

"It's a theory that describes why nothing works very well," she says. "The idea is that when people are good at their jobs, they get promoted. Till they finally rise to their level of incompetence. And that's where they stay. So no one's really good at what they do."

"The author's name was Peter something," I add, turning to Petros, "so think of it as the Petros Principle." Theo, who has caught up, is scowling. Petros looks pretty miserable too. Sometimes irony doesn't leap the cultural divide.

"It's just an amusing idea," I say. "If it were always true we'd never have walked on the moon."

"Right," says Theo as Petros nods.

"Why are we walking on the moon?" says Alex.

Tino's wife has made fresh *tarama*, and the feta is soft and sweet.

"Let's get some more *tarama* and pita," I say.

"Even the retsina's good," says Alex, dropping the moon. "Can't we give up and come here every night?"

"I've got another tour for you tomorrow morning," says Petros. "A bunch of Americans off a private yacht."

"Morning? What time?" Her second assignment and she's already negotiating.

"Eleven."

"Perfect."

"And don't worry too much about the facts."

This is a smitten man.

Many carafes later we're still waiting for Tomas to play. I get up to use the bathroom. Monika follows me in. She's putting on lip gloss when I come out to the sink. I'm expecting her to ask me something about Petros.

"Are you and Alex a couple?"

"No."

"You and the doctor?"

"Theo? No."

She turns to look at me. "You and anybody?"

It's a very small space we're standing in. I have no trouble feeling the heat.

"No one."

She has no trouble kissing me.

Whatever was left of Julian dissolves in her arms. Neither of us speaks for a while. We're going to be gone too long—this much time I can tell.

Then there's Alex, who's always the first to know what's happening. A violin starts to play. Really.

"Let's go," I say. Now I know what *tearing yourself away* means.

"Just a minute." She puts on more lip gloss and takes some off me. My heart is making the same racket as when I eat chocolate late at night. She takes my hand.

"Later," I say softly as I drop hers.

Music loud and giddy. Tomas and Takis are rocking back on their flimsy chairs, people are shoving their tables away to make room for dancing. Monika gives me a little push from behind as we wind through the action. You'd think it was a hot embrace for the effect it has. The trouble is I blush easily. Our friends look up as we arrive. Petros and Alex, and Theo, John the Baptist, Arabella, and Aldo '98 at the next table. All drawn by the fiddler. All as flushed as I.

24

"I'll lose my job." Flatly, from the praying mantis at second breakfast.

I've devoted my morning's meditation to rehearsing my news—this being the first woman in my life since Alex. I'm prepared for a display of emotion: confusion, anger, latent jealousy; prepared to be gentle and compassionate.

"Don't be ridiculous," I say.

"Petros will blame me."

"No he won't. If anything he'll blame me. He'll think I was chasing her, which I certainly was not. I don't have time for this."

"Oh please . . . time?"

I dribble some honey on my yogurt.

"And what's wrong with Theo?" she demands. "I thought something was beginning to happen there. Those eyes, the black T-shirt . . ." She's looking for help and boy would I like to oblige. Being with a guy makes life so much simpler. And a doctor! Speaks in the present tense only, but I can see my family overlooking that. So he didn't go to Harvard. Neither did Hippocrates.

"I admit something was shifting. And I'm not rejecting him, but then Monika . . ." I spread my arms. *"I can't tell you why . . . ,"* I sing, right on key with the Eagles.

"Smart, original, artistic, nautical," she helps. "Body by Dance France. More or less perfect for you."

"Nautical?" I say, dropping my guard.

"Her father owns a shipyard in Malmö. According to Petros."

She *is* perfect for me.

"We're old friends, I'll talk to him. But I think you're wrong. It's Monika and I he'll be mad at. And maybe not . . . it'd be much worse if she left him for another guy."

"It's Monika and *me* . . ."

Thank you, Lord, for making her a Virgo. I can pause to think.

"He'll probably laugh it off, Alex. He's got a great sense of humor. It's almost as big as his ego. Think about it. Petros can't afford to take this seriously."

"That's true." She looks at me from what feels like neutral territory. "Are *you* taking this seriously?"

"Too soon to tell."

She nods.

"I'll make you an omelette . . . " I offer. "If you've got time before your tour." Will the truce hold?

"Not too runny and don't burn it."

I skip down the stairs. We've just crossed a bridge—one of those tricky high-altitude swinging kind. But we're out of cheese.

"We're out of cheese! Be right back!" As I leave I drop a bit of toast at the base of the jasmine where Diana usually hangs out.

Whom should I meet at the store? But probably she always shops at this hour. On seeing me, all the parts light up not naturally lit. I notice the actress's habit of moving her eyes first, then her head.

"Hi. How are you?" She's putting eggs in a torn-off fragment of egg carton.

"*Yasoo,* Monika."

I open the door to the yogurt fridge. "*Kalimera,* Maria. I'll have five hundred grams of *gravura*—Greek Parmesan—please."

"*Entaxi.*" Maria, behind the counter, sees two girls stocking up on dairy.

"Don't you work in the morning?" Mischief is rearranging Monika's eyes and mouth.

"Yes, but I ran out of cheese in the middle of an omelette."

"Ah . . . you're a cook," she says, smiling for the dress circle. I'm sure there's a mantra for this situation if only I could think.

"Not really." It's too soon to lie.

"Four hundred drachma," Maria addresses me. Monika was here first, but I'm the old customer. This iron protocol usually works against me since almost everyone else in Kastro has been here forever.

"Can we meet later?" says Monika, no longer shopping. "Maybe you'll take me to your beach?"

"I don't know where you're staying," I say, no longer working on my article.

"Behind the bicycle shop. But I'll meet you at your boat. Just say when."

"I've got a few errands in town. How about two thirty?" How did we get here from the cheese?

"Great."

"I'm tied up next to the . . ."

"I know where."

She knows where I'm tied up. *Ham sa, ham sa . . .* finally kicks in. "Good."

"Do you want anything else?" Maria hands me the packet of cheese.

"No thanks, Maria."

"See you later," says the Malmö heiress.

Alex finishes her omelette. She chews deliberately—all that remains of a long (translation: unbelievably tedious) macrobiotic side trip. It's now too warm to sit on the open terrace, so we're down in the courtyard where the bougainvillea weaves through a bamboo canopy, shading the table. Diana's devoured the toast and she's washing up in the stone sink. A flowering jasmine branch floats beside her. It would be great to have Monika sketch that.

"I ran into Monika at the grocery store. Funny isn't it?"

"*Small and funny and fine,*" she sings. (Barbra does it better, but she'd kill for Alex's nose.)

"But what does your Christian Science friend say?" she adds as she gets up. "There are no accidents in God's kingdom."

"Not *my* friend. That's the ski instructor you picked up at Alta." Not a deliberate attempt to change the subject; I just hate adding any more confusion to my database.

"It's not that I disagree with that philosophy," she says. The subject *has* changed. "I just don't see how a skiing instructor can believe it."

"Maybe it makes him feel better as he goes along collecting pieces of his clients."

"That's it, of course." She takes my plate and messes my curls. "I really don't mind about Monika if you don't mind about Iannis."

"Mind what about Iannis?"

She flings me the Nurse Ellen smile as she turns away.

"Just be sure you're protected; and remember he's Greek," I deliver a little too loudly, given our location.

"Meaning?" from the kitchen.

"The opposite of Swedish when it comes to possessive."

"Oh yeah?" She returns for the glasses. "I'll bet he's got fewer designs on me than Miss Ocean Blue's got on you. Da . . . da . . . dada da da." She scoops up two glasses of crisp bougainvillea and pours them over my head.

"Out of the question," I say, picking petals out of my hair.

"Then as my granddaddy would say, they're both fishing with a straight hook."

"Would that be your granddaddy the fishing neurosurgeon?"

"No, that's my granddaddy the fishing Chevy dealer. Which reminds me, what time's my American tour? Oh God! Petros'll kill me."

Which is where we came in . . . She picks up her bag and her sandals and flees. I stare at the door thinking of a better way to have started that conversation. Then a much better way. Why didn't I pause after her provocative opening, say the mantra a couple of times?—that's what it's for. Because I forgot it. Maybe I need a phrase a little closer to home than *Ham sa* for domestic quarrels of the twenty-first century. But what? And will *Yoga Journal* still be in print when the article's finished?

And then there's real life, which has just become a lot more complicated. I collect my windbreaker and stuff it in my boat bag. Tula will be coming any minute to drown the terrace; better to think all this over on dry land.

25

On the first bend of the road to town I'm stopped by a herd of goats ambling from one side to the other. The heat of the morning has stirred millions of cicadas, unseen in the tall fragrant eucalyptus trees that line the road. Their whirling racket mixes with the goat bells in a deafening collision of sound. Even the dust rising off the road seems loud. I shut off Ernie Banks's engine and let myself drop into the fierce cacophony. When the goats have passed and the dust settles, I walk among the trees collecting some spectacular gold and white and umber bark peelings that lie scattered beneath them. Maybe someday I'll write a poem good enough to copy onto the back of one.

I smash my ankle on Ernie Banks's kickstand as I'm parking in the town square. Stephanos as usual, is instantly at my side.

(How does he do it? I used to like turning dinner parties into metaphysical speculations on coincidence and destiny. Until Gina came to one of them. "His office overlooks the square.")

He puts his lawman's weight against the No Parking sign.

"How are you, *Saraki*?"

"Fine," I say, rubbing my ankle and cursing sublingually. Actually I'm in shock; that diminutive is not for the likes of Stephanos.

"And Shakespeare he's good?"

"Good, as far as I know." I hop back; Stephanos can turn fresh air rancid. "I want you to play Sebastian."

"*Ti?*"

"Sebastian. The king's brother."

"No king?" He comes off the sign, which continues to lean.

"This is an artistic decision, Stephano." As if I'm talking to James Agee. "It's the character, not the title, that's important. Sebastian is a strong man, and very important to the story."

"Big part?"

"Very big." As in, if you're going to lie, lie *big*.

"Strong." He glances down at his Goodyear belly. The idea appears to take hold. He leans back against the sign. Maybe that's why it's there.

"The first reading is Friday night; I hope you can come."

"*Malista.* You know I find Vovo?"

"*You* find Vovo? Volvo?"

"Yes, you know. Vovo of the mayor." His pats his pistol handle.

"That's great news, Stephano. See you Friday . . . must go." I hobble away.

John the Baptist can't be in jail because we saw him at Octopodhi last night. Maybe Alex persuaded him to handle it discreetly, leave an anonymous note for Stephanos. A miracle on a par with, say, renting a motorbike that has working turn signals. Unfortunately the subject slipped my mind at breakfast: Shakespeare, Monika—my two front burners are already occupied. I head for Nikos's café. "What's the story on the Volvo?" I ask as Nikos serves my *sketto*.

"Stephanos found it . . . right near his house."

"Hmm. Was he alone?"

Nikos sits hastily and leans across the table.

"You know about the mistress?" he says in a loud sotto voce.

His mistress? . . . John the Baptist in drag?

"No." And I don't want to.

"Popi the barber. But I don't think she was there . . . so close to the house! His wife Natalia lives on the porch. Your coffee . . ." He points. He knows I like it hot.

Popi the barber. Why no feminine noun for barber? Did all those ladies cut their own? I just can't picture Cleopatra—Greek, according to Barbara Tuchman—snipping over the sink. As for the mistress news, I guess Lucky Steve got all the gossip software. Plus this is dangerous info.

"Niko, you didn't tell me this. Seriously." He sits back, looks skyward, spreads his sycamore arms, looks back at me intently and pulls down the inside corner of his eye.

"Dhen birazi, koukla." Softer, "You know something about this?"

Here's where I line up with the great Buddhist masters, not to mention cowards of all persuasions. "Nothing."

"Niko!" comes from somewhere thirsty. He departs.

The coffee's cold, and I'm meeting Monika soon. I get up.

"Kalimera, Sarah!" Theo's sisters gently push me back into my chair.

"Kalimera sas," I reply, remembering the polite form, but not their names. This is the wrong end of town for caryatids.

"Kala, kala."

"I was just leaving." I smile apologetically. But it's a meaningless gesture in the Mediterranean.

"Your coffee," they sing.

"It's cold." Best I can do. They raise their arms to signal Nikos. I stand up between their teased capitals, which are touching—a spider would have no room to spin in there.

"Sisters, excuse me, I have to run."

"Ti?" They're shocked. Nobody has actually run in Greece since the last Marathon.

"Dhen birazi," I call back. "See you at the rehearsal Friday."

Monika takes off her water shoes, rolls her shorts up higher, and comes aboard without stepping on the side pontoon. She sits in the middle of the fishing bench and doesn't try to help me get under way. When I throw the painter to her, she coils it. A few minutes into our trip she stands up, strips to her bikini, and stows her stuff without losing her balance.

We slip into the silence of the morning. No sound but the engine as we glide along the coast. No shadows on the sea except for a fleeting patch of indigo when a solo cloud skims beneath the sun. I steer between barely submerged rocks, dodging shallow razor-edged reefs. Multicolored dry-stone walls run like hedgerows across the green hills still covered with wild sage and sunflowers. Their jagged tops are crowned with prickly twigs that keep goats and sheep from leaping into a neighbor's fields or tumbling down cliffs to the sea. Our reverie is suddenly broken by a riotous clanging of bells; a big herd of goats, chased by a dog, is racing over the nearest hillside. As we turn to look, the piercing whistle of an unseen goatherd stops the dog cold. An instant later the herd is scattered and quietly grazing. And we sailors are back in the present.

"This is the perfect boat for here, isn't it," Monika says. "Light, maneuverable, low maintenance."

"Exactly." I nod. Light, maneuverable, low maintenance—my heart's desires in a nutshell.

Keep it light, keep it light, I repeat silently as we sail on a blue diamond sea under a fresh-swept sky.

"Did you buy it here?"

"No. I brought it from France. Now everyone wants one."

"Why don't you import them?"

"Because I'm a writer." Too abrupt. "But it's a good idea. Maybe *you* should?"

She shakes her head and smiles without taking her eyes off me. "I'm a painter."

Our arrival at Sandsoon causes an uproar among the lunching pigeons. Monika keeps out of my way as I perform the anchoring dance, then mimics my rock technique as we spread out our stuff. Except that her towel is three inches thick with a gorgeous seashell print.

"Hermès?"

"Yes. I know it's more Saint-Tropez than Pharos, but I like it too much to leave it behind."

"Why should you? Reverse snobbery is my least favorite kind."

"What's 'reverse snobbery'?" she says as she takes off her bikini and stretches out.

"Well, what I mean is people who make a show of not making a show. Like rich people who talk about buying their clothes from a catalog. If you've got a beautiful, thick . . . "

". . . expensive."

". . . expensive towel, why lie on a rag?"

"Exactly. My uncle Anders smokes cheap stinky cigars and insists they're better than my father's Havanas. We open all the windows and freeze whenever he comes for dinner. And he wears horrible drip-dry shirts. 'Who needs linen,' he says, 'I just have to pay people to iron them.' My cousins are horrified." She begins applying sunblock. "I tell them not to worry; they'll inherit a lot more than I will."

"Is that true?" I lay my naked body on a faded stringy New York City Ballet towel.

"Well, sure, it must be. But I'd rather enjoy it now. I doubt they serve beluga in heaven."

"Good thing I didn't pack a picnic." I laugh at my own joke, a trait I detest. Her laughter's easier.

"That's OK; I don't usually eat lunch. And it looks like you don't either," she says, smiling.

"I tend to forget it. But I never skip chocolate. There's some in my sack when you need it. I'm going for a swim."

This is what Jung calls a diversionary activity. I mean, I'd go swimming anyway, but after I'd stretched out under the sun for a while. When I come dripping up the beach she's asleep with a hat over her face. I'm so relieved I could kiss her. Doesn't this prove I'm not relationship material? I take out my notebook and make some notes for Friday's reading. After the doodle of a sleeping beauty.

When she wakes up she just smiles and wades in. No comment about the water temperature, which isn't warm yet, or the slippery rocks just below the surface. I look up once to be sure she's a strong swimmer. And once more to confirm the Dance France body.

"What are you working on?" She's drying off. Drops of light are sparkling off her skin. There's no phosphorescence at noon so I must be in a transcendental stupor. Luckily I can still talk.

"The first reading is Friday. There are a few parts we haven't cast yet."

"Is that difficult?"

"Actually it's great fun—picturing all these people in other roles."

"Petros tells me it's your first time." Her towel rustles the wheat sheaves.

"It is." I put down pad and pencil. "But it's theirs too. These aren't actors playing kings and monsters; they're butchers and cabdrivers."

"And you know most of them."

"All of them. That's what's hard. I've discovered everyone thinks he can act."

Monika stops drying and cocks her head. "Because most people do, don't they?"

I've just been watching her. "Yes," my brain surfaces.

"For instance, you're acting at being a director."

I've been living in England a long time. This sort of frank observation was outlawed by Queen Victoria. I'm delightfully shocked that she's risking her neck.

"That I am. What do you think constitutes acting?"

"I meant being something you're not. But thinking about it now, you are really doing what you're doing, it's not a pretense, you're sincerely absorbed in it, so there's no deception in that."

A person who speaks in compound sentences is running on my inside track. "You're right in a way. I've been producing plays for years so I know something about directing. But I haven't studied it. I'm kind of imitating directors I've worked with."

"Nothing wrong with that. At the academy we learned to paint by reproducing the masters. I'm sorry if I sounded rude."

"You didn't sound rude. Would you like some wine?"

"Is it retsina?"

"I actually love it."

"You must have been Greek in another life."

"Yeah, that is the only plausible explanation." I pour from my thermos.

"I'll have some. Do you really believe that?" she asks, sitting closer.

"That there's no other excuse?"

"No, in reincarnation. Because I do, and most of my friends think I'm crazy." She's watching me to see if I'm in the friends' camp. Her eyes aren't just blue, they're dark New Mexico twilight blue.

"I believe in it passionately. I'm making plans now to come back as a dictionary. I was probably a white birch in the last life." She frowns, thinking I'm kidding her. I rush on. "Really, Monika. I'm serious."

"No you're not. A white birch?"

"Uh-huh. More retsina?" I ask because she's actually drinking it. She extends her glass.

"OK, why?"

"I figure I must have just stood around last time, being admired without doing much, just bending with the wind. So this time I can't stop moving and doing."

She rolls right next to me and puts her hand on my foot. I hadn't noticed it was wiggling.

"Do you think that's progress?"

The short heavy coughs of a diesel engine are followed by the appearance of a small fishing caique.

"Not necessarily." I draw my towel around me. "The only progress I care about is understanding my deepest self."

"But a dictionary?"

"Well, a rhyming dictionary. Poet is several lifetimes away."

The fisherman ties his stern line to a rock on shore and begins unfurling his net as he backs his caique away.

"Hmmm . . ." She wraps up too. "You should write about that."

"It's already been said perfectly by lots of people. Emerson, Shakespeare, Merton, Hafiz."

"OK," she says, smiling, "but Shakespeare didn't stop Merton and Emerson didn't stop . . . who's Hafiz? Maybe you're afraid of failure?"

I sit up straight. "No. I don't measure failure, or success, that way. It's not that important to finish a book. It is important not to want to swim out there and cut off his shore lines. Which I still do. So even rhyming dictionary is probably a hopeless dream."

26

"We get money from the government last year and buy these lights. You work them from the organ loft."

Theo is standing with Alex and me in the doorway of St. Christopher's, an ornate vaulted chapel that was defrocked many years ago and is now the island's theater, exhibition hall, court when the circuit judge comes to town. Early-morning light sends fingerlines of spinning dust beams from the clerestory to the tiled floor. A pantheon of gaunt Byzantines with flaking halos and sooty bits of iconography look down fiercely from their dim kingdom in the rafters. I see rows of dyspeptic theater critics.

"Can we get rid of them?" I ask Theo.

"Almost two hundred people can sit here," he says, ignoring my question. "Only a few behind pillars. Costas builds a platform this high"—he indicates—"so everyone can see."

"Costas built it? How did you manage that?"

"Father Stavros tells him it's quicker than saying ten thousand Our Fathers." He laughs. "Don't ask me how he earns them."

"Well, it's a great space, Theo," I say as he leads the way to the transept. "But where's your backstage? Or do people enter from outside?"

"Oh no, the nave is perfect for that; the curtain goes there . . . air . . . air . . ."

"What's that sound? . . . ound . . . ound . . ." Alex cocks her head.

"Well, there's a little . . . how do you call it? Once you move to the center . . . enter . . . enterrrr . . ."

"Echo! . . . o . . . o . . . o." Alex spins around, looking incredulous. I'm not too happy about it either.

"Theo," I whisper, "you play here with that noise?"

"Yes . . . sss . . . sss." He stops at the altar and raises his arms in a shrug. Good thing they took down the crucifix or he'd be perfectly lined up. "It's the best place we have."

Have doesn't echo, I notice.

"But . . ."

"*Signome, Saraki*, I must open my office. You pass by later."

"Ay . . . ay . . . ay . . . !" I cry after he's left, and the echo goes on and on.

"Oy . . . oy . . . oy!" declares Alex in sympathy, and to hear the wonderful results. "Is there a musical *Tempest*? Or how about Gilbert and Sullivan . . . ann . . . ann. *HMS Pinafore* . . . Isn't there a shipwreck in that . . . at . . . at?"

"We're doing a play full of words, Alexi *mou* . . . ooo . . . ooo. We have more than a shipwreck on our hands. *Guru om* . . . *uru om* . . . *u ru om* . . ." My first mantra does sound great in here. Plus I need divine help.

"So what happened with Miss Malmö yesterday . . . ay . . . ay?" Alex asks as I'm contemplating a singing Caliban.

"What!" I growl, with reverb.

"Sorry. I guess it was the mention of ships . . . ips . . . ips."

"Nothing happened," I whisper. I figure those guys in the vault have nothing better to do. "We swam, we read. A fisherman came along and set up at the tip of the cove. She liked *Dishy* and she has a great body."

"Like a Nicolson '42 . . . tytoo . . . tytoo . . . tytoo . . ."

"Yeah." My voice rises. "Without the wooden decks . . . ex . . . ex . . . ex . . ."

"And nothing happened . . . appened . . . appened . . . ?"

"Nothing." I walk back down the center aisle. "Please lower your voice."

"I don't see a confessional."

"The Greeks don't confess."

"No wonder you love it here!" We've reached the stone font at the back of the church. "You've never been baptized, have you?"

"This would be a great place to play the pastoral scenes. Plenty of space and no echo."

"You're changing the subject."

"No, I'm reintroducing it. We're discussing the play, remember? And anyway I don't like talking about personal things in a church."

"Really? But this isn't a church anymore."

"Only because St. Christopher was decommissioned. Which is crazy considering this is a country of travelers. What are you doing?" Alex has opened her water bottle and is pouring it into the font.

"I've always been worried about this. Suppose there *is* a hell; you'd end up there."

"Alex"—I assume the principal's voice—"stop pouring. You're not a priest. If there is a hell, it's you who could wind up there."

"Shhh. God could be listening. And he sure wouldn't have any trouble hearing us."

"Actually it's not God I'm worried about."

"That's exactly my point. You should be. The thing about your do-it-yourself yoga . . . in the name of the Father . . ." She's actually dipping in.

I back up.

"Don't move . . . the Son, and the Holy Ghost," she says in a rush. She lunges at my forehead and lands two wet fingers on my third eye. "Voilà!"

"What? I'm saved?" I say ungratefully.

27

Walking down to town the next day we see fresh flowers in the little roadside shrine to a truck driver who went over the cliff. It's perched on a hairpin bend above some loose boulders. As we're passing it the bus goes by and we step onto the rocks to make room. The bus driver recognizes me and nods as he takes his hands off the wheel to make three quick signs of the cross. Through dusty windows you can see everybody on the bus doing the same thing.

"Wow, that's dangerous," says Alex, stepping back on the road. "Why is he doing that?"

"The guy who was killed was his brother-in-law."

"Great. And now he's going to take all those people to visit him."

"That's probably why they're crossing themselves. But it's much worse in the late afternoon when the sun's setting in the sea—then he's totally blind."

"I've taken my last bus ride."

"Do you want to be buried?" Alex asks a little later. We're having the usual at Nikos's and the proximity of death is still fresh.

"I haven't decided; I used to think no, but whoever put those flowers there just had a vivid experience of their love for that guy."

"But buried? Taking up precious ground? How about a nice little roadside shrine on some steep curve in San Francisco?"

"That would do it. Remind me to rewrite my will."

"Also, I know you don't care, but I'm hugely relieved that you're baptized."

"But Alex, you're not a priest," I say as I check out the prophecy in the dregs at the bottom of my cup. "You're an actress . . . a tour guide . . . a fake priest . . ."

"Anyone can do it."

"Oh well, that's impressive."

"Hey." She's offended. She squints at me across her orange juice. "Isn't that democratic thing the whole point of your yoga practice? 'See God in each other,' 'God dwells within you as you.'"

I'm caught. "You've been reading my books." And a sore loser. I re-arrange the prophecy with my finger. "You're right, of course. "But heaven and hell . . . it just seems like superstition."

"It probably is," she says brightly. "And what exactly are you doing with your cup?"

Just as John the Baptist finds his prey. An amazing coincidence.

"Alex! Vovo is gone!"

"Again, Ianni?" I say. "Then there must be two."

"What?" says Mother Alex. I haven't had a chance to fill her in.

"What?" says Iannis, in what could be considered his life's refrain.

"I saw Stephanos and he told me *he* found it. The one you told us about at lunch the other day."

"But *I* show him where."

"Then how can it be gone, Ianni?" In this late sunlight, with his indigo blue eyes and grapevine shadows crossing his troubled brow, he belongs on a frieze.

"*I* find it!" His neck veins are filling.

"I believe you," I say.

"Me too. Absolutely," Alex says.

"Now is gone."

"What a busy car," I note.

Nikos is heading our way.

"Did you tell Vassilis?"

"Yes."

"Well, he probably moved it."

The penny drops with a deafening clang.

"What would you like, Ianni. Something else, *Saraki*?" Nikos asks. But we've all gone missing with the car.

"Ah!" says Iannis eventually. *"Dhio portokalades . . . ke mia Coke."*

"Sit, Ianni," I say compassionately. Soon after, I leave them, deep in fantasy about the mayor's reward.

Silence as I enter the bakery for a *kourambyes*. So I gather someone has died.

"Has someone died?" I ask softly, recognizing all three women at Maria's counter.

More silence. Very odd, I think. Meanwhile another bit of brain is struggling to surface.

"What would you like?" asks Maria, using the formal *you*. Have I done something?

Rejected Mirandas! shouts a cresting brain wave, and I try to suppress the triumphant look this revelation is bound to produce.

"One *kourambyes*, please."

As she's wrapping it, unnecessarily, I turn to them. "Thank you so much for coming to the audition. You were all so good; it's just a shame (*ti krima!*) that there's only one female part in the whole play." Their shoulders drop; they make sorry faces and murmur things. "My mistake. But I've decided we'll have a chorus. You should all come back to the church for rehearsal . . ."

"Yes, good, *entaxi*...," they say all together. They're already rehearsing. "How much, Maria?" She waves me off and I depart unwrapping.

On my way to the dock it occurs to me I'm no safer now that auditions are over. But, I tell myself, at least I've still got a butcher a baker and a cleaning lady.

Soapdish is waiting with restless pontoons. I'm just untying her when a fisherman puts his big dirty shoe on the bow pontoon. "*Kalimera, Kyria Sarah.*" As I'm reaching for the sponge. "My Georgaki is so happy." He takes off his cap. "*Efharisto para poli.*" I recognize the father of the boy in Theo's office; Ariel's dad. I reach out and take his hand.

"And me, I'm so happy to have him. He's wonderful. Thank you for bringing him."

"Nothing, *Saraki.* What a beautiful boat."

What dirty footprint?

"*Grigora dhen eine? Kai dhinato.*"

"Quick and strong," says Monika, appearing, as they say, from nowhere.

"*Kalimera, kyria.*"

"*Kalimera,*" she replies with barely an accent. And to me, "May I come aboard?"

"Do."

She takes off her shoes and the fisherman hands her in.

"We'll see you Friday night at eight," I tell him.

"*Kala. Adio,*" says Ariel's dad. "*I panghia mazi sou.*"

"You don't mind?" says Monika. "I know you work out here."

We're rounding the port seawall and I'm considering which beach will still be in sunlight. "No. I'm happy to see you," I say, as she can plainly see. "I will do some work, though."

"Good. I don't want to be in the way."

You don't? You do.

The shadows are long on Sandsoon, but in the tiny cove next to it, a half-moon of pebbles is still bright and burning beneath us. The other day nothing happened. But that can't be true. When finally we roll down into the sea our skins have been shed on the sand and a heart line cast.

28

"The funny thing is, the last thing the fisherman said was '*I panaghia mazi sou.*'"

"Which means?" Alex is on her elbows, propped up on her travel guide.

"May the Virgin be with you."

"And you thought I was?" Monika is in the hammock with a cup of coffee.

We all laugh. We're having second breakfast in the courtyard the next morning. There's a slight breeze, a treat this late in June, and bougainvillea blossoms are swirling on the tiles.

"Who wants more toast?" I ask.

"We all do," Alex says. And, as I head for the kitchen, "I may as well get fat."

"Would the Baptist like that?" I call from the door.

"Please stay in there till it's done," she replies, showing off our intimacy. But I don't mind. Must be this universal love I'm feeling. *Ham sa* is perfect for this state.

"She burns *everything*," I catch on the obliging wind. Not bridges, I tell myself. If your ex-lovers don't become your friends, you're dancing on a dark stage.

"This is really good coffee," says Monika as I refill our cups.

"Thanks. But you should know"—before Alex tells you—"that I used up all my cooking skills learning how to make it."

"Is that true?" Monika turns to Alex. Here's a neat domestic drama, with each character feeling her way into her new part. As for me, I can feel love like deep breaths flowing through my body.

"*Yasoo,* Sarah!"

"Now what?" says Alex, as conscious as I that a spell has been broken.

"*Kalimera,*" and Theo walks in. "*Signome,* it was open."

"*Dhen birazi.* Would you like some coffee?"

"Yes please. I like to talk about the actors. Now is OK?" he asks tentatively as he takes in the scene.

"Now is perfect."

We go up to the terrace, leaving Alex and Monika in the courtyard. When we finally come back down Alex is still reading but Miss Ocean Blue is gone. I see Theo to the street. He gives me a quick kiss but I'm too distracted to react. "*Na ta ksana pumay,*" till we meet again, I say as I close the door. And I head back into the courtyard.

"Where'd she go?"

Alex looks up from her book and shrugs.

"Did she say anything? When she'd be back?"

"No. 'Good-bye.'"

"Right."

Days pass without a sighting. I must have created that soap opera all on my own. An ache begins to invade the silences. *So what* is the mantra I adopt.

29

The street outside Theo's office is empty when Alex and I arrive for the first rehearsal. I thought there'd be a crowd waiting. Instead we're greeted by Theo arranging meatballs on a bandage tray and the caryatids pouring little cups of juice. It's a sort of rerun of audition day, which was a rerun of Theo's name day. I'm not sure how to handle this.

"You can't have Greeks without food," says Theo, seeing my discomfort. "Sophia and Elena want to stay and help, if you don't mind."

"Of course not," Alex jumps in. "We've got groupies," she whispers to me, "we're legit."

We put scripts on the folding chairs and I pin a rehearsal schedule next to the No Smoking sign. Then I move it. Nobody ever looks there. We wait. I drink some terrible juice and regret I didn't bring a thermos of retsina.

"Where is everyone, Theo?"

"*Dhen birazi.*"

They all arrive around eight thirty. If everyone shows up late, I must be early.

With the juice and the *mezedes* and the buzz of neighbors, the air isn't exactly charged with tension. Not like a West End rehearsal, more like my last production at Lincoln High. I try to adjust to the tempo.

What tempo? runs my inner voice.

"OK, everyone," I say at eight forty-five, "may we begin please. Those are scripts on the chairs."

"Ena lepto," says Stephanos stepping in front of me, *"to avtokinito tou dhimarchou . . ."* The Volvo is missing again and he wants to know if anyone has info leading to its re-disappearance. No one does. I offer to help him track it down tomorrow so we can begin rehearsing tonight.

"Entaxi."

I quickly assign parts. Only Stephanos complains; he still wants to be king.

"There's no atmosphere here at all," I complain softly to Alex.

"I brought some," she says. And she unscrews all the neon lights and puts on a tape of a howling wind.

"Excuse me, *Kyria* Sarah." Evdhomada the music teacher makes a breathless entrance. "Forgive me not to come to the *akro'asi* Wednesday; I could not find my shoes." She looked better wet, but anyone who has to search for her shoes has a reserved space in my heart.

"That's OK, we're just starting. Or, we *were* just starting. Would you all mind just waiting a few minutes while Evdhomada reads for me? There's plenty of . . ." I trail off. They've already gone back to the meatballs. Alex turns off the wind.

We go into Theo's examining room. All the chairs are outside, so she sits on the desk and Alex and I perch on his metal bed. All our legs are dangling, not the most energetic posture. I have a momentary vision of us dockside at Kima.

"Try this." I hand her Miranda's speech to Prospero in Act I. She starts out carefully, internally, but then her throat opens, her face assumes an unfamiliar expression, and she jumps down to the floor. The speech becomes her own.

"You're Miranda!" I shout when she finishes.

"Bravo," says Alex.

"Thavmasia!" says Theo.

"Our Miranda!" I introduce her to the waiting cocktail party . . . mouths and hands too full to applaud, they make encouraging noises.

"Before we begin, I'd like to go over the plot. I know you've all read it, but you probably concentrated on your own part. It helps to have a feeling for the whole thing."

"*Kala, ne, entaxi*—good, yes, OK.*" They turn to face me.

"It takes place in Italy. Prospero, that's Priftis, is the duke of Milan. His brother Antonio, our Manolis, decides to overthrow him."

"What means overthrow?" Stefanos asks.

"Get rid of him, become duke himself."

"Ah!" He makes a slicing gesture across his throat.

"Exactly. And Antonio gets Alonso, the king of Naples, played by Gerasimos here, to help him. They kidnap Prospero and his young daughter Miranda, put them on a raft, and leave them to die at sea." Several people gasp. Gerasimo turns to Priftis. "*Signome, Prifti,*" he says.

"But," I say brightly, "Prospero and Miranda survive. They wash up on an island . . . small and rocky . . . like Pharos. It's called Arcadia. Prospero's taken some special books with him. He studies them and becomes a powerful magician."

"Oooohhh," says Georgaki.

"More Sprite?" says Sophia.

"One day," I continue as she fills uplifted cups, "about twelve years later, King Alonso—along with his brother Sebastian . . ."

"*Prince* Sebastian!" Stephano roars.

"Correct. Prince Sebastian, and Antonio and the king's butler and his court jester, are on a ship passing by Arcadia. Prospero uses his miraculous powers to create a terrible storm."

"That's the tempest of the title," says Alex, passing out *tiropitas.*

"Their ship is wrecked. Everyone survives, except the king's son Ferdinand is missing and they all think he's drowned."

"But I'm not!" cries John the Baptist. "I find the girl!" He's read the play. Alex is working miracles of her own.

"I forgot to mention that Prospero and Miranda aren't alone on the island. There's a kind of monster called Caliban who's Prospero's slave. Of course that's Tino, who's meeting the ferry right now, and also

Prospero's magical assistant Ariel, our wonderful . . ." I look over at Georgaki, who's fallen asleep in Theo's lap. If I don't wrap this up soon, they'll all be asleep.

"OK. While they're all wandering around, Antonio—remember that's Prospero's evil brother—and Sebastian plot to kill the king. And Caliban decides to kill Prospero. All the plans fail because Prospero's got them under a spell. He torments them with demons and scary visions, then he forgives the bad guys, reforms the monster Caliban, and sets Ariel free. Miranda and Ferdinand, the king's son, fall in love and get married. Love triumphs. Prospero magically restores the ship so they can all go home. It's a very happy ending."

They're all looking at me intently. "Very hard to believe," says Manolis shaking his head. There's a general murmuring.

"Yes. Well, it's really an Elizabethan fairy tale about good and evil, love and redemption. And there are some very funny scenes that I haven't described, but you'll see. And the language is absolutely beautiful."

"*Ne ne, sosto . . .*" Yes, yes, true, they all smile and nod.

"So let's begin please."

By the time we've read through the shipwreck, I know we can't work here. Heart diagrams and eye charts and the strong smell of disinfectant are all wrong on a magic island. I take Theo aside, hoping not to insult him. "I think we need to rehearse where we're going to play it. Do you mind, Theo? Is St. Christopher's open?"

"Of course, Sarah, no problem. Let's go."

Act I—Scene 1

"Heigh, my hearts! Cheerily, cheerily, my hearts! Take in the topsail!"

Iannis the postman/boatswain opens the show. The wind is howling. He shouts to the crew to pull on their ropes.

"You mar our labour!" he yells to Manolis/Antonio, Prospero's brother. *"Keep your cabins. You do assist the storm!"*

The royal passengers—that is, the entire taxi department—curse the crew and go below. The storm rages, the ship goes down. It's an auspicious beginning.

Alex appears at my side. "Isn't that his mailbag he's wearing?"

"Be glad he keeps track of it."

The rehearsal zooms along. People stop eating. Maria Milos's Chihuahua doesn't bark. And except for constant *"signomes"* as actors reading scripts collide with one another, everyone stays in character. There's definitely a mystical atmosphere in the church. Talents vary widely, but I avoid looking up at the critics. You can tell they're speaking English, and Omiros keeps up a steady translation, so nobody's laughing at tragedy or crying at the jokes. Of course, I'm not sure how accurate he is, but everyone seems to think Shakespeare's a Greek, which is good enough for me. If it weren't for the echo, I'd be giddy.

When we finally stop, Alex and Theo and Iannis and I walk to Alpha, the *ouzeri* on the port. It's a place I love, not a scrap of plastic, except for the ashtrays. I catch myself hoping Monika will appear.

"The Volvo's missing again," Takis our waiter tells me the minute we sit down.

"Are you sure, Taki? Stefanos said something tonight but . . ." Is everything Swedish this hard to hold on to?

"Does anyone have a garage?" Alex asks Theo. "Maybe it's just been put away?"

"How about the rehearsal tonight?" I'm determined to move on.

"Isn't Evdhomada a great Miranda?" says Theo. "She's the music teacher, you know."

"Actually she's a deep-sea rescue squad," says Alex.

"Signome?"

She recounts the tale with Irish flair. I'm amazed he hasn't heard about it. Are there secrets on Pharos after all?

"And she's very pretty," he says, midway through our second round.

Is he already picturing a piano lesson? And isn't he speaking in iambic pentameter?

"We knew she was gutsy when she leaped off that dock." I hear myself raising her stock. "And here's to Manolis! The perfect snake!" I raise my glass.

"As anyone knows who rides in his cab," Theo contributes daringly.

"Where's Monika tonight?" He asks between rounds.

"Somewhere else," I reply.

We all fall silent, as if Prospero's woven a spell.

A few boats are strung out evenly on the horizon, their fishing lamps winking and disappearing in the waves. The rest of the fleet is tied up around us, fishermen on decks, curled in their jackets, sleeping among their nets.

We stay until the waterfront is empty and the taverna awnings are rolled up. Theo and the Baptist walk off, chatting softly. I hear the mantra "Volvo." Ernie Banks roars to life. As we wind up through the narrow streets a few people are still sitting in candlelit bars, jukebox tunes trickling into the shadows. If I were alone I'd be ducking in to explore the probability that Monika is with someone else. Alex, riding double, has her arms tightly around my waist. Her warmth invites me into the moment. I notice that *So what* isn't working that well.

30

"There's a cake here." Alex calls up to me from the courtyard. Tula's noisily watering the pots down there. I'm at my desk bringing the mantra article to a pithy if sudden conclusion.

(Do I only manage to finish something when I've started something else? Didn't I accuse Copper of that?)

"Stick it in the fridge please."

"And the woman holding it?"

Merde. "Be right there. Give her something to drink. Do we know her?" Another Miranda hopeful? I cover my computer with Tula-proofing and go down.

This tiny old woman holding Alex's hand isn't instantly familiar. She's wearing a long faded sunflower dress, like a field in bloom seen through a summer haze—with a blue scarf, also flowered, covering her gray hair. It occurs to me how rare it is to see a woman her age not in black, on account of the Greek mourning protocol. Her smile spills over her webbed face.

"*Kalimera, kori mou.*" Good day, my daughter. She beams over her apple juice.

"*Kalimera ygeia sas.*" Good day to you.

"*Eime i mitera tou Christodolou.*"

"Mother of Christodolous," I translate for Alex.

"*Kala.*" I wait for further clues, silently repeating *come on, come on*—the baggage-carousel mantra. Alex refills her glass. She looks down and I remember where I've seen her. She's one of the old women who sit on the low wall beside the school. Three or four or five of them, perched like ravens every afternoon, calling to passersby and gossiping the sun down. Their daughters cook the dinners now, their husbands have departed, for heaven or Astoria, and this is their precious retirement. I used to think they were sisters, their headscarves being identical. Until I shopped at the village store—Leonidas's brightly painted pickup that parks in the square on Saturday mornings—and discovered that he carries just one bolt of cloth. His Saturday mornings begin with "*Elate na dheite!* Come and see! Brooms, pots, dresses, canaries," blasting the neighborhood with an electrified bullhorn. "*Elate na thite!*" Just what Jesus called out in the fields of Palestine.

"*Dhoxe sto Theo,*" thanks to God, she crosses herself and I realize it's *that* Christodolous. "The helicopter took him to Kalymnos . . . the doctor fixed him . . . we're so happy . . . it's wonderful . . . you saved his life . . . *Kyria* Kassoula tells me you like cake."

"She's the mother of that fisherman we stuffed into the taxi," I inform Alex.

"It's a funeral cake?"

"He's thriving."

I tell her we're so happy too. I picture the schoolhouse wall and don't sit down. She asks how long I've been coming to Pharos. The morning is slipping away.

"Four years, thank you very much for the cake, excuse me but I have to go back to work." Tula, who stopped watering long ago to listen, is shocked at the brevity of this reply. She drops the hose and sits down beside her. A raven in training.

"*Kalimera,* Maria *mou.*"

Alex looks like she's going for more juice.

"Don't. Please. Let's leave them. Can I read you the article? *Adio, kyria. Efharisto poli.*" I start upstairs.

"You've finished it!?"

I ignore the feigned amazement. I really do care what she thinks.

"I've decided it's over. Will you please have a look?"

"*Malista.*"

"It's a triumph," Alex says, handing it back. "And I think you should give me a real mantra. *Gin and tonic* isn't that much help."

"You actually liked it," I say, impressed with her discernment. Of course "triumph" is over the top, but a convert is nothing to sneeze at.

"Yes! You've got a really good point about keeping the mind busy with positive ideas."

"Well, it's not that you actually want to keep the mind busy," I say, coming right off my high. "The idea is to replace all that constant chatter with a powerful phrase that induces a state of mindfulness."

"Yeah, I got that."

"You did," I say not altogether rhetorically.

"Uh-huh."

"You're trying to achieve a state of alertness that doesn't attach to passing thoughts or become distracted by your senses."

"Right. So let's can *gin and tonic.* It just makes me want a drink. But please, nothing in Sanskrit. There's a reason I was born in America."

"Alex, you've just read the article. I suggest lots of different mantras, and most of them are very simple. You should choose the ones that resonate with you. That's what the whole thing's about."

"Oh no, I want an all-purpose one. I have enough trouble choosing lipsticks."

Can a triumph be so misunderstood? Was the article a complete waste of May?

"OK," I say, letting compassion get the upper hand. "*Ham sa,* I am That. That's the best all-around mantra."

"I am that what?"

I reflect. Alex has Leo rising. The fire in her heart can't be extinguished. (Too bad I didn't think of exploring the astrology angle of mantra selection; I too could be lying on an Hermès towel.)

"That everything. It helps you to see that you're not really separate from anything, or anyone. You are everything," I say, spreading my arms wide. "And it flows very easily with your breath. You keep repeating it to yourself till you actually *have* that experience."

"That could take a while."

"Don't worry. There's no timetable for enlightenment." Pretty good. Did I make that up?

"Well, that's a relief."

"So why don't you try it? There are whole libraries written about it; it's been test-driven for thousands of years."

"I am That," Alex says thoughtfully. "As in that and that and that. I am everything."

"Yes!" I nod vigorously. As in *yes*, the article was useless.

"I like it! Thanks."

"Feel like coming to the beach with me? I want to get in a swim before rehearsal."

"Sure. Unless you're meeting up with Monika."

"Nope. I think she's long gone."

Which shows how tuned in I am. The missing Miss Malmö is sitting on the dock beside *Dishy*, dangling her legs in the sea. That romantic nonsense about the heart skipping a beat turns out to be scientific fact.

"I'll see you guys later," Alex says, idling her motorbike.

"No, wait," I say. "There's plenty of room for three."

"I'm not coming," says Monika. "I just wondered if we could meet up later."

"How about Alpha after the rehearsal?"

"Fine."

"Well, she's back," says Alex, once we're beached and lying on the sand. "Must be getting pretty serious."

"She's pretty, and serious, but we? Us? I'm never sure about that."

"About what?"

"We or us in that context."

"Mmm. It's nice to see you've got your priorities straight."

I roll over and look her in the eye.

"Is *anything* more important than grammar?"

"I am That," she says, beaming.

"Go to the head of the class," I say in my Indian accent.

"OK, you don't want to talk about it."

"What 'it'?"

"Wanna sing about it? You must've moved on from 'I Can't Tell You Why.'" Her affectionate tone invites me to drop my guard.

"I've definitely missed her."

"Mmm."

"And there are plenty of songs that cover these summer heat waves, if that's what it is. 'Breaking Up Is Hard to Do'? She's probably brushing me off; it's a lot easier to be monosexual."

"True. But what about 'I am That'? Don't you think she understands that?"

"It's not the same as practicing it."

31

We start rehearsing around eight thirty. It's a festive atmosphere. Prospero's wife has brought her notorious *tiropitas* (cheese pies), Stella's made rice pudding, and Peros, the waiter at La Venezia aka Vendetta, is passing around a box of apricots that must have gone out the back door of the taverna. The caryatids have set up a camp stove and the works for Greek coffee.

"I have a feeling this could get out of hand," I tell Alex.

"You do? Have you got a match? Let's light the candles. We've got the best restaurant on Pharos."

A problem arises with the first group scene; you can't really understand what anyone's saying. All that echo gave a spectacular effect to the shipwreck and lent a kind of otherworldliness to Prospero's opening soliloquy. But there's no way to set the intricate plot lines with all this loud crossover dialogue. I take Alex aside at the next coffee break.

"Can't hear a damn thing anyone's saying . . . aying . . . aying."

"Do you care? . . . air . . . air? The cast doesn't seem to."

"Of course not. To them it's a perfectly normal Greek conversation. But it matters to me. Thanks," I say to Elena, bearing a *metrio café*.

"Well, we could play it around the font," says Alex as we walk down the aisle. "It'd be crowded though."

"Sarah, *parte.*" Maria the baker has brought her son Foti, my gofer, and a tray of cookies.

"A murder conspiracy hatched around a holy bowl? I don't think so." The camp stove catches my eye. "But if we had a campfire in the font—you know, like the three witches in *Macbeth*..."

"That's a great idea," says Alex, chewing. "Could it get us kicked out of church?"

"Out of Greece," says the chief of police, wiping powdered sugar off his chins.

I collect the cast in the back pews, and that's where we rehearse for the rest of the evening. King Alonso aka Gerasimo, the postmaster who can't remember addresses, has memorized his lines. (Like T. S. Eliot, a late bloomer.) Evdhomada/Miranda gets the hiccups laughing at Kostis/Caliban. Actually we're all laughing at Caliban, which is wrong; Caliban's the bad guy. And Kostis, with his black eyebrows the size of hedgerows and his handlebar mustache, looks ferocious.

"What's he doing that's so funny?"

"I think he's lisping," Alex says. We've stopped for what West End unions would call a dinner break.

I listen intently during Caliban's next nasty exchange with Prospero. She's right. But is that a real speech defect or is Kostis creating his character? To be wrong would be unwise; public notary is the highest official in a thicket of bureaucracy. And then, mocking a handicap is bad karma; it practically guarantees a reincarnation as slime. I take Omiros behind the altar during an apricot break.

"It's him, he, his," he informs me.

"Good grief, why is everyone laughing at him?"

"They always do."

"Thank you, Omire."

"Everyone, listen please. I'm making a change in the cast. Kostis is so funny he must play Stephano. We will find another Caliban."

"Stephano? What means funny?" Columbo is at my side in a flash.

"*Vlakas*... fool," says Omiros, helpfully.

"*Oxi, oxi!*" I shout loudly enough to wake the icons. "Stephano is the king's butler. He tells great jokes, he's very clever. Translate *clever,* please, Omire."

"Not *vlakas.*" Stephanos glares, first at me, then all around the company. I decide he should have the last word.

"Places, everyone."

Monika comes by as we're wrapping up.

"I thought you might want to go somewhere to eat instead of meeting at the bar."

"Eat? After a dinner party?"

Alpha has a few small tables right on the beach, under the night sky.

The fishing boats' diesels are coughing distantly, the sound magnified by a drumhead sea. There are nets piled high against the seawall. I order the retsina I've been craving all night. It comes in a tin pitcher and has petroleum overtones.

"*Ik ock,*" says Monika. Takis departs. I wait for Monika to speak.

"How are you?"

"You disappeared," I say.

She looks away, out to sea. Not her usual style. We both watch a fisherman silently slip his caique off its mooring. Our drinks arrive. "I had to think about this. About you."

"What about me?"

"I've only been with men."

"Uh-huh." I sip my wine. "But that's not about me. Listen, I don't hold it against you. You're very broad-minded in other respects." I laugh—alone, so it dies quickly. "And what've you decided?"

"I haven't. It's a big issue. But I wanted to see you again."

"Ahh." I try to cover my disappointment.

"I don't really understand how you go back and forth," she says, "Julian, Alex . . ."

"That was a sequence," I say evenly. "Do you mean back and forth between men and women?"

"Sorry, yes."

I stop playing with my glass. "You love who you love. My heart doesn't notice anything else. It only knows that it's happy."

"And your brain doesn't interfere?"

I shake my head.

"It really doesn't?"

"Well, it notices all the usual things: beauty, intelligence . . . towels. But it doesn't get in the way. At least not until I notice something seriously wrong. Like he throws stones at cats. Or she thinks Sondheim's a town in Austria."

I sit back. *Guru om, guru om.* I haven't had to explain this for a while, maybe because in the theater world there's a very wide range of acceptable behavior. Whereas the Swedish shipbuilding business . . . Monika is leaning in. I suddenly wonder if she's listening or mentally drawing my face.

"But you know how unusual that is," she says softly, though it's just us and the moon.

"Not unique, though," I reply. "Shakespeare has a much simpler explanation: *It's all one.* The wise fool says it in *Twelfth Night*."

"Too profound for me," she says.

"I don't believe that."

We drink for a while in silence. Not really silence; there's a goat herd grazing on the hill just above the port and every bell rings out.

"But I've just realized there's no difference between *It's all one* and *I am That*," I finally say.

"What's 'I am That'?"

"A really useful mantra. I gave it to Alex today."

"Maybe you should give it to me?" She smiles. "Unless you know a better one . . ."

"Maybe I should burn my article. It's finished by the way."

"Is it? That's great. More time for fishing. But why would you burn it?"

"It's all about choosing different mantras and I end up giving everybody the same one."

"Hmm . . ." she smiles. "Why were you all sitting back there on the benches?"

I'm happy to change the subject. I haven't made my mind up either, though for different reasons. The alcohol and the moonlight pretty much guarantee that nothing will be solved tonight.

"There's a tremendous echo under the vault. It sounds like Shakespeare for magpies."

"Can you take out the pews and play back there?"

"No." She's an alto, I register; just one more ideal feature. "It's kind of tricky. The church is deconsecrated, but it's not entirely secular."

We listen to all the village church bells, cascading over one another, marking midnight.

"I wish I could cue those at the curtain—*Our revels now are ended.*"

The village bells are overrun by others on distant hills. Their peals are a long time fading.

"It's a beamed vault, isn't it?"

"Mmm." I'm drifting in her offshore eyes.

"How about some sort of baffles?" she says. "Something to contain the sound."

"What?" I land abruptly. "That's it! Blankets."

"Sailcloth."

"Yes!" I lean across and kiss her. "We'll rig the vault like a giant schooner."

The moon is nearly full. We drive down to the dock and sail away.

The gulls are sleeping when we pull into Sandsoon and anchor so quietly they don't fly off. In the bright starless night we trace each other's bodies. Many lightstarved places to discover. From time to time we slip into the water, then let the warm breeze dry us off. The sand still holds the day's heat and so do the cove's rocky walls. Moonlight turns our movements into shadow play. Just before daybreak we fall into the boat and skim along the coastline to the harbor. As she swings her gear ashore I lean across and touch her arm. "Take your time, Moni," I say. "In Shakespeare I trust."

32

"I'm going with you to Tina's." Alex comes into the kitchen dangling her sandals. Tula is banging around inside the house and Monika is painting on the terrace, which is where Alex just discovered her. "I see Miss Malmö's up there with her easel and paintbox."

"She says she always carries them on her motorbike." I empty a bag of French roast into the grinder.

"You believe that?" says Alex.

"What do you mean?"

"I *mean* that she knew she'd be spending the night."

"She paints; it's normal," I say abstractly. Is that the last bag? The possibility of running out of coffee puts everything else in its proper perspective.

"Oh yeah. And Yo-Yo Ma takes his cello fishing."

"You don't need to come. I'm just asking Tina if she can find some sailcloth."

"Oh no. You'll end up talking about the show and her cook will bring out zucchini blossoms in truffle oil and caviar finger sandwiches . . . Plus I want to see this paradise you describe."

I interrupt Monika to tell her our plan. The beach where we spent last night is taking startlingly evocative shape.

"Like it?" She doesn't look up.

"Mmm . . ." I'm impressed. Did I assume her painting was a hobby?

"I'm having a show in December," she says, reading me coolly.

Would I have made this mistake if she were, say, ordinary looking? Or a guy?

"Not in Malmö," I say, attempting to recover a tiny strip of land.

"*Oxi.*" She turns and smiles. "Stockholm."

"Sarah! You coming?"

"Just a sec! I hope you'll be here when I get back," I hear myself say.

"No other plans," she says, touching her brush to the canvas. My heart skips. But probably everything sounds romantic to a romantic.

I change into something my mother would like. Not that Tina reminds me of her . . . except that she's always chic and pressed, whereas island to me means anything that covers.

Tina loves the baffle idea.

"And it will make the church look so beautiful. The rafters are there, we'll hang them like sails. You are brilliant."

"Actually it was a friend's idea. She's a painter . . . and a shipbuilder, as a matter of fact."

"Her family are shipbuilders," Alex clarifies.

Lukia glides in with a tray of fresh orange juice and miniature almond croissants.

See? says Alex's triumphant smile.

The amphorae in the courtyard glow in the fractured morning light—so do our crystal glasses. Clusters of young grapes are crowding the vines on the bamboo awning, casting dimpled shadows on the blue tiles. Tina's reclining in another gossamer djellaba.

"I think I can get the material today," she says. "If you call me later, maybe we can put it up tonight. Get Maria's son Foti to help us, and

Omiros. And you have chosen the cast. Send them to me soon. Alexandra, you like these croissants. I'll have Lukia wrap some for you."

The cobblestones are warm beneath our bare feet as we stroll home. Thick white branches of night-blooming jasmine and prickly tendrils of blood-red bougainvillea spill over the whitewashed walls that line the narrow lanes.

"Maybe this is going to work out," I say to Alex.

"The play part or the Monika part?"

"It's all one, isn't it?"

"According to whom?"

"To Shakespeare of course."

"Don't patronize me, I'm your dialogue coach."

Monika's still there when we return. She's having a drink with John the Baptist and they seem to be conversing.

"He wants to take you fishing this afternoon. Apparently there's some special fish out there today."

"Much *melanouri*. We must go," says Iannis. He too shines in the morning sun. It's almost too bright up there on the terrace.

"I've got to collect some stuff for Tina."

"But that's your favorite fish. And shopping can't take long," says Alex. "It's Sunday. The shops will be closed all afternoon ... We *are* here on vacation."

"OK, let's meet at the café on Iannis's beach at three. Monika?"

"*Ik ock.*"

33

Stephanos shades me as I'm parking Ernie Banks.

"No here."

Enforcing the parking regulation? "I show you where. Follow."

He heaves himself into his police jeep and waves for me to follow. Could there be a new parking lot somewhere on Pharos? A field some sheep have rented to the municipality? We leave the village and drive along the coast road. Suddenly he turns into a field just above a small rocky cove, flinging an arm out to signal me over. He wouldn't molest his director, would he? Big deal; let him be king.

"There my house is." He indicates a big stone villa a few fields away. "There was Vovo."

"Ahh."

He stalks to a patch of brownish greasy grasses. We survey it together. I didn't spend my formative years as Nancy Drew to be outsmarted by a restless coupé.

"Let's track it." I also didn't spend them on Pharos, so I have no idea how to communicate this except by example. I walk around hunched over in concentration until I spot the matted tire tracks.

"Here."

"Bravo, Sarah *mou*." He unsnaps the cover of his holster. The treads lead us down a gentle slope and end at the cliff above the shore. We look down. It's in the water, tipped to one side, the hood just below the surface.

"Uuhhh," he gasps.

"Wow," says Nancy. It's a beautiful sight. The slightly undulating sea is distorting the windows and metal shapes into pliant tactile abstractions. From up here the perspectives are flattened and sizes askew. It looks like the toys I pushed around the kitchen floor before my cars had engines. Whoever let the hand brake off also left the front windows open. Now the myriad bright small fry of the Aegean are test-driving the mayor's wheels. They wriggle through the spokes of the old leather steering wheel, circle the accordion gearbox, and flash across the rearview mirror. There's a thin sandy beach swirling slowly on the deep front seats, already occupied by snails and starfish.

"*Ella.*" Stephanos—I hadn't missed him—is back, and kneeling on the ground over a rusty metal case.

"From the Volvo?" Maybe it's a tainted ballot box; he's *always* re-elected.

"From *my* car. My crime box." He begins littering the ground with keys bullets cookie wrappers handcuffs broken pens battered notepads. Finally he extracts a one-inch watercolor brush and a little tin of powder. "I dust for fingerprints," I think he's telling me. (Sadly this isn't in my phrase book.)

He gets up, and we stand side by side looking down into the crime scene. It glitters in the sunlight. Some yellow-and-black-striped angelfish are tapping their snouts on the mayor's dashboard. He stares hopelessly at his little brush.

"Not possible," I say sympathetically. *Not possible to* think *this way*, I don't say. He looks back down into the sea.

"We never know who steals," he moans.

"But we know who finds!" I exclaim.

"*Sosto!*" He claps his hands triumphantly.

I remember Alex, waiting for me at the café on Archos beach. It's after three, but that's not really a problem yet; solitude is not a planet in her solar system.

"Stephano, sorry. I'm late for something. See you at the rehearsal." And I run uphill to my bike.

"*Saraki*," he shouts after me. "*I* tell Vassilis."

"*Malista*." I salute.

34

"Pushed into the sea? An amphibious coupé with fish behind the wheel?" Alex loves it too. But miss me? Six hunky sailors have joined her table, unless it's the other way around. One of them gives me his chair.

"It's a beautiful sight, just below the surface. So silent and ephemeral. Even the starfish have moved in. I've decided I want to be buried at sea."

"Uh-huh. This is my friend Sarah," says Alex. "This is Andrew, Steve, Lucien, Kuo Chun . . . sorry I forget . . ." She's looking over my head. Last wishes can wait.

"Helmut," says the ruddy blond musclepack standing behind me. "What would you drink?"

"Retsina, thank you, Helmut." Does it come from *helmet?*

"They're off that stunning sportfisherman at the end of the pier."

"*Sweet Leilani,*" I say, reading off their chests.

"And they've invited us for a day trip tomorrow."

"Have to check the weather," I reply. "I think they're expecting the Meltemi at seven to eight Beaufort."

"No problem for us," says Helmut.

"Really?" says Alex. "Sarah's boat isn't safe when it's blowing that hard." She can kiss *Dishy*'s pontoons good-bye.

Of course they want to know what sort of boat I have, how long, and all the rest. I don't make a big deal out of it.

"Zodiacs are great," says Kue or Klu. "One of our tenders is a Zodiac."

"Yah. The Brits use 'em as lifeboats," Helmut chimes in. The back of my neck must be turning him on. I look up into his boy-blue eyes.

"Please sit down."

Our waiter appears with my retsina and another chair.

"Thank you for bringing your tour group here," he says to Alex. "That was the biggest woman I've seen in my life. Like this—" He spreads his arms to their limit. "Maybe pregnant?"

Alex shakes her head. "American."

"Or German." Helmut laughs. "Did she order beer?"

"I ordered retsina for all of them, just to taste it. They've been traveling around Greece for a week and none of them had tried it. Or anything else Greek, as far as I could tell. Except olives, which they said were too small."

"My God, did they drink it?" I picture Alex looking for a new job.

"A little."

"They hated it, yes?" says our waiter, who was there. "Everyone ordered something else."

"Well, yes. But I don't think they minded trying it. They just have to be bullied a little. Otherwise what's the point of going anywhere new?"

"Yes, yah, absolutely right," says the *Sweet Leilani* chorus. So Alex can always be a deckhand.

"How did they like the monastery," I ask, "and the old village? You did take them there?"

"They've already seen lots of churches and the women hate putting on those old skirts. But they all loved Kastro. I took them into some houses." *Ours*, says her bright grin.

"*Ella!*" Iannis is waving from his pier.

I see Monika up at the bow untying his forward lines. I get up.
So does Alex. "Sorry, guys. We have to go."
"What about tomorrow?" says Helmut.
Alex looks at me like she's actually asking.
"Our revels now are ended," I say with Priftis's accent.
"I guess not. Thanks, though."
"Tipota—nothing," says the waiter as I wave him over for our bill.

From the way I'm enjoying myself, you'd never know how much I dislike
fishing. Iannis has brought us to a turquoise cove off a deserted end of
the island. Golden Eleonora's falcons are nesting in the yellow cliffs, invisible except when they're flying. Then they circle and squawk about
our being there. Otherwise the only sounds are ours—singing, laughing,
quoting Shakespeare. Iannis has a little pile of dough balls on the deck
(*melanouri,* like *sargoss,* are attracted to bread), an ice locker for the
catch, and an ice bag full of retsina and beer. Once we anchor he starts
pouring.

"*These sweet thoughts do even refresh my labours,*" says Alex over and
over. Why don't you just leave him in his element, I'm thinking. And
what costume could improve his looks? I watch Monika play her line
over the side. Even this simple action is arrestingly graceful. Do I love
her the way I love my cat? I wish I had more time to explore this, but at
that moment Iannis shouts: *"Ella!"*

Suddenly the surface all around us is dancing with silver glittering
battalions. All our lines jump. Iannis swiftly brings his in, unhooks the
fish, and slaps it in the locker. We imitate him as best we can. Alex and
I, that is; Monika knows how to fish.

"*Grigora,* quickly!" he shouts, handing out bread balls. We bait and
cast, over and over. The locker fills up. Then they're gone.

We celebrate with retsina and my emergency chocolate. Monika produces a bag of cashews.

"Yum," says Alex to her new best friend.

I'm about to jump overboard for a swim when Iannis extends a godlike arm across the bow. Glistening lines of small fry are arching through the water ahead of another school of *melanouri*.

"Look! They come."

"Where shall we eat?" Alex asks. It's just after sunset, that pale vermilion light, when we tie up and step onto the dock. Iannis has his arm over her shoulder—in public. Doesn't she see her forehead flashing *engaged*?

"Eat? We're rehearsing in two hours."

She looks at me quizzically. "But we're not in the play."

"Alex, this isn't a play. It's a feast in four acts."

"Oh no. I want something substantial—don't you?" She turns to Monika, but Monika's laughing.

"You remember the cheese pies Priftis's wife made?" I say. "And it just gets better every night. We'll be lucky to get through the first act before dessert."

"*Sosto,*" says Iannis. "*Oi adelphes tou Theo psahnoun andres.*"

"What was that?" says Alex irritably. She can tell he's agreeing with me.

"Those caryatids are fishing for husbands," I explain. "And that's just part of the chorus. Tula's daughter Stella isn't married either and she makes great *dholmades*. Forget about dinner. Monika, can I shower at your place? And please come to the rehearsal. You could help us hang the sails."

When we rendezvous later, the church is buzzing.

"I didn't eat either," Alex whispers in my ear. She has Iannis in tow. Omiros is passing sails up to Foti on a ladder. Tina's kneeling on the floor on a pile of white cloth, cutting big squares. Next to her a tiny old lady in a flowered dress is sewing ropes along their edges. She smiles up at me. It's the mother of the risen Christodolous. I look around for cake.

"Thank you everyone. Have you been here long?" I say guiltily.

"*Dhen birazi, pedhi mou.*" Tina makes a dismissive gesture; the rest just carry on.

"I think you should move here," says Alex in a stage whisper .

Stephanos arrives with another ladder. Monika runs right to the top, a deckhand trimming sail.

The caryatids are setting up their coffee works on the altar. Also up there, a large ceramic bowl. It looks ceremonial, but it could be soup. Tula's daughter Stella has arrived with her famous stuffed vine leaves, just as Iannis predicted. And a cucumber salad.

"Mama . . . ama . . . ama." Foti waves to his mother from the top of his ladder as she walks in carrying a tray of zucchini fritters.

"Foti! Come down from there!" Behind her is Tino's wife with a box of plates. I look out and see the back seat of his taxi covered with boxes of glasses and silverware. Napkins are flying out the door. Theo arrives and starts laughing.

"Café Tempest!" he explains.

I feel a little heart throb.

(The sign of Pisces is two fish swimming in opposite directions. I'm just running true to type.)

He spots Tina working on the floor and bends over her.

"Making a sign? Stella's fresh *dholmades*?"

I explain the baffle plan.

"*Thavmasia!*" he says, shaking his head; it's the Byzantine mentality—yes and no at the same time.

Iannis takes Foti's place on the ladder. The church is quickly being transformed into a six-masted schooner. Another big benefit—those critics in the vault can no longer scowl on the proceedings.

Monika climbs down with a rope in her teeth. "Why don't we make a couple of sails that actually hang down from the rafters and flap around during the shipwreck?" This is what comes of being born into a sailing dynasty.

"That's a terrific idea, but we need a way to get rid of them."

"Well, we could tie ropes to the lower corners and run them through rings on the ceiling."

"Is that OK?" I turn to Theo.

"It's deconsecrated."

"Great." So I'm still not baptized.

Iannis and Monika keep rigging while everybody else eats *dholmades*.

Alex comes over to the pew where I'm making notes. She hands me a glass of retsina. "That *is* a great idea," she says, watching them work. "We've made very wise choices." And she pops an olive in my mouth.

The rehearsal goes smoothly, except for the burping in Act II, after the dinner break.

"The cucumber salad," says Alex.

"That's what happens if you start at eight thirty," says Theo.

"But if we start earlier they don't come; we tried that."

"*Sosto.*"

"I have a solution," says Alex. "We outlaw cucumber salad."

"And *gigantes*"—lima beans, says Tina.

"Call 'places,' Omire. Or we won't get to Act Three before dessert."

"No, wait," says Alex. "We don't have a Caliban."

I see Tino standing in the kitchen/nave talking to Elena. I pull a few curls rakishly over one eye and approach. "*Kalispera,* Tino. Please just read this for us so we can rehearse."

Act III—Scene 2

"The isle is full of noises, Sounds and sweet airs that give delight and hurt not." At first he just reads the lines, but gradually, little slithery gestures creep in. *"Sometimes a thousand twangling instruments Will hum about mine ears."* His posture changes, his face contorts. *"And sometimes voices That, if I then had wak'd after long sleep"*—his voice resonating in every niche—*"Will make me sleep again; and then, in dreaming"*—the rest of the cast has folded around him spellbound—*"The clouds methought would open and show riches Ready to drop upon me that . . ."*

"Ferry!" someone sticks his head in and shouts. It's around midnight. Caliban bolts for the door, leaving us breathless.

35

I run into Theo at the post office, where I'm mailing off my article. Now that I'm dispensing *Ham sa* at all hours in all situations, I realize it's entire premise is thinner than a communion wafer.

"You *finish* it?" says Theo. Is my sister-in-law Marjorie moving his lips?

"Yes."

"We celebrate!"

As we walk into Nikos's the regulars look up from their ouzos and backgammon to greet us. Nothing unusual about that. But as we sit down I can feel their eyes lingering on us. Nikos comes over to take our order. He's wearing a silly smile and humming.

"*Saraki*, what will you have?" Theo asks.

"*Café sketto*," Nikos answers for me.

"The same," says Theo, and Niko backs away. I look around and see that the guys behind newspapers aren't turning pages, nor is anybody snapping chips on their game boards. Theo is leaning toward me and the table is very small. It occurs to me we've never been alone together in public. They could be waiting for him to stick a tongue depressor in my mouth. But it looks more like they're waiting for a kiss. I stare down a few of them but nobody blinks. Obviously Greek mothers have skipped over this point of etiquette. Nikos, still humming and grinning, leaves our drinks on the table.

"How do you think it's going?" Theo asks.

"How what's going?" I demand.

"The play." He raises both hands to emphasize the obvious. I'm too relieved to speak. So whose idea was the kiss? You never know when your imagination's going to sneak up and hijack reality.

"Everything's fine except we still don't have a Caliban. And he's so important. Are you sure Tino never leaves his taxi?"

"Never." He sips his coffee.

"Not even for the star part?"

"I think no. When his daughter marries they have the party in his garage."

"OK, it's hopeless. Can you think of anyone else?"

"*Oxi.* So many more women like to play, too bad there's only one woman part," he says.

"Yes, I've been thinking the same thing. But maybe there's a solution. In Shakespeare's time women weren't allowed to act, so men played their parts. We could turn that around."

"Turn around how?"

"We could have women playing the men. Vienoula, for instance, would make a good king of Naples."

He stops drinking. I think he's thinking it over. I begin recasting in my head. Then I think he's also stopped breathing.

"Theo?"

No response.

"Are you OK?"

He just stares at me, eyes wide.

"Theo? What's wrong?" I jump up. We've been popping olives and pistachios. A pit? A shell? I'm trying to visualize the Heimlich maneuver.

"*Oxi!*" he explodes. "Women cannot be men! Vienoula the king? No, no, *Saraki.* We are not Hollywood, we are Pharos!"

For a moment I see him taking his job back, and I don't like the feel of that at all.

"It was just an idea." I sit back down. "Forget it. Really. Let's go back to Caliban."

His face returns to normal, and he reaches for water. "But maybe we make Caliban a woman . . .?"

I'm anxious to humor him, but I've still got principles. "Can't rewrite *The Tempest, pedhi mou*," I say sweetly.

We sip in silence.

"I have it!" I practically shout.

"*Ti?*"

"There's hardly any business at night till the ferry gets in."

"*Sosto.*"

"And that's around midnight."

"Around, or after. Yes."

"So I'll shorten a few scenes and we'll bring it down by eleven forty-five."

We consider. Then Theo leans across the small table, grinning, and pats my hand. "You can't rewrite *The Tempest, pedhi mou.*"

Says who?

36

"Great," says Alex when I tell her that afternoon. "Cut away."

We're walking along the beach where I hunt for starfish. "I mean, if *you* don't think Shakespeare's sacred . . ."

"I do. Sacred and flexible."

She shakes her head and laughs. "Now, *that's* an oxymoron."

"No it's not." I reject a curly specimen with a broken leg.

"What's your criterion, then? What's this?" She hands me a small green spiky carapace.

"Nobody prays to him. That's a baby sea urchin—and it's perfect."

"I think you're wrong."

"They make the perfect clasp for a shell necklace."

"About Shakespeare, I mean. There's probably a huge cult that worships him, swears on the First Folio, wears a ruff . . . names their kids Cymbeline and Bottom." She stops. "That's a scary thought."

"No it's not." I lay the still prickly urchin in my collecting box. "Christianity was a cult for several hundred years. I'll bet if you put his book of sonnets in every hotel room instead of the Bible there'd be millions of people praying to Shakespeare."

"You've lost your mind. Julian come and take her away."

"Look!" Brushing away some dried sea grass, I uncover a whole bleached starfish. "They get tangled in this stuff and can't get off the beach." I hold it up to the hollow at my throat. "Beautiful, isn't it?"

"Death is tragic."

"Death is inevitable. Please don't spoil my main hobby."

"Death be not proud . . ." Alex addresses a dried sea urchin.

"That happens to be John Donne. Another god."

A wave breaks over our feet and scoots up the beach to our camp.

"Hey!" Out in the bay, Iannis appears in his speedboat. A person can be seen waterskiing behind it.

"That's amazing," I say.

"Not anywhere else, it's not," says Alex. Then they're out of sight. "Are all the shells we find dead animals?" she asks as we're wringing out our towels.

"No. Mostly they're houses that are outgrown. I'll bet they only drink Falstaff beer."

"Do you think they suffer like the fish?"

This topic isn't going away. I pick up a tiny conch at her feet. "See this hole? Put on your glasses."

She obeys. I should memorize that tone.

"OK, that's where she escaped when she needed bigger digs."

"Really?" Alex takes it, then drops it in the sand, where it's lost forever. "Oops, sorry."

"It's OK, there are trillions more. It's starfish that are scarce." I'm walking ever so lightly in my search trance. It's amazing how the lens of your eye adapts its focus to whatever it's looking for. I see two tentacles in the sand. "Freeze!" Very carefully removing the sand around it, I reveal another perfect starfish. Which I don't hand over. "Wow. Two in one day . . . auspicious."

"I'll bet they're a secret order," Alex says as we're celebrating with retsina from the thermos.

(*Celebrating with retsina* isn't an oxymoron to *me*.)

"Alex . . . we know they're secret—we haven't heard of them."

"How long are you going to keep the Monika thing from Theo?"

"What?"

"It was the word *secret*, I guess."

"It's not a 'thing' and I may never tell him."

"Why not? You're not embarrassed are you?"

"Embarrassed?"

"About being with Monika?"

We've stopped hunting. I lean against the rocks. "It never occurred to me. But I *could* be embarrassed for people who tune out half the population."

"Yeah, but that's a very sophisticated concept."

"Is it? I don't think love's a sophisticated concept. It sure doesn't take brains. That's why they call it 'falling' in love."

"So have you fallen in love?"

"Falling in love again; never wanted to . . . ," I sing.

"What am I to do," she joins in . . .

"I can't help it." Together.

The search continues. A north wind the night before has washed up lots of tiny spiral shells with intricate coral and black patterns. They look dazzling just beneath the surface.

"Here's my problem." I scoop a handful out of the sea. Alex comes over. "These are so beautiful in their natural habitat. Then you take them out of the sea and look, they lose their shine, the colors fade. I think there's something wonderful about Monika, but I'm not sure it wouldn't disappear if we were somewhere else."

"And you aren't willing to take that chance."

"I might be. I don't know. But at the moment it's not my decision. This affair's on probation till she decides if she can be with a woman." I'd rather not be discussing this with Alex, but it wouldn't be fair to leave her with the impression that it's only up to me.

"So you're just talking all night?"

"I guess *probation*'s not the right word."

"I guess not," she says. I have Alex's full attention, which has the effect of getting my full attention.

"Not everyone's as versatile as we arc. We're swimming against the tide of human history. I seem to be stuck in aquatic metaphors."

"It's certainly a direct threat to daytime television," Alex jumps in. "Boy gets girl . . . or whoever."

"Whomever. Anyway, it takes time for some people to accept it."

"Some people in Ohio maybe. But she's Swedish! Ingmar Bergman must be turning in his grave."

"And he's not even dead. I'm going for a swim."

"I'm happy for him," I hear before I dive in.

The small bay is home to a galaxy of tiny fish. Whoever painted them had a dazzling palette and a limitless imagination. I glide around with snorkel and mask watching the action below. The sun sends fingerlings of white light through the glassy surface to the rippled sandy seabed. Fat yellow-and-black angel fish poke their snouts against little rocks speckled with plankton. Sleek blue-and-red-striped models with green circles on their bellies slide between waving braids of sea grass. Swimming silently above them, I spot an iridescent blue *cipoura* and follow it till it outruns me. When I turn my head to the side I discover that I'm surrounded by silver small fry skimming just below the surface, checking me out. I reach out my hands and they nibble at my toes. Sometimes I wish they were fins.

We're lying out on the hot stones when Alex abruptly looks up from her book. "This is amazing." I think she's about to read something to me. "You're not in charge for a change. How do you feel?"

"I feel great, thanks." Which is absolutely true, though my precarious relationship with Monika is ruining my ability to predict the future. (This is only a problem for people who want to know what's going to happen next.)

"Uh-huh." She closes the book. "Want to run to Theo?"

"You mean for a Band-Aid? OK, what do *you* think?"

"I think you're off the hook and maybe for the first time you'd rather be on it," she says, smiling and very pleased with herself.

"Now you're fishing for a metaphor."

"Yeah, and I've found it."

"A fisherman is what you've found." I pick up a towel and start drying my hair.

"OK," she says, "the subject is closed."

"*Efharisto.*"

"So is Theo completely out of the picture?"

"You really know how to close a subject."

She turns over and picks up her book. I try to meditate but the guru's face keeps turning into the chief of police. I finally give up and open my eyes.

"Alex, we've got a problem."

"Mmm . . ." She doesn't stir.

"We're rehearsing Act Two tonight. It's the act where Stephano rides ashore on a cask of wine."

She looks up.

"Drunk and singing," I add.

"Is that a problem?"

"If you're the chief of police with the same name it might be."

"Unless you have a sense of humor," she says. "Yeah, we have a problem."

"Of course everyone knows it's just a play."

"Of course."

"I mean," I continue, "if the public notary, who's totally humorless, doesn't mind playing that part, it can't be that offensive."

She sits up. "I think you should cut it."

"You're kidding . . . the king's butler? The guy who plots with Caliban to kill Prospero? Damn! Why didn't I think about this earlier?"

"Because it sounds just like the real Stephanos?"

"That *is* why. Did we bring any chocolate?"

She brings out a Valrhona bar—dark chocolate with caramelized almonds. "There must be lots of calories in these," she says, hoping to influence the division.

"I've just had a long swim," I point out.

"What? You think you can work off calories in advance?"

Sunlight, beach, Valrhona. We chew reverently.

"Well, if you're not bothered about the First Folians, why don't you soften Stephano's character? Have him ride in on a cask of lemonade."

"Can't. He's the low comedy that balances the high tone of Arcadia. He represents everything base in Elizabethan society. Somehow I don't think lemonade conveys that."

Mare's tails drift in and the sun winks out behind the hills as we devise ways to change the part and, when that doesn't work, the story. Which doesn't work either.

"I'm getting cold. Aren't you?"

We pack up and push off.

"We change his name!" I shout as we're rounding the headland. "We'll call him . . . Mandino! And we sail back in silence, amazed at my genius. At least I think that's the reason.

Monika's propped up against a pillar on the dock, reading, as we pull in. "Let's have a drink at Alpha." She takes the painter and ties us up.

"Bug off?" Alex whispers.

"*Oxi.*"

I jump on Ernie Banks. Alex and Monika kick their bikes into gear. We have the town to ourselves as we ride through the narrow lanes that run uphill to Alpha. It's the tail end of siesta. The air has cooled a little but not enough to chill our bare arms and legs. The shops are still shuttered; business will wait until dark. We zip by an ouzo bar on a small *platia*. Two young waiters still in their T-shirts and jeans are playing backgammon under a shade tree, piles of paper table mats stacked on the empty chairs beside them. One of them lifts his glass and smiles as we pass. His friend turns and nods. I don't recognize them, but for sure they recognize us—three girl gringo musketeers who've ridden in from another universe.

"I just broke the news to Petros," says Monika when we've settled at Alpha and our ouzos have arrived.

"What news?" I wonder.

"That I'm not going out with him again."

"How did he take it?" Alex jumps in.

"Fine, I think. He's meeting us here after he closes."

"Fine? He was fine? What did he actually say?" says Alex.

Monika looks for my reaction in case this is privileged information.

"It's the American interview style," I say; "rottweiler on ankle." I realize we've never discussed my relationship with Alex—among a million other things we've never discussed. I try looking completely relaxed . . . drop a couple of ice cubes in my ouzo.

"Oh, sorry . . . really," Alex says. "Of course you don't have to tell us." Us?

"That's OK," Monika laughs. "I come from a country with *no* interview style. People don't ever talk about things like this. They just kill themselves. Anyway Petros said he understands. He said he knew I wasn't really right for him. We don't have much in common."

Takis interrupts with a bowl of pistachios. They don't serve pistachios at Alpha.

"You need one more pirate, Sarah?"

"*Ti?* Ahh, o*xi*, Taki, no pirates." I give him a look that says 'thank you, please go away' and he does.

"What reason did you give Petros?" Alex wants to know.

"I told him I may actually prefer women."

"Why did you tell him *that*?" I say, practicing what I preach against.

Monika looks surprised. Then she half smiles and turns up her hands as if collecting raindrops. But I'm too well defended to jump to any assumptions.

"What did he say to that?" says Alex, moving right along.

"He asked if I'd sell him my drawing of Nikos's place."

"Yes!" I shout.

"Right!" cries Alex.

Monika's startled. I lower my voice. "We're of the opinion that most guys find the idea of women together unthinkable, or unbelievable. It goes against all their conditioning."

"Mine too," says Monika.

"Hi," says Petros, very sunny. Alex scoots over so he can sit between us. I'm alert for a different attitude, a change of temperature. Nothing. So I'm not under suspicion. He starts describing a busload of Italians who insisted on stopping for an ouzo en route to the Church of the Virgin.

"It was eight o'clock in the morning! And the women were in shorts. I told them they'd miss the service if—"

"Petros, you're not Orthodox, are you? You never go to church."

"*Yasoo!*" Arabella calls. There is no Aldo '98 trailing her.

"Hellooo." Petros turns so fast he pulls something in his neck. "Ow! Damn!"

Not that she notices.

"Sarah, you pick the music teacher for your play!"

This moment had to come. "You know, Arabella"—I drop my voice—"I thought it was more diplomatic to have a Greek play Miranda. It's the only female part. Don't you agree?"

Her eyes wander off. When they return they look sad and serious.

"*Vero*, you are right. Is too bad." For them, she means.

Alex isn't moving over to let her in. Petros, one hand grabbing his neck, is nevertheless tucking in his shirt and fixing his hair. The more the murkier, I figure, and get up to fetch a chair.

"Can I buy you a drink?" Petros asks Arabella's cleavage as he takes the chair and wedges it in next to his. He signals Takis.

"*Grazie, caro.* What you are having?"

You, he says, but not out loud. "*Dhio* Campari, Taki."

Monika's a fling of the past.

"And you, Sarah? Would you like to drink?" says Takis, leaning in to me. "Where a bee socks there socks I."

"No, thanks. Taki, I'm really sorry, but auditions are over."

"Too bad," he says.

"Handsome," says Alex sotto voce.

"Next year, Taki," says Theo, just now arriving. Cast complete.

"What's wrong with your neck?" he asks Petros, who abruptly drops his hand.

"Nothing," he chirps. He wraps his arm around the back of Arabella's chair. Arabella turns to me with a dazzling smile.

"I could under . . ." She hunts for the word. ". . . copy Miranda, no?"

"That's a very good idea," I hear myself saying. I don't look at Alex, but it is.

"*Ouzaki?*" Theo offers.

"*Si,*" say Alex and Monika.

"No thanks," I say. "I'd better stay sober for the rehearsal."

"Do you think that's a good idea?" says Alex.

37

We rehearse the storm scene right after dinner. The burps and various other digestive asides are drowned out by the sound effects. (I congratulate myself. Do you think they teach that in Directing 101?)

"Owwwllllll . . . uuuuuueeeeeuuuuuu . . . shhhooooooowww . . . rrrrrr . . . Oeeeeeeeooooo-eye eye eye eye . . ." Stella and Maria Milos and Vienoula and Arabella (direct from Alpha) and the caryatids are roaring the storm from the transepts; Foti bangs on a metal sheet; Georgaki rattles both light plugs; Monika and Omiros, on ladders in the wings, are flapping the sails. (The saints must be covering their ears.) The effect is spectacular. We all stop to marvel at it, including everyone on stage.

"Great, everybody. That's enough!" I yell to the chorus, who've ignored Alex's cutoff cue. "Let's do it again with all of you staying in character." Omiros comes down the ladder.

"Stain in character, *Saraki*?"

"Do it like actors."

"Signome?"

"Don't worry about it now," says Alex at my side. Right.

"Call dessert, Omire." Because a storm makes everybody hungry.

"The sails are terrific," Alex says between bites of walnut cake. "We can flap them whenever Maria's dog barks."

Tina comes over with her coffee. "It's wonderful, Sarah. Maybe I could be in the chorus?"

"*Malista!*" A pro in the cast; my planets must be trining.

"But how many performances? I have to be in Athens in August for *Orpheo*."

"Just six. The last weekends in July."

"Perfect."

"Alex, will you catch her up?"

"Sure!" She's picturing Lukia's tea cakes. They go off to the transept to echo.

"How about a few props?" says Monika during Elena's baklava break.

(There's nothing on the altar anymore that isn't food-related. I think of them as offerings.)

"You could ask the carpenter, what's his name, and I could paint them."

"Costas, sure. Let's get together tomorrow and figure it out."

"Anything wrong with tonight?"

"Uh . . . no. OK, everybody! Omire! Places!"

I've marked up the floor, as I do before every scene. Stephanos stalks the tape.

"Stephano, you're so clever," I tell him at arm's length, "you always know your spot. Do you think you could take off your gun, though? People keep bumping into it and—"

"Don't worry, *Saraki*, if king dies, I know where he goes."

Dies? We can't open if the postmaster washes up on the beach.

"He can't be serious," Alex says. "Ask Theo." Which I do when he comes by late, after a delivery.

"How do you call it? Kid?"

"No," I say. "A kid is a baby goat."

"Yes, it's that—*katzika*. The baby sticks inside so the mother will die."

"You're an animal doctor, too?"

"We are an island, Sarah *mou*."

Talk about handy around the house.

"Theo," I whisper, "do you think Stephanos is capable of murder?"

"No." An unexpectedly short answer.

"Why no?"

"He does not see. To kill you must see. This is why he talks to your face."

"Aha." I'm enormously relieved. Of course it was a far-fetched idea. But here we are in a low-lit echoing Byzantine church watched by smoke-stained icons spurting blood.

We're in the beginning of Act Two; Antonio, Prospero's usurping brother, is conspiring with the king's brother Sebastian to murder the king when I notice that both Antonio and Sebastian are lisping.

"Hold it please! Alex?"

The dialogue coach is missing.

"Omire, have you seen Alexandra?"

"I think she's out looking for Iannis."

"*Signome?*"

"He gets lost in town."

"You're kidding, Omire."

"He has trouble with landmarks," says Theo, laughing as he hands me a glass of retsina. "Maybe we should move to the lighthouse?"

I see Evdhomada sitting alone in a pew marking up her script. Her close-fitting soft sleeveless dress shows a long delicate neck and slim sculpted arms. One naked hand is absently pushing hair away from her face. I realize that any lines I was dangling in Theo's direction dissolved in the moonlight on Sandsoon. "Do you think Evdhomada would like a retsina?" I ask him.

"Yes, of course." He jumps up.

Since we've stopped, and my cast is already snacking, I decide to explain the transformation of Stephano into a new character called Mandino.

"Stephano, the king's butler, is a very important character. He's very funny, but he's also evil—stirring up trouble with Caliban and even plotting with him to kill Prospero. Of course he's a character of the writer's imagination, and nothing like our real Stephanos."

Omiros has been translating at a good clip. He stops, chokes theatrically, and throws me a look that could shorten his life. I stare him down during my wrap-up.

"We don't want to confuse the real with the imaginary, so I've decided to change the character's name."

You could slip the Rocky Mountains through the holes in this argument. I wait for reactions.

"Elena, *toso nostimo afto to baclavas,*" such tasty baklavas. *"Poli gliko,"* very sweet. *"Bravo, kori mu." "Toso orea,* so wonderful, Elenaki," they say as Elena passes around seconds and thirds. Not even Stephanos is the slightest bit interested.

"OK! Everyone! Open your scripts. Wherever you see the name Stephano cross it out and write Mandino."

"Yes, fine, good." Mumbling, chewing, scribbling, purpose.

"Bravo," says Theo softly as he refills my glass. "This is thinking like a Greek. Also, you have no rehearsal tomorrow. It is Agios Stavros day."

"Oh no, Theo. We play in less than three weeks."

He shrugs. "Agios Stavros is special to Pharos. Tomorrow night we eat and drink."

"Oh, *that* special." But my sarcasm is lost on him.

(The Greek Orthodox calendar is really a birthday book. If you took off every saint's day, you couldn't stage a chicken barbecue.)

Alex eventually returns with Iannis, looking gorgeous in his wet suit and introducing a bold fishy smell. I realize he could make an interesting Caliban if it weren't for all those lines. He's already an expert at wandering around the island.

When we break for the night, the caryatids invite us for a St. Stavros feast. So do Maria and Tomas and Priftis and Gerasimos and Evdhomada.

"*Efharisto,* but we're staying home," says Alex, skillfully.

"I meant it," she says. We're lying on the roof watching shooting stars. "I'm starting to hallucinate baked potatoes."

"I can make a special Swedish dish, if you like," says Monika. "Oh! Over there, did you see? Two at once!"

The stars are raining down tonight and the slightest breeze carries night-blooming jasmine. We lie under a black canopy; the moon hasn't risen yet, and no lights reflect from the sleeping village.

"As long as it isn't fish," says Alex.

"It is fish, but I promise you won't recognize it."

"Why does it have to be . . . ?" Alex persists.

"Shhh," I say, "we can't hear the stars falling."

38

I'm winnowing some scenes in search of an eleven thirty curtain when the front door opens. For a second I imagine Shakespeare's ghost. Looking down into the courtyard I see Alex, back from an early round of shopping. She's not alone.

"What is that?"

"You don't recognize a dog?"

"See no evil, smell no evil . . ."

"A wet nose, pink ears, a tail . . ." She smiles up at me. "We don't live together anymore."

"We do here." I love dogs, but I'm very allergic. It's hard to sneeze and blow your way through a short life.

"He looks like he's starving and he followed me home. He can live in the courtyard."

"What's his name?"

"You're so good at that, I thought you'd name him."

"That's so transparent."

"Come down and have breakfast with me."

"So what happened with that scene?" she asks as I brew.

"Omiros decided if all the guys lisp we won't notice Kostis doing it. It's crazy."

"But it works," she says.

"It works if we're doing a gay *Tempest*."

"Voilà! Your West End transfer." She makes an unladylike gesture with the banana she's about to slice onto her yogurt. "Oh what a wogue and prevant swave . . ."

"Stop!" I'm laughing. "And that's *Hamlet*."

"Well a lot of people think *Hamlet*—"

"Bananagravel bananagravel," I yell with fingers in ears. She begins slicing.

"What's going on?" Monika appears in a sarong, pushing sleep-spun hair out of her eyes. The dog follows her in. She reaches down to pet it without noticing that it's new. So far there's nothing about her that's difficult to live with.

"We're rewriting the play a little," I explain, "to appeal to a narrower audience. Sorry we got loud. Can we take this beast outside?"

"We're moving it from Saint Christopher's to Christopher Street," says Alex as we resettle in the courtyard.

"Ouch! Damn! Diana's bitten my toe." I swing my feet onto the table.

"But she's over here," says Monika.

"Not the dog, the tortoise."

"The what?"

"I guess she's been hiding in the bougainvillea since you came." I throw a bit of tomato in Monika's direction and Diana hurries over.

"Watch your toes," says Alex. "Ooh, nice polish, Moni."

"Hiding in the bougainvillea? Thanks, it's 'Carmina Burana.'"

I can't believe I've never noticed. Did she paint them while I was meditating? OK, she's a painter; but do I write on my toenails?

"It's nothing personal," I tell her. "She's very shy."

"My God, a real tortoise," says Monika, swinging her feet onto an empty chair. "She should be in the play."

"Wildlife on Arcadia," says Alex, who knows I hate polish and is beaming. "What a good idea." They both look to the director for approval.

"But we don't know if she can act."

We all look at her.

"She's a good eater," I admit. "She'll fit right in."

"And what about this dog?" says Monika. "Has it got a name?"

Alex looks at me. If I did have a choice, you could call this the decisive moment.

"Al Fresco," I say. "As in 'lives outside.'"

Monika and I are lying in the afternoon shadows on Sandsoon when I explain the reference to Christopher Street. Monika can't be expected to know it's the East Coast capital of gay America.

"You two are so great together. Why did you ever break up?"

My fault for mentioning it; or talking at all. I unwind from her and roll onto the sand.

"I can't explain that . . . the path love takes. Feelings change. That's their nature."

"Hmm." Her crystal eyes are working. "That's *your* nature."

"Right, OK. But if it's love, it never leaves me. We're still great friends."

"That's a good option," she says. She rolls over and instantly falls asleep. I'm left wondering if that's an exit line.

"Another essay?" she asks when she wakes up to my scribbling.

"No. Doing a little more cutting so that Tino can play Caliban. It makes me highly nervous."

"Why? Shakespeare had an acting company, didn't he? I'll bet he did it all the time."

"But not to catch a cab."

She laughs. "In Stockholm in winter?"

"It's true he was known to make changes till the curtain went up."

"So don't worry about it. What about your own writing? Now that the article's finished, what's the next thing? Did you say something about working on a novel?"

The cove suddenly fills with waves. Alex is heading right for us, on a rope behind Iannis's boat. *Soapdish* bucks on her painter; I wade out and grab hold of it. Iannis cuts an arc just in front of us and Alex does a perfect ski onto the beach.

"Hi guys!"

Talk about a *Deus ex machina.*

39

Theo is leaning on the No Parking sign in town as I swing off Ernie Banks. "Are you really at home tonight? I like to see you."

What's happened to Evdhomada? She's a natural Miranda, beautiful and warm, and she practically floats in Tina's diaphanous creations. Could it be she only respond to wet cats?

"Yes I am. *We* are. Monika's making a special Swedish dish."

"We thought Saint Stavros would like fish," says Monika, riding up and parking next to me.

"Though she's promised to disguise it," says Alex, shutting off her engine.

"We had so many invitations. We thought it would be rude to say no to anybody, so we said no to everybody."

"*Exipnos,* very clever." He puts his hands on my shoulders. "But me?"

"Aren't your sisters having a party?"

"*Oxi.* Elena and my mother are going to my uncle's. And Sophia"— he lowers his voice—"she is with Costas."

"Costas the carpenter?"

"Yes."

A new girlfriend. It's terrible news for his clients.

"Of course you're invited, Theo." I'd like to ask him to bring Evd-homada but that would require a leap of centuries in the careful dance of this culture.

"Iannis will be there," says Alex, who probably wasn't looking for a better time to tell me.

"And Petros," says Monika. "I ran into him at the fish market and he asked if he could come."

"*Thavmasia*," says Theo. "I bring my bouzouki. And some wine."

"OK . . . Great. What time?" I ask the cook.

"Nine o'clock," says Monika. "If we go home right now."

Home? Did I hear that? Maybe I missed something on the beach.

"*Entaxi*," says Theo.

"*Adio.*"

"You don't mind?" they ask me when he's gone.

"No, really, it's finc."

"*Ham sa?*" says Alex.

"Exactly."

40

Tina's left a note on the door saying she has some costumes to show me. I could leave it until tomorrow, but maybe she'd like some seafood risotto. Or a Greek doctor.

So there are seven of us having supper in the courtyard, plus Diana and Al Fresco, when the mayor raps at the door. He only speaks Greek and very fast.

"*O Stephanos . . . kephali . . . Boom!*"

A crime on Pharos? The Volvo thief? All I can gather is that Theo is needed to attend to Stephanos. Gestures suggest he's been hit on the head—with a heavy something.

"By whom?" we ask in waves.

Petros and Iannis are very excited, asking lots of questions, but not translating. "*Dhen pistevo*"—I don't believe it. Iannis's tresses thrash about.

"*Ti krima*"—What a pity! Theo keeps saying. He pours the mayor a glass of wine.

"*O Theos mou!*"— Oh my God! cries Petros the atheist.

The tale is very long, naturally; it's not by chance *The Odyssey* is Greek. I'm thinking Stephanos, aka Sebastian, may bleed to death before the mayor wraps it up.

Theo suddenly gets up and puts on his jacket. Of course Petros the harpy gets his. Then they all rush out. At least fifteen lifesaving minutes late. We all turn to Tina as the door shuts. She's wearing a spangled DK turban that nearly covers her ears. But she hasn't missed anything.

"Natalia found out about Popi and attacked Stephanos as he got out of his jeep."

"Oooh . . ."

"Natalia?" Alex asks.

"Stephanos's wife," I tell her. "Nikos told me she lives on the porch."

"It's true," says Tina. "She's the neighborhood spy. I can't believe Stephanos would try anything. Plus she's . . ." Her bird arms stretch as wide as they go.

"Wow!" says Alex. "What did she hit him with?"

"A frying pan," says Monika.

We all look at her. Iannis is the most astonished, and he *knows* what happened.

"How did you know that?" says Tina.

"From the movies. Plus the mayor did a pretty good pantomime. Why isn't he in the play?" Which I ignore. I don't need any more actors . . . yet.

"He's not dead, is he?" I ask Tina.

"Not yet."

"No, seriously. He's got a big part." My friends generously ignore the brazen self-interest in this remark.

Not Tina, though. "Very nice, Sarah," she says, laughing. "We can always play it at the graveyard. No, I gather he was just unconscious for a few minutes."

"So he probably forgot his lines," moans Alex, his dialogue coach. Solipsism must be contagious.

"Theo's lemon cake!" I remember, and I jump up to fetch it. This is my first directorial crisis and like any crisis it calls for sugar. I eat a piece while I'm looking for enough plates. The debate is sizzling by the time I return to the courtyard.

". . . and so would *I* if I'd caught my husband—" Tina's voice is rising.

"But that's crazy. All men fool around," Alex interrupts. "It's zoological." She throws a look at Iannis for confirmation, but he's watching the lemon cake advance. Not that he'd have a clue what she's saying at that clip.

"I don't live in a zoo! That's what civilization is all about." Size 4 is burning all her dinner calories.

"Neither do I," says Alex, "but I love . . . I live in the real world."

"Cake anyone?"

"Please," says Tina, to my amazement.

"*Efharisto.*" Iannis manages to get a word in.

"I wouldn't even call it fooling around," says Monika.

Hold on."You wouldn't?" I say. "They're married."

"And they're Greek," Tina says, meaning *extra* married, I gather. She picks up her cake in her fingers.

"So?" says Monika, doing the same.

"Scandinavian morality is very different." Tina swallows. "In fact I recently read that sixty-two percent of Swedish children are born to unmarried girls."

"Sixty-two percent?" says Alex, between bites. "With all those gorgeous men?"

"*Ti?*" says Iannis, passing back his empty plate.

"Can we stop, please," I say.

"What? Why?" says Alex.

"So we can enjoy this delicious cake. Plus no one's listening. We're all just repeating our fixed positions. Let's just stop and think."

Luckily there's cake to occupy us. And mantra. But I don't mention that; I'd hate to sound pedantic *and* sanctimonious.

"OK," says Alex, licking her fingers "Sarah's right. We've got three cultures here and maybe we can learn something."

"Not if we don't agree that marriage is sacred," says Tina. "Isn't it, Ianni?"

"*Malista!*" agrees the bachelor. But how hard is that?

"Plenty of things are sacred," I say. "Nothing to do with their legal status."

"Exactly," says my sometime lover. But I'm not claiming victory.

"What would you do if you were Natalia?" Tina turns to Monika.

"I'd never ask anyone to be faithful," she says, "and I don't expect anyone to ask me."

How right was I? And look how bad right feels.

"But if you promise to be faithful . . ." Alex, digging up her Connecticut roots.

"Yes," says Monika, "but why would you ever . . . ?"

"*Yia sas*," calls Theo as he opens the door, followed by Petros, who's brought Arabella. Just think, an Italian perspective.

"How's Stephanos?" we shout over one another.

"*Kalispera*, everyone," says Arabella, waving. She's dressed in a gauzy pink Indian kurta tucked into a red bandage-tight miniskirt. Two sets of prayer beads are wound around her throat. Jasmine is twined into her flowing hair. My mind comes to a complete stop.

"Fine, fine," says Theo. "Well, fine with a big headache. And I have to sew a little his ear."

I do hear this, however. "That's OK." Sebastian wears a cap in every act. "Hi, Arabella. You're in time for Theo's lemon cake."

"Cake? *Vero?* How you are clever," Arabella gushes at the doctor. No one corrects her.

"I don't suppose he threw his wife in jail?" says Alex brightly.

"Why?" Theo and Petros together. So we know where *they* stand.

"*Madonna, perché?*" chimes in Miss Sub Continent. "But maybe she throws him!"

"That's what I say," says Tina, who seems equally transfixed by the outfit. Iannis leaps from his chair to offer it to her.

"Popi is very lonely since her dog dies," says Theo.

"That would explain Stephanos," says Tina.

I'm losing track.

"It's pretty simple," says Alex later, when we're cleaning up. "The guys think he should get away with it. But if he gets caught, he deserves a smack."

"And Monika thinks," I add morosely.

"Swedes qualify as guys here." She stops drying to look at me. "You wouldn't want it any other way, would you? *Liberté, sororité . . .*"

"Actually I hated it when you slept with that mechanic."

"You did? You never said anything. He fixed your transmission!"

"What's 'transmission,' " says Monika from the doorway.

"I thought you'd gone to sleep," I say, wondering how much she's overheard.

"I can't. Too much cake."

"It's the part that lets you shift gears." Like I'm doing now.

"Ahh."

"I'm going to bed," says Alex. "Cake has never interfered with my sleep."

"Sit down, Moni, I'll make you some chamomile tea."

"Don't we have ouzo?"

"Sure."

"No ice for me. Where do you find chamomile tea on Pharos?"

"I don't. I find chamomile; it grows wild in the hills."

"Mmmm . . . Let's go there." A few moments pass while we visualize this. At least I think that's what's happening.

When no dogs are barking and the doves fall asleep, Kastro is as silent as the seabed. Whereas the soft noises we're making in the old stone kitchen seem as loud as rain on a rock pool.

"Shall we sleep on the roof?" I say.

"Sure," she says, and leads the way, stopping for a blanket.

"What did you hear before 'transmission'?" Our eyes are adjusting to the waves of starlight.

"You hated her sleeping with the mechanic."

"Mmm. Call me old-fashioned. That's a song, by the way."

"And a cliché, isn't it?"

I sit up and untangle us. "Clichés have a very bad rap."

"Any mechanics in your life?" she asks.

"No, but I lived with an architect for a few years. He was very clever at fixing things that *don't* move."

"A few years?" She sits up, surprised. "Is that what you call a long relationship?" she says seriously.

"My longest lover."

"Well, what happened to him?"

I start laughing.

"What?" she insists.

"I moved."

"Be serious. I want to know."

"I moved on. We didn't have a lot in common, mainly Bob Dylan and foreign films . . . and whatever project he was working on. We'd stay up all night pasting little models, drinking wine, making love. Then I got interested in Eastern philosophies. I started meditating. He didn't like it when I went off on a couple of retreats. I was leaving him, or asking to be celibate. I just wanted to explore this whole new way of seeing things. But he had zero curiosity about it. He didn't even want to *try* to meditate. Mostly he laughed at it all. I finally realized that what we mainly had in common was him."

We think about that for a minute.

"So how did you break it off?" she finally asks.

"I picked up my guitar and sang him a Dylan medley. It started with 'Don't Think Twice' and ended with 'It's All Over Now, Baby Blue,' unless it was 'It Ain't Me, Babe.'"

"In other words, you let Bob do the hard part."

"Very clever I thought. Anyway it was the language he understood."

"So if you ever start playing 'Sad-Eyed Lady of the Lowlands' I should know . . ."

I put my hand over her mouth. "Moni, let's not waste these stars."

We make love by the distant light of the Pleiades until they slip below the horizon. Then we lie awake, arms and legs tangled, drinking in the luxury of the moment.

"Why do you think we can't sleep, Sarah *mou*? Tell me, please."

I'm not rushing it. A feeling of no-time has spilled over me, light and quieting. In the now moonless night the sky surrounds us thick with stars. The wind has set with the moon.

"I don't get involved very often."

"What about Alex?"

"The romantic part was brief. I'm probably impossible to live with."

"Maybe you should look at me while you're saying this."

"I think better when I'm staring into space."

"It's not for your benefit, *Liebe;* I'm hooked on your eyes."

So I turn and meet her gaze.

"You think we're a summer thing?" she says.

"Well . . . seasonal."

"Aha! I'm a crop!"

Our laughter could wake the neighbors, but no lights come on and nobody shouts at us. I want to ask her if she's made up her mind. But it's like asking someone if they love you. If they do, they'll volunteer it. And if she has? I still like the sound of seasonal.

"I wasn't entirely honest tonight," she says, "when I asked why anyone would be faithful. I was faithful for several years. Then I found out the guy was still married. I was completely shocked. I dropped everything and went off to Paris."

"Well, at least you made the perfect move," I say. "I *know* I can be faithful to Paris." Is it possible I've never asked her about her past?

"Me too," she says, and sits up. "So I guess we could live there?" I look back at the stars. Arcturus has set and now Sagittarius is directly overhead. Monika follows my gaze. "Isn't that the hunter?"

"Uh-huh." His heart is beating in my chest.

She runs her fingers through my hair. "Are you thinking of jumping off the roof?"

An unstoppable smile is betraying me. "It wouldn't be the first time."

41

The flapping sails and raving chorus reminds me that we're lacking, as in desperately need, music. Arcadia's a magic kingdom after all. During the first run-through of Miranda's scene with Ferdinand I pick up Ariel's guitar and strum a melody. With these acoustics a tree frog could make the top forty.

"What was that?" asks Tina. "It's beautiful."

"Miranda's song."

The cast is crowding around . . . without food.

"Did Shakespeare write it?" says Omiros.

"He wrote the words. Katrin Campbell wrote the music, for a production in London a few years ago."

"And you remember it?" Alex knows I forget names, birthdays, dinner dates, the works.

"Well, it haunted me. Plus it drove me crazy; the musicians were rehearsing in the studio right next to ours."

"It's wonderful," says Monika. "Is there more?"

The attention's a little heady. I tune up and sing Katrin's rhapsodic "Come Unto These Yellow Sands." Group trance. Then applause, cheers.

"More! *Thavmasia! Ti orea!*" Just like for Elena's baklavas.

"No, no. Let's get back to work." Quick, before they get hungry.

"No, another one," cries my captive audience.

So I relent and give them her gorgeous arrangement of "Full Fathoms Five."

Then we eat.

"Why don't you sing during the show? You can be in the wings," says Alex, chewing a spinach pie. "It's only six performances."

"No, too boring, just me and solo guitar all the time."

Costas has come by with the props that Monika's painted. He's licking honey off his fingers. There's much more on the legs of his overalls but I don't point it out because I'm pretty sure he'd start licking there too.

"*Oxi* solo, *Saraki*. We get Takis and Tomas to play with you," he says.

"A great idea," says Theo, who's following Costas with some of the props. I realize he always looks better to me at night, when he's wrinkled . . . and I've had a little wine. "Bravo, Costa." He turns to me triumphantly. "Everyone loves a musical! And your voice, Sarah *mou* . . ."

"Theo, Siamese cats could cut a gold record in this place. But if we really can get a trio . . . I'll have to write Katrin to ask if it's OK."

"You do?" Alex breaks in, eyeing our postman, aka the boatswain. "As long as we don't have to wait for a reply."

Act II—Scene 1

"Sir, you may thank yourself for this great loss . . the fault's your own." Sebastian is raving at Alonso over his fate. It's a pretty convincing performance, and anybody not dozing in the pews is watching. Sebastian raises his sword to kill Alonso. They all gasp. Prospero drops his coffee cup on the tiles. *"Signome!"* he cries, ruining the spell. But Manolis as Antonio spins it again.

"Although this lord of weak remembrance . . . hath here almost persuade[d] . . . the king his son's alive, 'Tis as impossible that he's undrowned as he that sleeps here swims."

"Wow, that last scene was powerful," says Tina. "I think we should tape the gasp."

"Great idea," I say.

"I thought Sebastian was going for his gun," says Monika. "Can't you get Stephanos to take that thing off?"

"With Natalia on the prowl?" says Tina. "But I'll find a way to cover it."

"We're lucky it isn't a frying pan," says Alex.

It's midnight at Alpha, and the production staff is winding down.

"And one reason it was so powerful," Alex says, "is that Gerasimo was off book. Not holding a script," she translates for Monika.

"*Sosta*," says Theo. "The postmaster. And I never use him."

"Why not?" I ask.

"Because he never remembers anything."

"Right," I laugh. "I forgot to worry about that."

"No, seriously," says Alex. "Isn't he the guy who forgot his kid at school?"

"He's the one." Theo shakes his head. "The doctor has no answer."

Humility, as noted earlier, is my favorite extinct quality. I give him a long appreciative look. So does Tina. Longer. Aha! Theo–Tina could be better than Theo–Evdhomada. I give Monika my thumbs-up smile. She misreads me, and looks from me to Theo and back again. There's a chilly Malmö stain in her eyes. I'm surprised; just last night we were moving to Paris. And we know where she stands on monogamy. *Ham sa?* No, that doesn't work. But I don't know the Sanskrit for "nolo contendere."

"It's late, me hardies." I stand up. "Let's go."

42

"Knock knock." Alex is making her way to the roof with a tray of coffee. Al Fresco underfoot makes the climb potentially fatal.

"What's this?" I sit up. "Bad news?"

"*Oxi.*"

Al Fresco is licking Monika's face, which is still at bowl level.

"I've got an early tour this morning and I've made some for Petros."

"He's here early."

"Not exactly."

I don't need to look around to know I've got no moral ground to stand on.

"Ah."

"So why don't we meet this afternoon and figure out the music stuff."

"OK. Niko's at four?"

"Cut that out." Monika comes to life.

"*Kato,* Al Fresco. Four is fine," says Alex.

"*Kato* means 'down,' Alex, and he can't get any lower. Try 'sit'—*katse.*"

"I don't know why we're teaching Greek to this dog," she says, taking his chin in her hands. "He'll never use it." She pours the coffee and then starts down the stairs. Al Free Love is enjoying the view.

"Go with Alex," I say in English. And he does, but probably for reasons of his own.

I want to talk about last night and Theo. It's the new me, trying to communicate even when I'm uncomfortable. But I'm still not ready to ad lib. I rehearse some openings as I'm sipping my coffee.

"I think the trio's a great idea," says Monika, refilling my cup. "The music sounds magical in that space. Did you write to your friend?"

In America we know this is a diversion; if we didn't, millions of self-help therapists and their publishers would be filing for Chapter 11. But things may be different in Malmö.

"I think I'll try calling her."

"Wow!"

"Well, I've got all morning. And I can do some scene cutting while I'm waiting." We drink and watch a couple of sailboats slipping out on a light northerly.

"Theo's a friend. I'm not interested in him."

"I know that. But he's interested in you and you were playing with him." She looks at me. "So just at that moment I wanted to kill you."

No wonder Bergman shoots in black and white.

"But I wasn't playing with him. As a matter of fact I'm trying to steer him to Evdhomada. But I may shift to Tina. So far Evdhomada seems more interested in cats."

"You'd have more luck mating cats, given the insularity of this culture."

I give her a hug.

"What?" She pulls back.

"You have no idea how it thrills me to hear a word used in its proper context."

"Pedant!"

"Thank you!"

"We think Petros spent the night, right?"

I nod. "There's no other explanation; they both think morning is strictly for farmers."

"What d'you think happened to Iannis?"

"How much can you say about waterskiing? Or the beach-chair business. But she can't be serious about Petros. How about some yogurt."

"Mmm. Ask Al Fresco to bring some up."

"What a good idea," I say. "Now, that's a problem. What's she going to do about that dog when we leave?"

A beat.

"He isn't seasonal?" She starts down the stairs.

Out on the bay, caiques are laying glittering ribbons across the horizon, the sea so calm the waves fall back unstirred. Monika sets a tray on the tiles and peels the waxed paper off the ceramic bowls. The honey comes from the bees at the women's monastery; its lavender aroma sweetens the cool morning air. We drip it slowly over the fresh yogurt.

"This is why we're here," she says, licking traces of honey off her spoon and drawing an arc over our view.

And this is why I'm in love with you, says my intoxicated inner voice.

We can hear Tula drowning the flowers on the terrace when we finally abandon the roof. She's also having an agitated conversation with herself, I think—until I see a tortoise shell scurrying around her open-toed sandals. *"Fige! Fige! Eeeee!"*

Diana isn't normally up at this hour either. Maybe it was all that sugar in Theo's lemon cake. Monika's laughing on her way down the stairs. "Is Tula still afraid of her? She hasn't lost any toes, has she?"

"Who can tell under those thick stockings? Tula! Give her a bit of tomato."

"Don't laugh!" she cries, sending a stream of water in Diana's direction. Of course this just drives a tortoise crazy with happiness. And stimulates her appetite. I run into the kitchen to fetch a tomato. Then I pick up Arcadia's leading reptile and put her in the flower bed.

43

What's going to happen when tortoise meets Chihuahua? I've placed my call to Katrin and I'm sitting in *Kyria* Kassoula's salon waiting for the ringback. I have more important things to think about, but I can't when the butcher's mother is yelling at her son in Athens. I think she's telling him to come home fast because his wife's having coffee with the electrician. Unless she wants him back to replace the fuse for her coffeepot. I may have misunderstood the critical bits. Alex suddenly peeks in the doorway.

"Did you get through?"

"Sure, and I'm sitting here till it stops snowing." I can see a cluster of pale faces crowded behind her.

"We were visiting the Church of the Virgin and I thought I'd show them a real Greek household. Monika said you'd be here. Would you ask *Kyria* Kassoula if we can come in?"

But before I can, *Kyria* Kassoula herself throws open her door and her arms.

"*Ella, ella.*" She must recognize Alex from the Miracle of the Folding Fisherman on the *platia*. "Nescafé?" She offers, completely unfazed by the string of American chicklets pouring though her ancient doorway.

Not enough chairs, but the Greeks immediately get up and offer theirs.

"Ooh, Myra, look at that picture. Do you believe that hat!" Myra's friend is pointing to the portrait of the long-dead, thus revered, Captain Kassoula.

"Jasper, honey, don't sit on that chair! It's gonna snap!"

"Do you think she's got Sweet'N Low?"

If I could just crawl under the sofa.

"Are you the one who directs plays? I want to take your picture." A pudgy freckled plum with a midwestern accent scrapes her chair over to sit directly in front of me.

"What?" I reply graciously.

"You're famous aren't you?" She slings the camera off her shoulder and leans back to focus.

Famous for killing rude tourists. But before I can tell her, Alex steps between us.

"She's not the one, Lila."

"Oh!" Lila looks up. "Isn't that a photo of her on your fridge?"

The orange tabby comes to life. She hisses, arches her back, and leaps off the telephone directory.

Al Family Dog jumps on my lap. It's mantra time.

The phone rings. Is *Ham sa* actually working? I almost beat *Kyria* Kassoula to the phone.

"For you, Mikhaili," she says.

"Excuse me, I have to hear this," and I get up with my chair to move closer to Mikhailis. Which is plainly unnecessary since he's shouting over Neptune's aquarium.

The mayor's Volvo is sitting in the sea, he's telling someone. And he wonders why anyone would steal such an old thing. All the locals in the room wonder along with him.

"*Ti? Ti?*" The usual interruptions from other callers and fish.

"Insurance? So much?" Oops. It seems Vassilis has a big policy on that car. My neighbors are riveted. And they'll be the jury if it goes to trial.

"Which it won't. It can't," says Nikos, sharing our table in the afternoon. "Impossible to prove."

I've had a quick word with Katrin's answering machine. No one in the room took the slightest interest; too busy processing this godsend of a rumor.

"Her answering machine?" Alex says, brooding over her Nescafé frappé. "Will we ever know?"

"I'm taking it as a yes. I told her to wire me if she's opposed."

"To the music?" says Nikos. Why bother to ask how he knows. "It will sound fantastic in there."

So that's settled.

44

I call everyone together before rehearsal to tell them I've made a few cuts in the script so that their friend uncle cousin Tino can play Caliban. Directors usually prepare for this by wearing a flak jacket. And they've had a few drinks to render themselves heartless. Because actors hate cuts, unless it's something they can't remember or can't pronounce. It's a little easier if you're the author, as in authority. You can say—with false humility—that you've made a mistake. But a director is just a capricious egomaniac. You inevitably cut their favorite lines, never mind that they haven't learned them yet. Or you're destroying their nuanced character development. What's really happened is that (1) they knew they had more lines than he did and now they're not sure; (2) they used to pick up the glass on that cue and now the glass will have to pick itself up; (3) they hate change, in common with the whole human race.

No tears, no protests, no grief at all if you don't count Stephanos— "I am best king"—interrupting my preamble. I reckon it's the Byzantine mentality. On a windswept day you can see bits of Turkey from Pharos. With a pair of really strong binoculars you can see people taking it easy all along the Turkish coast. A few lines in a play? This is the considerable upside to the telegram problem, the phone problem . . .

I had forgotten to tell Tino (here Alex wags her head in despair), but he's delighted.

"*Efharisto poli, Saraki.* I love Calibani."

Wait till he sees the costume. At the next *kafedakia kourabydes* break, Tina calls for order. The costume department in Athens has shipped a box from her workshop and everyone needs to come for a fitting. Here's another chore that Western actors fuss about.

"When? Where?" They can hardly wait.

"Do we get costumes?" the chorus wants to know.

"*Oxi,*" I say. I've been told there's a shroud hanging in every Greek closet. "You just wear your own long white dresses."

"Oooh . . . ," they moan collectively. I wonder if Omiros has used the word for, say, "mummy wrap" instead of "shroud."

"*Saraki.*" Tina is at my side, in my ear. "May I say something?"

"Of course." Is there a euphemism for grave clothing?

"You will wear your white dresses," she tells them. "But you must make a ring of fresh flowers every day to wear as a necklace. You will look so beautiful." They actually applaud.

"They like to dress up," says the designer when we're off in a corner. "And by the way, Lukia's made a chocolate cake. You should pick some up tomorrow morning."

"Of course." I'll do anything to help her keep her figure.

After rehearsal, during dessert, Costas turns up with Tomas and Takis, carrying their instruments. Elena and Sophia rush to them.

"Sit." Out come the reserves of fish soup, spinach pies, and tomato salad. I hadn't noticed the bottle of retsina chilling in the baptismal font. Sophia uses the familiar tactic of a tough cork as she leans directly over Takis. She pulls and pulls but just can't get it out; it seems her muscles are in her butt. Takis, grinning, comes to the rescue. Elena simply hands Tomas a spinach pie. She lets her filo do the talking.

Eventually there isn't a crumb on the altar and it's very late. Theo manages to get his sisters out the door. We move to the nave and the guys tune up. Too bad I'd forgotten the little detail called sheet music.

"You sing we play," says Tomas. I'm skeptical.

Theo comes over to me. "*Dhen birazi*, Sarah *mou*. They don't read."

So we begin, and they really can play by ear. The reverb amplifies every dazzling run on the bouzouki, and the fiddle carves warm lingering lines. I walk around singing until we find a spot where my voice rides just above the waves. Dialogue would get lost in the wash, but for atmosphere and scene changes it's perfect. They're going to need some rehearsal, though.

The subject comes up later at Alpha. Since they work at the boatyard all day they can only practice when I'm busy rehearsing the cast.

"Do you know someone with an electric keyboard?" Monika asks Tomas.

"Yes, Adonis, my son. But so late at night."

"Can I borrow it?"

We all turn to look at her. She smiles shyly. So, painter sailor–piano player. "How many songs are there—three, four?" She turns to me. "You can teach them to me tomorrow."

"Great," I say.

"Just wave a white flag, a piece of sailcloth, and propose to her," Alex leans in and whispers.

45

Strike! No boats today. Maybe no boats tomorrow. Diana and I are listening to the radio. She's chewing a lettuce leaf with mayo but not so loudly I can't hear the background rabble as the reporter shouts the news from Piraeus. With no other way off the island, we're stranded. This is about the best news a person sipping French roast under a bougainvillea canopy overlooking the sea on a Greek morning with an air temperature of about seventy-eight and a wave temperature of eighty could hope to hear.

"It's a good thing that mantra article's finished," I share with Diana (who does stop and look up when you speak to her), "or I'd probably tear it up."

"Really?" Can't be Diana; she's still chewing. "What's wrong with it?" Alex says. She's not sleepwalking, but there's no pace in her approach. Nor any coffee.

"The world is perfect just as it is. There's no need to add anything to what's already here. It's called *sahaj samadhi*."

"Mmm. Is there any coffee left?"

"You passed it. And please bring it out here."

"But I'll be adding something," she mumbles as she turns around.

"So what is *samaj mahadi, maladi*?" She drapes herself over a canvas chair.

"Drink. It's too early to explain."

"Too early in the morning?"

"In your life." I pour myself coffee and take one of her biscuits.

"You can't steal from me and keep ancient wisdom to yourself. Why is Diana's mouth white? Is she getting old?"

"I put some mayo on her lettuce."

We sip in silence; only birdsong.

"God, what a perfect day," says Alex. And she doesn't even know there's a boat strike.

"That's *sahaj samadhi*"—I can't help myself—"the natural state of bliss. You're in it now, you're feeling it around you."

"Yeah, now, when everything's perfect. That's not natural."

"Right. But according to the yoga masters, it always exists, it's the nature of this world. The trick is to become aware of it all the time, even when everything seems to be going wrong. *Trick*'s the wrong word by the way."

"Don't worry, Professor Davis isn't up yet."

"Up and out. I think he's dead."

"*Samadhi!*" There must be lots of sugar in her coffee.

"That's the other kind. You have to die for it."

I fix some toast and jam and bring it out. A few caiques are slowly making their way to the fishing grounds. Others are skimming home with the night's catch. But the long wakes of the ferries are nowhere on the horizon.

"Ow!" I look down. Diana's out of lettuce. "Cut that out. Is there any of that fish risotto left?"

"She would eat that?"

"She'll eat anything."

We look at each other for a moment. "*Sahaj samadhi*," I say. I break off the charred edges and give her some of my toast. "Of course it's easier if you're a tortoise."

"What isn't?" she replies. "Have you heard back from the magazine? And what were you telling Diana about mantras?"

"I don't think they'll call me here. God, I hope not, I couldn't take another day of *Kyria* Kassoula's. I just meant there's no need to repeat a mantra when you experience natural bliss. But since you usually don't, you do."

"That clears it up."

"Good. There's a boat strike by the way."

"What! No tourists?"

"Not today."

"I'm unemployed! And look at that sea. Why don't we go with those guys on *Sweet Leilani*? It's not even blowing that hard."

"I don't feel like talking to them all day. You can go, of course."

"I'm not sure I—" A torrent of water hits us.

"Aye! Signome kyries!" Tula has knocked over an amphora up on the terrace and let go of the hose. We jump up to shake the water out of our eyes. A moment later my red espadrilles are washed overboard. Diana is spinning joyfully in a new pool.

"Saraki?" comes a soft call outside the garden gate.

"Come in."

Tina's in a maroon caftan cinched at the waist. "I was going early to market and I heard voices. Shall I bring the cake over?"

"No, no, come in. Have the world's best coffee."

"I shouldn't . . . *Entaxi.*" Her enormous cocoa-colored Panama brushes the canopy and rains down bougainvillea.

"Look out for Diana, she's feeding somewhere." Which makes me realize I haven't seen Al Fresco this morning. "Where's . . . ?" I ask Alex.

"I think he's curled up with Monika. He doesn't like getting up this early." Which means on my bed. "I'll just get a cup," she says to Tina; *and a dog,* her look tells me. They both appear moments later. Then Monika, dangling a cup. But the pot is empty.

"I'll make more," I announce. But if the boat strike lasts and supplies dwindle, my *samadhi* will be tested.

"I'm off," says Tina. "Will you stop in this afternoon? I want to show you the costumes. Everyone's coming tomorrow for fittings."

"Sure. Just knock on the door as you're passing by."

"*Entaxi.* Lukia will make us a late lunch."

"We'll be there." Alex speaks for all. "Plan B," she announces, when the door closes. "Forget *Leilani.* We can take *Dishy* out to Cannoli late this afternoon."

"You mean Kanela. Cannoli is an Italian pastry."

"With a great beach."

"You're sure you don't want to go sailing with Helmut and Co.?"

"And pass up a Lukia lunch?" says Alex. "That's my definition of sahaj . . . saladi."

That afternoon we huddle around an old steamer trunk in the leaf-lit courtyard while Tina flings things at us. Her cohorts in Athens have sent several seasons' worth of rags and finery that we hold up, sniff, and otherwise consider for a postmaster playing a king, a fisherman prince, et cetera.

"Ooooh this is wonderful. Oh! And it's my color!" Alex starts pulling on a feathered turquoise sweater. She's left the costume department to shop for herself.

"This robe's perfect for your eyes, Monika," says Tina, instantly corrupted.

"How about our Miranda?" I venture. But Monika's zipping it up.

"O brave new world that . . . ?"

" *. . . has such people in it,"* says the dialogue coach, now twirling in a sequined tutu. A boater with red and blue ribbons sails across the courtyard and lands on a priceless amphora. Good thing it's straw. Monika plucks it off.

"From *Oklahoma.* Ado Annie," says Tina. She extracts a green feather boa and tosses it to Alex, who wraps it around her neck and perfect collarbones.

"Thanks. I've always wanted one of these!"

"We used it for *Hello, Dolly.* You'll see it's a bit thin where Maria Milos's dog chased it."

"Just the thing for Caliban's drunk scene," I say to no one listening.

"*Saraki*, you should have this blouse." Tina throws it at me. "It's for the gondolier in *Cosi.*" Navy with white stripes, my favorite colors; what the hell . . . I pull it over my T-shirt.

It's only when a tray of freshly baked spanakopitas—spinach pies—arrives that a fragment of purpose returns.

"No problem with Prospero and Miranda and the crew, but I don't know what's happened to some of the royal costumes. I thought we had lots of them in wardrobe; there isn't even a crown."

"Could this shipment have gone through Stephanos's office?" I mumble through a spinach pie.

"Hmm. He's probably wearing it around the house. That blouse looks great on you, Sarah; keep it."

"But wouldn't it look good on you too?"

"No, wrong scale," says Tina, who isn't eating. No doubt *her* scale lives in the kitchen.

Lukia brings out stuffed red peppers and tea. We sit on old Berber carpets on the marble ground. Monika in her gorgeous embroidered robe falls silent. Along with the rest of us. The magic courtyard is bedecked with thespian finery.

"No ermine, no crown. I'm really sorry."

"That's OK," I say. "The king could wear a crown of leaves."

"That'd make Stephanos happy," says Alex.

"He might even take off his gun," says Tina. "Ok, let's make some notes." We go to her worktable and she sketches while we talk. When Lukia produces an orange flan, in actual flan dishes, the costume party in the courtyard comes to a halt.

"You can't go out on the street like that," I have to tell Alex and Monika when we're ready to leave.

"Uh-uh. And where's your gondola?" says Alex.

"How about Cannoli. Is there still time?" says Monika as we're walking back home in mufti.

"Kanela." I check the angle of the sun. "Sure. After we pick up the keyboard."

"Not me," says Alex. "I just remembered Iannis is teaching me to slalom this afternoon." We stop.

"Iannis?" I say.

"Yes."

"But what about Petros?" Monika is developing an interview style.

"Petros? . . . Ahhh . . . *Frailty, thy name is woman.* Hamlet." She grins.

"So nothing happened?" I say. I've heard that before.

"Nothing of note."

A few minutes later we're at our front door.

"Alex," I say, as Al Fresco lets us in, "you *know* how to slalom."

"I've forgotten," she beams.

46

Tomas's house, where we're picking up the electric keyboard, is a farm on a quiet cove, far from any village. His fields run right to the water's edge; only a low stone wall separates bushy rows of tomatoes and potatoes from the sea. Out in the bay, a tiny caique with bright red freeboard is nearly submerged. Not capsized; its new hull is curing. A scruffy oily-eyed donkey tethered to a fig tree greets us with deafening friendliness. No need to ring the copper goat bell dangling from Tomas's doorsill.

"*Ella Toma! Ella dho!*" Tomas's wife rushes from the terrace. Small wooden chairs and a sun-stripped table sit under a tamarisk in the front garden. A hen and her chicks are scrabbling beneath it. Two kittens are wrestling on top. She grabs my arm to pull me toward a chair. "*Cafés me zachari?*"—coffee with sugar?

"*Oxi, efharisto,*" says Monika sweetly.

"Toma!" With a long sweep of her bulging naked forearm she clears the table of leaves and beasts.

"*Fige!*" she shouts at the chicks, waving a kitchen towel at them. "I am Eleni, you're Sarah aren't you? And . . ."

"Monika," I tell her. "Happy to meet you."

"*Nai.* Sit, sit . . . *cafés.*" She disappears into the house.

"Can't you say we've just had tea?" Monika asks.

"It wouldn't matter."

We sit back and succumb to the beauty of this idyll. I'm imagining that it's ours. Is she imagining the same thing?

Eleni brings back Greek coffees and little things wrapped in yellow foil, which she immediately begins to unwrap for us.

"Toma!" she yells, and the donkey picks up her call. The coffee's delicious. I never put in that much sugar. The cookies are stones, covered in milk chocolate. Experience tells me we'll hate them if we ever break through.

While we sip and wait for Tomas to appear, Eleni fills us in on her family tree. She's a Kallitsis, which means she's related to everyone on the island: sister to Alonso the king, second cousin to Caliban, aunt by marriage to Ariel. And sister-in-law to Popi who's been fooling around with Sebastian.

"*Trelli*, Popi." She shakes her head and smiles. "Crazy, but what can you do. Her dog died."

No family peccadillo is simple or sacred or beneath her radar. Words flow in an unbroken stream. Woodwind players spend years mastering circular breathing; Eleni should sell that keyboard and take up the sax.

Her voice is high, low, lilting, grating, whiny, husky, and accompanied by the dramatic facial expressions of a silent film star. Her elbows arms fingers dance in punctuation. By the time Tomas appears we are numb with amazement and information. *Information*'s the wrong word; I understand a quarter of what she's saying. And Monika . . . but it's the performance that counts.

"What has Eleni been telling you?" says Tomas, twinkling. And we have one more coffee for the road.

Eventually the keyboard is strapped across the back basket of Ernie Banks and we head for the port. The cookies we didn't eat are blocking my headlights in the front basket. Luckily I don't need them yet.

Kanela ("cinnamon") Beach is partly in shadow by the time we anchor. Rust-colored stones freckle the sand, and the shallow clear water is filled with yellow-finned small fry. They scatter through our toes as we wade in. The sea is so warm now, you can stay in for hours.

"Sing to me," says Monika as we're floating out in the sun pools. Which I do; the whole score of Katrin's *Tempest*—a cappella except for a few sporadic bells on goats grazing on the bushy shore. Finally we stretch out on the ledge where the rocks still catch the sun.

"I think privacy is a luxury more precious than any material thing," says Monika.

"Agreed."

"I grew up in a big family, but luckily we were on the coast. I could always escape to a rock. You?"

"I had a tree house . . . it overlooked the sea. But my sister and brother used to invade it."

"Ah, no. I always picked a small rock. And high"—she laughs—"so I could rain stones down on my brothers if they came to bother me."

When the shadows reach our perch, it's time to go back.

"Let's break up these cookies for the fish," says Monika, unwrapping them. "God, they're hard. What do they taste like?"

"I think stale is the flavor they're after."

"No wonder she's toothless."

"Oh no, they're just for visitors."

"I wonder if that's how these stones turned brown," I mutter as we're grinding down the hulls.

"I'll bet you're working on a chocolate field theory to explain the whole universe," says Monika, bashing away at a cookie.

I look over at her. "You've been reading my diary."

Eventually we scatter all the crumbs, creating a whirlpool of small fry that tickle our ankles. They follow in a wide glittering fan as we wade in deeper to launch *Dishy*.

Monika leans back against a pontoon and covers my bare feet with hers. "What's on your mind?" she says, the engine speed low enough for conversation. The sun sinks quickly toward the horizon as we sail directly along its dazzling path.

"The lighting rig for the church."

"Why don't you leave that to me."

"Because I really like doing it," I say. The sun drops into the sea. The low thinly sketched coastline of clouds glows intensely pink, and we watch for the green flash that sometimes follows a watery sunset. Not tonight. Silently we round the headland. I notice that Monika is bringing out the underdeveloped side of me that's fearlessly direct. How is she doing that? By being the least self-absorbed person I've ever met?

"OK." She drums on my toes with her heels. "But maybe I can help?"

"That would be great."

A fisherman waves at us as we slow down to pass without creating a wake. A line of red doughnut-shaped floats trailing behind his stern is barely visible on the surface of the water. I tip up the engine to drift across it. The deck of his tiny circus-striped caique is crammed with cans and floats; nets are coiled in big reed baskets; oilskins and a sweater are flapping at the entrance to the low cutty; an upturned pair of boots is lashed to his ship-to-shore antenna. From a hook on the salt-caked transom, an old copper briki rocks in time to the sea. His universe in the wingspan of a gull.

"I'd love to paint that," says Monika.

"Take a picture with your mind," I say.

"Mmm," she nods.

I set the engine back in the sea and scan the horizon for other nets.

"Another thing," says Moni as we're coming in to shore, "and don't jump over . . ." I turn to her. "I'd like you to share my rock."

47

Tina's sitting cross-legged in one of the pews stitching a crown of olive leaves. Her costume department surrounds her. Maria, my favorite baker, is sewing some gray gauze onto wire hangers that she holds up for my inspection. "Wings for Georgaki."

"Bravo, Maria."

The caryatids are stretching a tape across Stephanos's chest, even more puffed up from the attention. He seems to be mouthing his lines. Stella and the tiny cake maker have tattered blouses on their laps. They're frowning and mumbling as they sew leaves over the holes. Now and then they hold them up for Tina's inspection and look mystified each time she says "Beautiful!" Evdhomada has spirals of ribbon around her arms. Theo the surgeon is stitching them onto the shoulders of her cape. Is he leaning in a little close? Costas, who used to be a carpenter, is sanding a broadsword across the baptismal font. Omiros scurries around with coffees. Really dangerous with all that fabric. At least they're not eating sticky baklava.

"Where've you been?" Alex asks from the top of a ladder. She's got a spotlight in her hand and another tied to her belt. My crumpled lighting sketch is taped to the top rung. "I'm not sure where you want these."

"Right there is fine. But be sure they're low enough for their beams to clear the rafters." *Where have you been?* I ignore, since if ever there was a case of the pot calling the kettle black. . . Caliban is pulling on green tights with the help of Maria Milos's Chihuahua.

"*Katse! Fige! Fige!*" has no effect. Another non-Greek-speaking dog.

I gather Omiros and the rest of the spotlights and we rig from rafter to rafter. Until I start a small fire. One of the sails has slipped down and rubbed against a hot lamp. I try blowing it out. Since the front door's open and the Meltemi's gusting we get lots of smoke right away.

"*Exo,* out! *Exo* . . . oooooo!" Theo shouts.

"And take the costumes with you . . . ooo . . . ooo!" I cry.

Alex passes below me, her arms loaded with material. "Try not to burn your bridges," she calls up.

Monika runs up my ladder with a pitcher of water, taken from the coffee shop on the altar. I dip in the smoking sail and it fizzles out. Cast and crew return, chattering excitedly. It's a natural dinner break.

Takis and Tomas suddenly appear in the nave just as the kalamari salad is making way for *dholmades* and a *kolokithia* casserole. I'm stretched out on a pew scribbling some stage directions. Monika brings me a tall glass of retsina disguised as ginger ale.

"Is it olfactory or ESP, do you think?" I ask her.

"Neither," she says softly. "We'll start rehearsing as soon as you do and I didn't want them to feel neglected."

"It's a good thing too," says Alex, carrying a similar glass. "If they came any later we'd have to start eating all over again."

"Omire, call places."

"No coffee, *Saraki*?"

"That's Act Four."

"The boat strike's over," says Petros, arriving at Alpha and moving into the chair that previously held Tina's Gucci knapsack. "The road's been voted down."

"Is that what the strike was about?" I ask.

"I don't think so," says Theo.

"But there may be some connection . . . we think," says Tina.

"Over. Good," says Iannis, shaking his golden hair vigorously. Alex turns to admire it. I guess. It can't be his politics.

"So we should expect a taxi strike tomorrow," Petros continues.

"What? For how long?" If this were the West End I'd be leaping off the cliff. Petros smiles at Arabella before turning his sunny attention to me.

"Many days, probably. Saint Christodolous's feast day is Friday, and once they stop working . . ."

"Oh God." I take a deep breath.

"I am That, I am That," says Alex as I exhale.

"Could Stephanos do something about this?" I ask.

"Stephanos?" Petros and Theo repeat.

"Or Vassilis? I mean, is there any local government that might outlaw this or, I don't know, force them to sit down and discuss it?"

Theo seems to be thinking this over. So does Petros, but maybe only because Arabella is focused on him.

"We have many strikes in summer," says Iannis. Which is a complete sentence.

"Because of the good weather?" Alex encourages him. They've found a topic!

"I think," he replies. I throw her a triumphant smile, which she lets fly past. Then I turn to Theo, who has to have an answer by now.

"The mayor can ask people to talk about a problem. Only if there is danger he can do something. Otherwise he is not elected again."

"Boats or taxis, roads or sea—every year we have this," says Takis. He's balancing a huge copper tray loaded with another round of drinks, including one for himself.

"We call it holy war," Petros says.

I'm trying to follow this but the baseball players are throwing footballs.

"What makes it holy?" I ask.

"Holi-day!" says Takis. "*Stin yiamas*—to our health," he adds. "On the house."

"Holi-day!" Iannis laughs and we all join in. We're Takis's only customers at this hour, but he would never rush us or even appear interested in closing. It's a national trait worthy of an ode.

"No taxis. Damn!" says Arabella as the laughter dies.

"You could rent a motorbike," I tell her.

"I should die here?"

"I'll drive you anywhere," says Petros on cue.

"*Malakka.*" Theo is upset, but not Theo the Director, Theo the reformer. "A road that disturbs nobody."

"Except fishermen," says Iannis. We look at him. "*Ftohi.*"

"Poor," Tina translates.

"True," says Takis. "The taxi drivers are more rich. Enough there are roads."

Who wouldn't second *that*.

"For every taxi driver on Pharos, there's a cousin who fishes," says Tina. "Let it be."

We all recognize an exit line.

Alex is walking along the beach like a seagull in a crosswind. "Ride up with me," I say. "We'll pick up your bike tomorrow."

"What makes you think you're more sober than I am?"

"Because watching you walk makes me sick."

Candles are burning at the tiny church of Santa Barbara as we begin the twisting climb to Kastro. Otherwise the road is dark, sweet with eucalyptus and jasmine. Tina waves as she passes us in her pale blue minimoke. You just see the gold bracelets catching moonlight. That answer! Maybe I should have showed her my mantra article. Never underestimate small people, I decide, no matter how covered with labels their little bodies.

Monika's caught up with us; her headlight appears in my rearview mirror. I've put this afternoon's conversation on a high shelf, where I beg it to stay till the show opens.

"We open in ten days, right?" Alex calls into my ear. Am I thinking out loud?

"Right," I say, wondering what else she's picking up.

"And the taxi strike might last through July." The wind is wailing as we pass the shrine at sunset curve.

"Aye aye!"

"So!" she shouts. "All that cutting you did for Caliban and now Tino's out of work!"

"Let it be!" I yell. Quick study, no? Only now, it's a prayer.

48

The electricity cuts out while I'm brushing my teeth. At least I wasn't soaped up in the shower. It happens a lot because the underwater cable that feeds Pharos is no thicker than dental floss. If a big fish bumps into it, or gets something caught in his molars . . . Luckily the stove runs on gas so coffee is possible, and fried bread, which, as everyone knows—not Tina—is the reward for a primitive life. (The electricity company supplies candles free of charge for these romantic moments.) It's not all good news, though. When Iannis comes with the mail he tells us it's not the cable. The electricity workers have gone on strike for the day.

"Why, Ianni? *Yiayti?*"

"*Yiayti?*" He looks at me sweetly, then slowly shakes his head. "Sarah *mou* . . ." The class dummy. He hands over my neighbor's latest forwards: a postcard from Marjorie tripping with my nephews in Disneyland, eight credit card solicitations, the spring seed catalog from a Devon garden center, and an invitation to a wine and olive oil festival next week in Surrey. When I get back I'm changing neighbors.

"Let's go on strike too," says Alex helpfully at second toastfry. "Whaddaya say, Diana?" Our leading tortoise is blinking in the sunlight, stepping and chewing on a buttery crust. It's another crystal-blue morning in a breezy courtyard dancing with bougainvillea.

"Are you crazy? The shows opens in what—ten days?"

I look over at Monika, stretched out on a bench painting her toenails. She feels the glance and smiles back, but doesn't vote.

"It's going to be impossible to rehearse without electricity."

"It is? Shakespeare didn't have any."

"He didn't know any better." She flips the toast with a nifty gesture. "Aldo '98 is sailing to Turkey today, coming back late tomorrow. On that gorgeous boat with the wine cellar. We're all invited."

"How do you know this?"

"Shakespeare didn't have to rehearse at night," says Monika, casting her ballot.

What the hell. "We've got to tell everybody."

"Not everybody," says Alex, "just Omiros."

49

A couple of hours later we're stepping aboard the long sleek blue-hulled walnut and teak (as in forty hours of polishing per week) motor yacht *Sirena,* tied up practically alongside *Soapdish.* I try to sneak past her.

Standing next to Aldo's captain is Arabella, holding aloft a glass of bubbly. Hot pink fingernails are glistening around its stem. She's had a manicure. By candlelight?

"Welcome *cara,* welcome *tutti,*" she says waving from the stern in a tight white T-shirt and capri pants. The tips of the blue anchor on the T-shirt come to rest exactly over her nipples and rise and fall with every gesture. Yesterday those moves were for Petros, but *Arabella* must mean "flow with life."

"Sarah, Alex, I am so happy you're coming." Aldo '98 appears in the gangway with a sweating green bottle of Taittinger and a handful of crystal flutes. He looks past us to the blond bonus.

"Aldo," I say, "this is Monika from Sweden."

"Bellisima." He beams with uncluttered enthusiasm. I should jump ship now and drag her to my dinghy. He fills the glasses and passes them around. Arabella disappears belowdecks.

We're out of the harbor and setting sail before you can say *andiamo,* because *Sirena* has roller furling, roller reefing, power winching, global satellite positioning, autopilot, loran, and a gimbaled ice bucket.

(If Columbus had had loran, you'd be reading this in Portuguese.)

"You're a sailor, *si*?" Aldo says as he refills me. "Maybe you like to see the works?"

"*Grazie,* Aldo, I would." Because when I win Big Lotto and *Soapdish* is swinging from the tender hooks of my Concordia '38, all this will come in handy.

"I would too, please. I also sail," says the natural blonde.

"*Certamente!*"

Suddenly I notice how muscled and handsome '98 is, in an ordinary Latin god sort of way. And I consider: It may be spiritually evolved to be unimpressed by outer beauty, but it's also pretty stupid in terms of global social positioning. I try to decipher the tone in Monika's "please."

Aldo stretches out a lean tanned finger to push a button on the pilot's console.

"*Bella,* we come down."

"Aye aye, *caro mio,*" comes the voice from below.

"And Alex?" Monika turns to me as we start down the companion-way. But Alex is stretched out on the foredeck chatting with Aldo's Irish captain.

"She'll find her way," I say.

The galley is stainless, gimbaled, and fully equipped to turn out Michelin stars. At this very moment Arabella is making a *quattro formaggio frittata.* A bowl of fresh strawberries sits on a stainless shelf inlaid with rubber buttons.

Monika puts her hand on Aldo's shoulder.

"May I take a few pictures?"

"Of course," he says, touching her hair.

Is the ship lurching?

"Pictures?" The chef lifts her dripping whisk, one anchor point rising, and kisses Aldo on the mouth. Good!

Across from the galley is the pilot's station. It trembles with red, green, and yellow screens and resembles the cockpit of a stealth bomber (but how would I know?). A chart on the fold-down table shows this precise bit of the Aegean.

"Sit down, Sarah." I do. *Ham sa, ham sa* is being drowned out by *cool it, cool it.* I run my hands over the consoles, but I don't push anything because who knows which button launches the missiles. Aldo turns up the gain on the loran and presto, there's the coastline of Turkey.

"Our present position is the green circle. We can never be lost."

Oh yeah?

"How often do you update your charts?" I say.

"They send me everything new," he replies to Monika.

We move to the main salon, an elegant semicircle of dove-gray leather sofas and chairs, and teak teak teak. It's a crime against Africa.

"Wow," says Monika.

"This is beautiful, Aldo," I ad-lib.

"*Grazie.* You like my paintings?"

"Mmm, great taste," says Monika, circumambulating the cabin.

"All Italian. No very expensive but I like so much to collect."

I can misinterpret everything he says.

He takes us along the corridor, opening the doors to three gleaming, cleverly fitted double cabins. "You sleep here tonight. Any one you like."

Scusi?

We arrive at the sumptuous master's suite—with a huge art deco bed and mirrored walls. Monika doesn't seem to like it. (I'm no longer interested in my own impressions.)

"How do you keep this clean?" she asks.

What a weird question!

"What a weird question," I say when we're back on deck having pre-lunch Bloody Marys.

"I felt weird."

"How?"

Alex arrives with the captain. Her body language says they've developed a real rapport. Maybe I'll lose two birds in one night.

"Michael's from County Armagh. He went to school not twenty miles from my grandmother's cottage."

"Amazing." Especially as Alex isn't one to flout her Irish cottages.

"Aye. That place was on my newspaper route."

Michael's Irish smile drills into me. I'm speechless and thought-free. No mantra anywhere.

"Cheers," says Mike, refilling my tumbler. "So how d'you like our equipment?"

"What?"

"The GPS and loran. We could dock this lady between a chicken and her egg."

My God it's true; all Irishmen are poets.

"I don't doubt it, Michael, but let's aim for Turkey instead."

"Ha ha . . ."

"Why weird?" I try again as the frittata is being passed. Monika's sitting next to me, but that could just be habit. I take a tiny piece because I've lost my appetite.

"It's just so self-conscious," she whispers. "What about all those mirrors? When we're in bed together I don't see a thing. I am *out* of my mind."

"Aldo," I say, "could you pass that back here?"

I'm back at the console after lunch, relaxed and getting a lesson in GPS from the paperboy. The tannoy is alive with Greek fishermen trading fish sightings and their fishwives trading recipes.

"Bloody hell, that's the international distress channel," says Michael.

Inside the cackle you can just make out Turkish bulletins. They become louder and more frequent as we get closer.

"What are they saying?" says Alex.

"Damned if I know."

"What if they're trying to communicate with us? Does anybody aboard speak Turkish?" says Monika, perched on the edge of my chair.

"Hell no."

"What if they're storm warnings?" says Alex.

"For storms I look up to the sky." Auden? And he's right, isn't he? We're sailing in a robin's-egg sea with a limitless horizon, doing a steady seven knots. But Alex has Virgo rising.

"Have you got a dictionary on board?"

"Aye." He pulls a thin book from the shelf above the chart table.

"This is a phrase book, Michael," Alex says as she opens it. *"There's too much starch in my collar."*

"Oh, sorry . . ."

"I need a diuretic," she mumbles. *"Is this a vegetable?"*

"What's going on here?" says Aldo, coming over with a plate of fresh purple figs. Arabella's anchor points are dancing behind him. We're living an Italian operetta.

"May I take some of these?" says Alex, her fig-sticky fingers plucking recipe cards from a box in the galley. "I'm going to make some vocabulary cards."

"Oh that's wonderful," says Arabella.

"But why do we need to speak Turkish?" says Aldo, screwing his manly face into a question mark. He must have gone to a British public school. But who cares . . . if that's where he learned to pour Dom Perignon.

The steering wheel on the upper deck sits behind a neat semicircle of blue-and-white-striped cushions. We settle back with drinks in hand and let the breeze and the pale blue sky transport us. Monika opens her case of pastels and props her sketchpad on her knees. The shoreline gives way to open sea, flecked with fishing boats and a few other sailing yachts. A light wind leaves a string of bubbles on every wave. Nurse Ellen soon appears with a stack of little cards. "Turkish 101," she commands. Monika obediently closes her sketchpad.

Alex takes us through the cards a few times, then comes the test.

"OK, Aldo, 'Yogurt'?"

"*Yo-ar-ta.*"

"Close. *Ti. Yo-ar-ti.* Good. Michael, 'I come from Armagh'?"

"Who bloody cares about that?"

"OK. 'Honey.'"

"Yes?"

"Honey the food."

"Oh." Laughing. "No idea."

"*Myeli.*"

"Uh-huh."

"How about 'Thank you.'"

"*Tush a cur* . . . blah blah blah."

"Monika?"

"*Shesh a kir* . . . sorry, that's a hard one."

"Sarah?"

I'm trying to see the ink through the back of the card.

"*Shush a cur air a dream.*"

"Air a dream?"

"Well, what's 'no'? That comes up a lot more."

"Than 'thank you'? Where were you brought up?"

"Not in Constantinople."

"That's Istanbul, if you don't want them to burn the boat behind us."

And so on until we pass the headlands and sail into the harbor just at dusk.

A uniformed party of three is waiting for us as we come alongside. They're standing casually but attentively around the only unoccupied bollard on the pier.

WELCOME TO KUSADASI says the banner strung high between light posts behind them. It's dusk but the lights aren't on.

Just like that, my old *Midnight Express* reel begins to play, and I'm writing my memoirs from a moldy Turkish prison cell.

"Ahoy!" calls Aldo and throws the bowline. The guy whose shoe it hits looks down and kicks it away. It slides into the water.

"Christ!" cries Aldo, as he dangles over the freeboard to try to haul it in.

"Throw the midships!" yells Michael, who's cut the engine.

"Reverse!" calls Monika. We're a moment away from colliding with the dock. I grab the midships line and jump ashore, then push us off. Aldo, in the bow, is readying a second throw.

"Tesshacur air a dream," I call to the welcoming party. The shortest one stretches out his arm to take the line.

"And *this* time . . . ," Aldo growls as he throws.

"Cool it, Aldo," Alex say softly from the bow. I sprint to the bollard, take the line from our host, and tie up. Then I jump back aboard.

"Here at last! *Bravissimo,* Aldo," cries Arabella, waving her arms above her head as she passes me. "I'm going downstairs to dress."

I reach out and snare a bare arm. "I think you should stay in your T-shirt."

"What?"

I beam at her like a stupid person and cock my head toward our hosts.

"Ahh." A light goes on. So she knows the power of those anchor points.

The gang of three boards *Sirena* and asks for her papers. Aldo hands over a couple of stuffed envelopes. One begins to read as the other two walk through the cabins. After half an hour we're keen to go ashore.

"What do you need?" says Alex in Turkish, reading from the Hotel Check-In section. The reply, which we repeat to each other several times to get the right pronunciation, is not to be found among "a bigger bed," "is that a bar beneath us?" "what time is breakfast?" The leader shakes his head and disembarks with Aldo's entire file.

"Shall we get off and let them figure it out?" says Arabella, who has a contact in town to buy kilims.

"They may shoot us in the back," says Michael.

"Santa Maria!" She smooths her anchors and starts setting up for cocktails.

Alex brings out her vocabulary cards. Sadly, her student body is busy mixing drinks. But there's fresh blood! She pulls up a deck chair opposite the two officers, just inches from their heavy stinky cigarette smoke . . . the sea breeze makes it possible. She opens Aldo's book and flips through to Meeting People.

"What is your name?" Silence.

"Are you married?" They look at each other. Too personal?

"How many children have you got?" Classified information?

"Do you come from this village?" Nothing.

"Maybe they're not Turks?" Alex turns to me. But you can see they're enjoying her attention.

"These guys seem awfully stiff," says Monika softly, passing by with a Bloody Mary. "They've got pistols. We should get them to relax."

I look at Arabella, but she's absorbed in Aldo's lemon zester. (What does she do with that?) So I take the phrase book from Alex and find the chapter titled Going Out.

"May I get you a drink? Whiskey?" They understand me perfectly. Monika fills their glasses. En route back to Meeting People, I happen upon Personal Pronouns.

"Alex, here's the trouble: You're using 'I' when you mean 'you.'"

"I'm *what*?"

"You're saying 'What is *my* name; how many children do *I* have?' They think you're crazy."

"Aye aye aye."

"Exactly."

With that cleared up, the three of them are soon laughing and chattering away, though Alex can't have a clue what they're saying. Another hour passes before their leader returns with a tall guy wearing lots of stripes. He orders us, in plain English, to leave the port at once. Aldo begins to fume. In Italian. But fuming doesn't really require translation. I'm about to take control when Arabella opens her arms and throws them around Aldo.

"Caro mio, amore . . ." He has no air to continue. Then she turns to the chief, tugs at her anchor points, cocks her finger, and pirouettes. He follows her down the companionway. Minutes pass.

"How is she communicating?" says Monika.

"Hand signals?" says Alex with a grin. I check out Aldo, who's oblivious. Back comes the chief, trailed by anchors aweigh.

"We can spend the night here," she says.

"That's great!" we all say. *"Tesh a dir air a dream,"* I throw in for goodwill.

The chief looks at me suspiciously. "We go with you for dinner," he says in not what you'd call a conversational tone.

The six of us squeeze into the back of two squad cars and are driven to a barren hillside overlooking the town. We stop abruptly, Keystone Kops style, and walk to a low strung-out brick building with a huge iron-studded wooden gate. "Prison contemporary," Alex mumbles next to me. I'm studying the pistols and handcuffs decorating their belts as two of the policemen push open the doors.

We walk through a paneled arcade lined with fish tanks out onto a torchlit terrace. Polished old fruitwood tables are set among blossoming almond trees. The earth is covered in pink petals. There are no walls, only Grecian columns scattered throughout the garden. These are entwined in vines heavy with bunches of ripening grapes. The place is humming, and not with a Sing Sing clientele. We sit at the edge of the hill; the lights of the town are glinting below us, the air so still our candle flame looks painted. It's obvious that lots of people aren't as discouraged by a hideous facade as I am.

The chief, now relaxed and cheerful, orders for us. It's a hit parade of Turkish dishes. While we eat like ravens he tells the miraculous tale of ancient Ephesus. He regrets many times over that we cannot see it tomorrow, but our papers are not in order.

"What is order?" I finally ask. Alex and Monika shoot me looks of alarm. But we've emptied so many bottles of wine, with so many toasts to friendship that a samurai war cry would bounce off his epaulettes. Not that I want to push our, make that Arabella's, luck. But we need to know; the plan is to return someday.

"Order, my American friend?" The chief beams, and then raises his decorated shoulder pads and opens his palms in the universal gesture of mystery.

50

"What a terrible waste of time." Aldo is pouring champagne as we dine in the stern of *Sirena* the next night, back on Pharos. "I'll never go back there."

"Yes you will, *caro*. It was fun after all."

"Fun? *Per piacere, Bella . . .*"

"Arabella's right," says Monika, chewing on a sirloin from the ship's freezer. "I'm glad we went. The sailing was great, that fish place, the sky last night . . ."

"And think of the fortune we saved not getting to those bazaars," says Alex. "Don't you agree?" she says to me gently. Alex knows I've wanted to see Ephesus since before I was born.

"I absolutely do. *Locananda samadhi sukam*," I say, enlightened by the tiny bubbles.

"Where's that?"

"Right here. It means the bliss of *samadhi* is wherever you happen to be. I've always wanted to see Ephesus, as Alex knows. But this experience was terrific—the trip, the company, even the guys last night."

"I will never understand women." Michael laughs, throwing his arm around the closest one, Alex. They click glasses.

"Malakka!" John the Baptist appears on the dock as if by radar. He leaps aboard with his shoes on. Michael jumps up to intercept him, unconscious of the greater danger to his person than his deck.

"Your shoes, mate!"

"What?"

Alex scurries between them and gives Iannis a preemptive kiss.

"What have we here then?" says Michael, turning to us.

"A heat-seeking missile," I reply.

"Come have something to eat," says Alex. "Aldo has steak!" She attempts to lead him to the table. It's clear Iannis would rather bite into Michael. He doesn't move. Alex drops to the deck and begins untying his shoes. I am wildly impressed at her abandonment of principles.

"Aren't you the waterskiing instructor?" says Michael. "The guy who found the mayor's car?"

"Is me!" Iannis crows to his new friend.

51

"Why do we ever forget this?" says Alex from the stove where she and Monika are making omelettes. I'm sitting on the counter near the fridge in case they need anything. "One little compliment is all it takes." She's waving her whisk. "If Brutus had just said, 'Nice speech, Mark Antony,' we'd be living in the Roman Empire."

"Oye! oye!" I cry, since there's no other rabble around. And then, because I can't help it, "Alex, this job has really brought history into focus for you."

Her whisk is too drippy to swing at me.

"But wasn't Aldo '98 amazing?" says Monika. "I think we should upgrade him."

"How?" I ask.

"Give him a new year. Next year, for instance."

"I don't think Arabella will keep him," I say.

"Because she's an adventurer?"

"No. More like an explorer," says Alex. "Think Vasco da Gama."

"Vasco da . . . ! Whatever happened to Petros the Conqueror? History is truly infecting your brain."

"Give me some parsley," says Alex. "And more *gravura* if we've got it."

"A great adventure," says Monika, "no matter how she did it."

"But I still want to see Ephesus," I say from inside the fridge.

"Why don't we go when the show's over?" she says. I turn around slowly and hand things to Alex. The future has just invaded the present —a move that's not in my playbook.

"That's a good idea," says Alex, looking at me innocently, if that's possible. She garnishes the omelette while I collect silverware.

"Maybe we should learn Turkish first." I say as I head into the courtyard.

"You're not serious," says Monika, following me out with plates. "You've traveled all over the place. How's your Japanese?"

So fast, so smart, so fearless. Am I ready for this? *"Mir i druzba,* Moni *mu."*

"Peace and friendship," says Alex, dividing the omlette. "In Russian."

"All my Russian," I say.

Breakfast passes without the subject reappearing. But I'm not kidding myself. My life is changing minute by minute, and I need to be there. *"Ham sa, ham sa,"* I repeat as we ride down to town.

Except the taxi strike means there are local women walking on the road in the heat (not that they ever pay—only foreigners do that), and of course we offer them rides. The first one I come to outweighs me three to one, not counting two huge baskets of vegetables. Like all Greek women her age, she rides sidesaddle. Her husband must not have a bike because she's no good at gear changes or shifting her weight on corners. With a big dead load taking all traction off the front wheel, steering is impossible. Every turn has *amen* written on it. Instead of contemplating life with Monika I find myself contemplating life after death.

Alex goes by me with a frail old lady nicely balanced on the back.

"You're all over the road," she shouts. "Your rear tire's almost flat.

Slow down!" If I slow down here the baskets will spill out and we'll skid over a cliff on a track of beans.

"Why aren't you coasting?" Monika yells as she flies past with a wiry widow wrapped around her waist.

"Because it's only second gear that kept me in touch with that road," I explain, gasping for breath at the end of the ride. They're looking like they've been waiting hours instead of minutes for me to arrive with the church key. "I'm lucky to be alive," I say emphatically.

"I'll set up the keyboard while you find the guys," says Monika.

"Next time pick up somebody your own size," says Alex.

And I thought they were rivals for my affection?

Takis and Tomas are playing backgammon outside at Nikos's—a game they probably started in kindergarten.

"Don't interrupt them," I tell Alex as we head for their table. "It won't take long." So we stand and watch their warp-speed smack stack and rattle.

What's wrong with this picture, I ask myself as the four of us enter the church. Monika has set up the keyboard in the back, away from any echo, and is tuning my guitar. The critic saints are perfectly hidden by sails. Light beams crisscross the wooden floor and pool around the pillars. Iannis the Baptist walks in behind us carrying a can of beer.

"*Yasoo, Aleex!*"

Food! That's what's missing. We've never worked here without an altar of provisions and a font full of chilling retsina. The atmosphere is still and sacred.

"*Yasoo,* Ianni." Alex takes a sip from the can. "We're practicing the music."

"Stay if you like," I tell him. What's he doing here at this hour? It's the height of the tourist tanning season.

"*Oxi;* I'm working at the dock. I hear you and I think to say hello."

"I thought he was going to tell us the Volvo's missing again," says Alex when we take a break.

"I thought he was going to tell us Petros is missing. Forever."

"Your flair for the dramatic."

"Or Michael," I add.

"What are you doing?" Theo is standing sunlit in the doorway.

"Rehearsing the music. Will you stay and listen? I'd really like your opinion."

"Of course, Sarah *mou*."

We all tune up with Monika and play through the score. It sounds pretty good to me, though the guitar is drowned out by Takis's bouzouki.

"*Thavmasia*," says Theo, standing up and applauding.

"It really works," says Alex, grinning.

"Can you hear the guitar?" I ask.

"No." Together.

"Then I won't play it. These guys are so much better than I am, anyway."

"But the songs! We must hear."

"OK. Taki, can you follow me?"

"I try," he says, smiling. We run through the first two songs.

"This does not work, I think," says Theo.

"Theo's right," says Monika. " 'Full Fathoms Five' sounds really weird with the bouzouki. Arcadia needs a guitar."

"Most people think Arcadia was in ancient Greece," I say. "In which case we need a lute."

"Swell," says Alex. "Moni, you wouldn't happen to have one?"

"Well what do *you* think, Alexi *mou*?" I say sincerely.

"The guitar," she says. "Ariel's song will be much sweeter, and more mysterious. You just need to rehearse a little more."

"That can be arranged," says Monika suggestively. The soft lines of Theo's sunny face harden. He looks at me and cocks his head as if to spill out a question.

"Let's all have some lunch at Angira," I say, getting up and grabbing my notebook. "We'll set all the music cues so we can put them in the scripts tonight."

"Good idea!" says Alex, who graduated summa cum laude in Distractions and Diversions.

"I'm going to walk there," I say, as the posse revs their motorbikes. "Just order me the *horiatiki*"—the classic Greek salad.

I pull down my panama to shade my face from the midday sun. I'm also trying to disguise myself from all the Pharian wannabees who think I'm their ticket to stardom. Although this pale shredding brim, with more holes than reeds and a shape that's seen decades of abuse, is probably easier to spot than all my unconscious gringo ticks.

The road to Angira is one of the few that's paved, which means it's tar studded with crumbling caverns surrounded by tire shavings and edged with loose gravel. I realize as I'm walking that I've memorized the major holes, but only in my motorbike brain. So walking itself takes concentration, whereas the purpose of this stroll was unencumbered thought. "*Ham sa,*" take what comes, arises with every step. What's come is Monika, what's gone is Theo. Handle it gracefully. I arrive at *Angira* with a clear intention, but not with a plan.

"Is there time for a swim before rehearsal?" says Monika when we've spread the last bit of *tonnosalata* on Ari's fluffy pita. We've plotted all the music and it's time to play.

"We still have many things to decide," says Theo, turning to me.

I panic momentarily . . . is he going to propose? *Ham sa,* I breathe in, and exhale.

"We do?"

"The program, the time we play, the money we charge."

"Money?" I ask, laughing with relief. "I thought we didn't . . ."

"Yes yes. Not very much. For the school."

It doesn't take long to figure out five hundred drachmas for grown-ups, kids free, Saturday matinees at two PM and Friday and Saturday nights at eight.

"I'll design the program," says Monika, "unless you want somebody else."

"No no, you do it," says Theo. "Only we must say to Maria. She always makes it."

"Which Maria?" I ask.

"The baker. Foti's mother."

My feminist. I had no idea she was an artist. But then how would you know? There isn't a single art gallery on the island.

"But wait, Theo. Will she be insulted?" Monika may not be a crop, but Maria's a staple.

"What is 'insulted'?"

"Will she be angry, or hurt?"

Theo thinks it over.

"No I think. She has another baby in two months. But Sarah, you must say to her soon. It takes some time for the printing."

"OK. I'll go there now. Alone," I add as Monika gets up to go with me.

"The swim?" she says.

Theo looks at me. So do Alex and Takis and Tomas.

"This won't take long," I tell them. "I'll meet you at *Dishy*." If they all show up we'll have a drowning party.

Only Monika at the dock, sitting on the bow pontoon. "The others?" I ask.

"They decided to stay at Angira. Ari showed up with his homemade wine."

"Permission to speak," says Monika. We're floating in the shallows after a wordless cruise to Sandsoon. Not a forced silence, the worst kind, but an unforced one, the best.

"If you can keep your head above water," I say.

"I may not want to."

"Ahhhh." I could swim off, as usual. But I don't.

"You didn't exactly jump at the idea of a trip to Ephesus after the play."

I flip upright. *Ham sa, ham sa.* I can tread water for hours.

"*. . . Nevertheless I'm in love with you,*" I sing.

"What's the rest of that?"

"That's the punch line," I tell her. "*Maybe I'll win and maybe I'll lose . . .*"

"It's not like I'm saying I'm moving to London." So quick. Those treading muscles won't be tested. "Is that how you took it? Like I'm moving in on you?"

The swim-off's still an option, but then I really could lose her. "Haven't I sung enough for now?" I'm treading with no hands.

"Just talk to me, *Saraki.*"

"Can you work in London?"

"I can work anywhere. I'm a painter." Her treading technique's pretty good too.

A scream breaks the silence. On the rocky ledge high above us a falcon is dive-bombing a raven that's landed on her nest. She dives again and the raven shrieks and flees. The falcon lands and closes her feathers. Monika turns back to me, smacks the surface with the flat of her palm, and sends a stream of water into my face.

"You heard me." She's smiling. "Didn't you?"

"Yes. And I'm thinking it over."

"While you're singing."

"No."

"While you're saying a mantra?"

"Not exactly saying. It goes on like an undercurrent."

"Which one is it?"

"I am That."

"That what?"

I look at her. "That afraid of landing."

And *she* swims off.

52

That sacred atmosphere of the morning has been swamped by spanako-pita and *melitzana salata* and gallon jugs of *portokaladha*. Just as we're clearing the plates Maria the baker shows up with a huge walnut cake. "Let's save that for the break." I say.

"It's hot from the oven, *Saraki*."

"*Malista.*" I fold.

"Why don't we do the music stuff now," says Alex as Maria starts slicing.

"OK. Thanks, Foti"—he's handed me the first piece. I bite in. It's the best cake I've ever tasted. I can hear myself saying this before, about other cakes. Taste buds must be way ahead of the other senses in waking up new every day. I have time to think about this because it's impossible to think about anything else. Being in the moment is so much easier when the moment is fantastic.

"Maria, this is the most delicious cake I've ever tasted. Why isn't it in the shop?"

She holds up a hand to silence me and continues slicing. Foti continues passing. Elena has started boiling water on the altar. You can't have cake without coffee.

"Omire, please ask everyone to gather around with their scripts; I'm going to explain where the music cues come in."

They all manage to balance their cups and plates while scribbling in the margins. I attribute this to the tight mental focus that comes with a sugar high.

"And here at the end is a very famous song"—which I've nicked from Katrin's *Twelfth Night* score—"'When That I Was a Little Tiny Boy.' I think Takis and Tomas and Ariel will play after I stop singing, while we're doing the curtain call." The cast stops eating. Omiros turns to me.

"What did you say?" I ask.

"While we're . . . shouting at the window."

"Hmmm. Try 'Bowing to the audience . . . while it applauds wildly.'"

"Is that 'curtain call'?" he asks.

"It is when you have a curtain," says Alex. "Here we would say 'sail call.'"

"But we won't," I add.

"Let's hear it!" says Caliban.

"Hear what?"

"Your song about the little boy."

"Yes, yes," chime in the diners aka actors.

Monika produces the guitar. "It's tuned," she says. How far afield can you take a deconsecrated church? Does musical coffeehouse tread on blasphemy? I look to Theo in these matters. He's saying thank you to another piece of cake. Then he notices me—so we're still tuned in.

"Play, yes!" Chewing joyfully.

"*When that I was a little tiny boy, with a heigh and a ho, the wind and the rain . . .*" Tomas picks up his fiddle and looks for the notes. Takis watches my hands and begins to mimic me on the bouzouki. After a few repeats of "*Heigh ho, the wind and the rain,*" Tomas starts singing along. Then Alex comes in. Then Theo, a pretty good baritone. "*A pretty thing was but a toy. For the rain it raineth ev'ry day.*" Then everybody. It's not exactly the Vienna Boys' Choir, but the sails are billowing at Café Tempest.

" 'A musical is best,' that's just what you said, Theo," I recall as we're sitting around later at Alpha.

"And you've got a terrific voice," says Monika, ad-libbing. "You'll have to sing at the curtain call." She smiles at him, then at me. Who needs a formal peace treaty.

"Can you teach this to everybody, Moni? It would make a great finale."

"Sure."

"To me?" says Iannis.

"I'll teach you," says Alex.

"A pretty thing is but a toy," I sing.

Just then Aldo '98 and Arabella appear. We open the circle, and they wave Takis over.

"A round for everyone," says Aldo.

"We celebrate!" says Arabella, throwing her arms in the air. The tiny beaded bandolier that just covers her breasts can't take the strain. There's a zinging sound followed by a little scream. She recovers, though, and holds it more or less in place with one hand.

"Do you have a pin?" she asks Alex.

"We have the papers for Turkey," says Aldo. "You must come with us."

"Great!" says Alex. "No pin, sorry," she says to Arabella. "But maybe Takis has something in the kitchen. I'll ask him." She gets up.

"We can't go," I say, slightly distracted by Alex's warmth toward the Sicilian siren. Alex turns back, surprised.

"The play opens in what . . . a week?" I say.

"Eight days," says Theo.

"And we're eighty from getting it right."

"Oh. Wow! No, we can't." Alex sits down. Arabella will be holding up her bandolier till bedtime.

"We can go after, *cara,* don't you think?"

Not till you're stitched in, I'm thinking. And I've missed a golden opportunity. If Arabella had done the costumes we'd have a sell-out every night.

53

"Everybody," Alex agrees at second breakfast. "Dead people would rise up. Vienoula's mother. Of course we have no idea what Arabella's idea of a chorus robe might be. And I doubt she travels with a shroud."

"Well, what would Vasco da Gama wear?" I've come down from the terrace to forage for coffee. "Luckily we've covered up the saints."

There's scratching at the front door.

"Come in!"

Nothing.

"*Ella dho.*"

More nothing.

"Must be Al Pucho," says Alex.

"Why doesn't he let himself in?" I ask. "We know he can open the fridge."

"He doesn't want us to know that he knows. Just open it." But as I get up, the door swings open and a sandaled foot appears. It's Monika with a load of groceries.

"*Kalimera. Kalimera,* Tula!" she calls up to where Tula is drowning the hydrangeas. "I thought we'd have a big late lunch at home. I'm working with the chorus later so I'm going to get it ready now." We watch as she and her faithless attendant cross in front of us and disappear into the kitchen. Then Alex turns back and gives me what the Brits call "an old-fashioned look."

"*Indispensable, that's what you are . . .*," she sings. A hand reaches out around the kitchen door with a bowl of water. Al Fresco appears and starts drinking.

"Six months' quarantine," says Alex. "Can you live without them?"

"Come out here and have a coffee with us!" I shout as Tula's complete-immersion technique sends a wave of dead bougainvillea and assorted debris over the wall into the courtyard. I take a quick look: my espadrilles aren't in the flotsam.

"No time," Monika calls back.

"Six months," Alex repeats. "You might forget her. You know how absentminded you are."

"You're not jealous." I lean in. "You know nobody replaces anybody else."

"Oh yeah? Your heart just expands indefinitely?"

"Not indefinitely. Infinitely. Look at Irish Catholic families, Greek Orthodox families, Hopi tribes. . ."

"Oh no. You're not starting another article, are you? Farewell, Opus One!"

"*Dhen birazi*, Alexi *mou.*"

"I *do* birazi."

"Alex!—we've got one week till our show opens!"

"As the time grows closer it's 'ours.' "

"Absolutely."

"I *will* join you for a sec," says Monika, coming out with coffee and a plate of *kourabyedes*. "Whaddaya think Arabella's going to wear on stage?" She sits down beside me.

Parallel minds. Could this relationship be easier?

"We've just been speculating about that," I say, taking a cookie and blowing the powdered sugar onto Al Fresco's nose.

"And we haven't a clue," says Alex. "But we think we're going to love it."

I give the white nose a piece of my cookie. Diana scurries over and I feed her too. Al Fresco sniffs at her tail.

"Will you tell me something else?" says Monika.

It's early, it's breakfast, what can happen?

"Sure . . . what?"

"What does *Ham sa* really mean?"

"I am That."

"Not 'That afraid of landing.' "

"No. That everything. It's another way of saying 'I am one with everything.' "

"Isn't that Prospero's line?" says Monika. "It's all one?"

"Actually it's Feste who says it, in *Twelfth Night*. But I've been saying it long before this."

"That's true," says Alex.

Monika drinks her coffee, and I pretend we're all contemplating *Ham sa.*

"I'm just not clear how that helps you when you're in a tight spot," she says finally.

"You mean like treading water?" I say.

"Mmm."

"It reminds you that you aren't really separate from anything. And if you're not separate, how can you be afraid?"

"Not separate . . ." There's a knock at the door. "Has he learned to knock?"

"No he's right here, counting my every bite."

"Sarah *mou*!" It's Iannis Milos. I let him in. He settles his letter bag on the floor and hands me a telegram.

"You sing . . . so beautiful," says Iannis. Which probably means this letter's been in his bag since the Dark Ages. I rip into the envelope as if I could make up for lost time.

"Wow!" seeing the date pasted at the top. "Only three days old. It's from my editor at the magazine."

"How can you tell?"

"A lot of her name's here. In fact, the whole thing's pretty much in English." We drink in awed silence.

"We think your article's terrific," I scan aloud, "original . . . accessible . . . Wareham's very enthusiastic . . . Wareham's the editor in chief," I tell Monika and Iannis, ". . . would like your input on illustrations."

"Illustrations? *Ham sa* in pictures? What could he mean?" says Alex.

"I wonder if they actually read it," I say.

"Good news, *Saraki*?" Iannis takes a cookie. Al Fresco sidles over to his chair.

"Please don't feed him, he's getting fat. I guess so. Illustrations are expensive. They must like it. And they want an answer ASAP. Excuse me while I go and think about this."

(Even if you can't *do* anything on Pharos ASAP, you can think ASAP.)

"I wait," says Iannis as I head upstairs.

"Oh no, Ianni, I don't mean a few minutes."

"*Dhen birazi.*" He waves his cup.

Cookies, coffee, women. What am I saying?

I look back to Alex for help.

"Great," she says, then turns to me. "Think of it as a deadline."

"*Apo pou eise*?" I hear as I come back into the courtyard.

"*To* Greenwich, Connecticut."

"*Oxi, oxi. Apo to Greenitch Commetiput.* You must *apo* before *to*."

Iannis the mailman and Iannis the Baptist are sitting opposite Alex at the courtyard table. Al Fresco is sitting next to her and Tula is leaning on her mop, a footsore chorus girl from *Singin' in the Rain*.

"*Ti eine to onoma mou?*" says the postman. What is my name?

"Iannis," says Alex.

"*Kala!*" exclaim the Iannises.

"But you're using the familiar," I say, coming back to the courtyard. "You should be learning the polite form."

"Finished?" Alex looks up. "Gosh, that must be some kind of record."

"That's exactly why you should be learning the polite form. "*Ella, Ianni. Efharisto.*" I hand him my reply to the editor. "Where's Monika?"

"*Fourno.* Stove," says Alex.

"*Sto fourno.* Bravo Aleex," says the Baptist.

Every bowl and dish and knife we've got is littering the kitchen. Monika is wearing a faded tomato-stained apron tied tight around her bamboo waist, and her sleeves are haphazardly rolled up above elbows dipped in flour. My heartbeat goes *vivaci*.

"These smells are terrific. Why isn't Al Fresco in here?"

She turns to look at me. "He loves Alex more."

"He's a dog." And, hoping we're out of the courtyard's line-of-sight, I kiss her.

"Mmm." She stands back. "Dogs are loyal, even when they aren't obedient."

"I can do that," I hear myself say.

"Can you?"

"When and where are you rehearsing the chorus?" I leap right over that crevasse.

"At four in the church." She stands on my bare feet, pinning me down, and it feels good. "They might as well get used to the echo."

"OK. When you're finished with this, let's run through the music one more time."

The score has six songs, three with choruses. I've decided to make Vienoula the choir master. Evdhomada's a better singer, but she has a wispy blond personality, whereas directing an amateur chorus in a foreign language is a job for Margaret Thatcher.

"Vienoula has authority," I explain. "She's the only way off the island. People are used to showing up for her."

"That's such a weird rationale. Are you sure it's not her face?" Monika demands.

"It's not a rationale." I ignore the second part.

"But people *have* to be on time for boats," she says.

"Not here. The boat schedule's very flexible. Sometimes it leaves early."

"You're kidding."

"I'm not, Moni."

"C'mon. *Early*? You're taking poetic license."

"The whole country's got a poetic license. That's why I love it."

"OK, fine. Sing me through these lead sheets and I'll make some notes."

We fly through the score as best I remember it, with Monika embellishing on the Yamaha and penciling in choral lines on her homemade music paper. The last tune ends around the time the scents from the saucepot become irresistible.

Alex has set places in the courtyard. I'm glad to see one Iannis has left, the one with my letter.

"Beautiful," says the sea god.

"It sounded great from here," says Alex.

"Thanks. Can you take Diana off the table?"

"Sure. But the acoustics aren't so good at ground level."

Diana heads straight for Al Fresco's tail. He leaps into Alex's lap and settles there.

Monika serves up a fish stew that would keep Don Juan at home.

"Monika *mou, thavmasia*!" says his representative. I wonder how his "Mary Had a Little Lamb" is coming along.

"*Poli kala*," says Alex.

"This is divine," I say reverently.

"*Efharisto*," she smiles.

Several blissful spoonfuls pass before anyone speaks.

"So does Vienoula read music?" Monika says.

I consider. "Timetables."

"OK. I guess I could write sight cues in the margins."

"Why are we discussing Vienoula?" says Alex, licking her spoon. I'm wondering myself how she reappeared. Could Monika be slightly jealous . . . ? Terrific!

"Sarah's decided she should lead the chorus."

"Why?" Alex looks at me. "She can barely sing."

"Exactly what I said," says Monika.

"Beautiful eyes, though, and that classical nose," says Alex, "hair to her waist . . . "

"A small waist at that," says Monika.

"And she's a powerful woman," says Alex.

"You don't want me to chime in here, do you?" I say.

Alex raises a forkful of fish. "We're figuring this out for ourselves."

"Vienoula?" Iannis has been focused on the stew. "Pia?" Which one?

"The ferry ticket woman." I take a second scoop.

He smiles. Appreciatively, I think we all notice.

"What *is* the reason?" Alex turns to me.

"Her toenail polish."

I'm washing up and feeding scraps to Al Disposal when Theo walks through the courtyard. I didn't hear a knock.

"*Yasoo*, Sarah *mou*." He gives me a hug. "We are alone?" He takes off his coat and leans against the fridge.

"We are. Alex's taking a bunch of Americans around the island, and Monika's rehearsing the chorus."

"Americans? Must be from the yacht. Very beautiful with blue on the water, one big sail. *In die anna Jones* it says on the nose."

"The bow," I say.

"Bow," he barks, as in bow-wow. "Yes, of course."

"*Dhen birazi.*" I'm waiting. Why is he here? "Are you in a hurry, Theo? I can finish these dishes later."

"No, no. But please"—he smiles—"some coffee?" He's not in a hurry. I moan silently. With the house empty I was thinking of doing some thinking. Also he's looking awfully relaxed standing there. I put the kettle on and finish the dishes. Then the three of us go up to the terrace with pot and cups and the remains of Maria's cake.

"You like doing the play?" He kicks off his shoes and leans back on the cushions. Al Fresco picks up one shoe by its lace and then drops it. He's had a whiff of dessert.

"Oh yes." I nod enthusiastically and pour. Animation is one of my basic defenses. I hand him a piece of cake.

"Mmm, delicious, Sarah *mou.*"

"I didn't make it."

"I meant your coffee." He smiles.

"And you think the language isn't a problem?"

"Oh no! Everyone loves learning this."

"Good! Because I'm not sure they know what they're saying."

"Omiros is helping. And they know what they feel."

Maybe this *is* a production meeting. The cake hound makes his move.

"Down Al Fresco! Off!" Nothing. I'm about to sweep him off when I realize he makes a good barrier between us.

"He only speaks Greek, I think," says Theo, laughing.

"He speaks cake actually."

"Ahhhh."

We sip and chew.

"Are you looking in on Christodolous?"

"*Oxi*. I come to talk to you." He swings up to a sitting position, as close to me as Al Sandals allows.

"I like you very much."

Production meetings don't start this way. "Thank you, Theo." I take care not to move away. "I'm very happy to have your friendship."

"I think it is more than that, Sarah *mou*." He puts down his cup, which isn't empty. It's an alarming gesture. When can I politely stop him? It's got to be soon.

"You come how many years?"

"Four."

"Yes. And I watch you many times and I think you like it here. Even, you can live here. Not like *xenoi*—foreigners. Is that right?"

"Yes. I feel like I'm at home here. You understand that very well . . . not everyone does." He is nodding vigorously and nervously stroking Al Fresco. Since I am too, our hands touch. Heat. "But I couldn't live here, not for longer than I do." His fingers draw back. "I need to be in England, where my work is, and my friends. Of course I have friends here and they . . . you . . . all mean very much to me. But this is not my home."

He puts his hand over mine. It's a strong lean hand that's used to fixing people.

"But it could be, *Saraki*. And you would not have to work."

I get up. Al Fresco and Theo stay where they are.

"I want to work. I love to work." I look at him steadily and let him feel my affection. "And I like you very much, Theo." I reach down to touch his shoulder. "But I want to be your friend. Not your lover, not your wife."

He can't hold my gaze. His neck sinks into his shoulders and his shoulders collapse.

"I want us to stay friends, and I think that's the best way. I know it is for me."

Only Al Fresco is looking in my eyes. I shove him off the cushions, sit down, resist the temptation to take Theo's hands and go for his knees instead.

"Theo, believe me, I can be a much better friend than a wife. My coffee's the best thing I do." I laugh, hoping to ease the tension.

"It is not your coffee . . ."

"No!" I shout. Theo jumps. So does Al Fresco, with my whole piece of cake in his mouth. "Bad!" The dog is wagging his whole body, whereas next to me is a frozen man. "Not bad really."

Now he looks at me.

"I mean the cake; it's fabulous," I explain. "Now we *all* know."

"Yes." He almost laughs.

"Tell me something Theo." I'm hoping we can stay on this tack. "Why doesn't Maria make it for her shop in town?"

"Her uncle Theo is the baker here in Kastro."

"So?"

"He's famous for his cake. We all buy from him."

"You mean she doesn't want to upstage him?"

"Does not what?"

Ahhh . . . a real diversion. "Listen, Mister Director, this is a word you've got to learn. *Upstage* comes from the theater. It means steal the glory, make someone smaller. You know how when Stephanos is on stage he walks in front of Priftis or Iannis or anyone—getting between them and the audience . . . I mean, if we had an audience."

"Yes, yes, he is always doing it. In *Hello, Dolly*, Manolis steps on him!"

"Well, that is called 'upstaging.' "

"Up staging," he tries it.

"Yes. So Maria doesn't want to look like a better baker than her uncle. Is that what you mean?"

"*Sosto.*"

"Wow."

"Is so unusual?"

"Unusual? In America she'd be canonized." Another mystery to him. I'm going to remember this tactic. "A saint. They'd make her a saint."

"Ahhh, yes." And we laugh together.

I get up. "Do you mind? I told Monika I'd get to her music rehearsal. And I'd like you to come by if you can. You haven't had time to learn the curtain call song."

I walk him to the door and open it.

"I'm not sure I am right in the curtain call," he says, looking down.

"Oh yes you are, Theo." I kiss him lightly. "You must be there. You're the muse of Pharos."

"Am I?" He stands up straight. "Yes. *Adio*."

Al Fresco and I watch him walk down the hill.

"His heart's not broken and his ego's intact. I think we handled that pretty well," I say. "Don't look at me like that."

54

Dinner's in full swing at Café Tempest. The women's chorus is eating together so I guess the rehearsal went well. Except for Arabella, who's kneading Petros's shoulders in another pew. He's grinning like he could be Petros '99. When she spots me she jumps up and throws her arms around me; they happen to be bare.

"So much fun, *cara*!" She kisses me on both cheeks. "My mama would never let me sing. I was so sad. Now she is dead to hear me."

Monika, just behind her, is grinning too. I wonder just how bad Arabella's voice is. At least her mother will be spared.

"Try the goat stew, it's fabulous," says Vienoula, baring her great teeth.

"I bring you some. I make it," says Elena. "And some *gigantes* and *fasoulakia*." The column rises on red patent heels as the chorus wriggles to make room for me. Not *much* room, though; they're Eastern women and they collect like a harem.

"Where's Alex? Did she rehearse the curtain call?"

"Not yet. She's over there. With our audience." Monika points with her glass. I see her in the nave, surrounded by a bunch of fair-haired Yankees in windbreakers. They're also dining at Café Tempest.

"Audience?"

"They're off that big blue sloop. She's been showing them around the island all day. She's planning to ask you if it's OK."

"I think it's a good idea," Tina says to me. "An audience will be good now."

"*Entaxi*," I say.

We have something akin to a run-through, with almost everyone off book. Laurence Olivier might be mystified, but their heavily accented English probably makes better sense to Greeks. The Yanks laugh and react all through it. (They can't all be Shakespearean scholars, I tell myself.) And the cast swoon to their attention.

It goes amazingly well until Stephanos is attacked by the Chihuahua. It's the scene where Sebastian plots to kill the king. Stephanos raises his arm with a knife and the dog launches. She gets a bit of thigh with the pants and holds on in midair. Stephanos starts wailing and flailing. Maria grabs her tail. Stephanos's pants rip but the Chihuahua has great midair balance. The three of them whirl around until the dog finally loses her grip. Sebastian's murderous mates are going crazy. It's the sort of laughter that's contagious and pretty soon we're all flopping in the pews and rolling on the floor. The Yanks hooting, Stephanos howling, the dog barking, the echo rolls and rolls. I'm powerless to stop it, tears running down my face. Eventually we're exhausted, coughing and blowing. "Call coffee, Omire!"

The owner and crew of the *Indiana Jones* gather around, chirping about the show. I see Priftis spiking the cast's coffee. Meanwhile the ship's doctor tears a bit off Caliban's tail and wraps it around Stephanos's leg.

"Has this animal been vaccinated for rabies?" he asks.

"What is rabies?" growls Stephanos.

"A very rare infection from dirty dogs," I tell him, looking at the doctor prayerfully. I ask Omiros to ask Iannis, who asks Maria, who asks Manolis, but no one knows the Greek word.

"Theo will know what you mean," says Priftis. "Funny he's not here so late."

"Probably delivering a baby," says Sophia.

"Or a goat," says Elena.

I don't contribute to the speculation, but I'm not worried.

"Can't you just act it out for me?" says Omiros. I snarl and try to foam at the mouth, blowing a few spit bubbles. This starts everybody howling again, including the doctor. All of Stephanos's karma is coming out to play.

Under the moonlight at Alpha, Jack Ferguson, *Indiana Jones*'s owner and captain, orders a second round of Metaxa. "Why did you choose *The Tempest*? It's a great choice, by the way."

"Because I love it. And I thought if I'm only going to direct one play, it should be that one." I omit the part about seeing the title in meditation. That's sure to provoke another round, and the moon's already set.

"His last and his best," says Alex, raising her brandy.

"Aye aye."

"But why *your* last?" Jack asks in a handsome baritone that matches his rugged jaw. "You're doing a great job."

"And Jack knows what he's talking about," says Terence, the first mate. "He heads up an independent studio in L.A."

"Really, Jack?" says Alex, instantly dropping into her sexy Actors Studio register.

"Well, actually I'm the head of the company that owns it. But I see a lot of theater."

"What is he?" Arabella turns to Alex.

"My last," I say, "because I'm just imitating a director. I have no idea what I'm doing. I can also imitate a rock drummer, a cabaret singer, a cowboy . . . It's a gift. I can't explain it, but it doesn't last."

"What is he?" Arabella is her own echo.

They're all looking at me in disbelief.

"I think it's a spell," I finally say. That many silent people *is* a spell. We drink in the silence.

"Well, whatever you're doing next, I want to be there," says Jack.

"Ik ock," says Monika softly.

55

"He proposed? And now he's missing." Alex can still chew while she's agitated. Our trio is having breakfast in the courtyard; quintet if you add Diana and Al Omelette.

"He's not missing, he's absent. I'm sure he's absolutely fine."

"You're being awfully cool about this. Cold," says Miss Malmö. "How do you know he's fine."

"Because he's a man. He's going to be sad for a day, because I do make great coffee. Then he's going to decide I've made a big mistake."

We listen to Tula knocking over an amphora and scraping up the dirt.

"How does she do it?" says Alex. "They're incredibly heavy."

"Not if everything in them's dead," I say. "She's only growing espadrilles and bits of tile."

"So what did you tell Theo?" Monika wants to know.

"That I thought we'd be better as friends. Longer, better, that sort of thing. That I didn't want to be his wife or his lover."

"Good, *Saraki*," says Alex. "Very direct."

I hear an insinuation of past crimes that I choose to ignore.

"Then I was saved by this cake hound."

"And you parted on good terms?" says Monika.

"He's not at the bottom of the sea. He may be drunk, but I doubt it . . . too responsible. I'll bet he shows up at rehearsal tonight. I told him he's our muse. Ow! Damn!"

"That's why you should leave Diana on the table while we're eating."

I make a second pot of coffee while I'm icing my big toe.

"I've got an idea," says Monika on the second round.

"Turtle soup?" says Alex.

"I'd like to do the artwork for your article. Some watercolors, inspired by the mantras. What do you think?"

"I think it's a great idea . . . maybe," I say.

"Why maybe?"

"I think so too," says Alex. "They did say they wanted pictures."

"Maybe, because it involves a phone call. I don't want you to do them on spec."

"Well, I'll go with you to *Kyria* Kassoula's if you like."

"No no, too big a sacrifice. Then I'm committed to you for life." Direct, no? "Besides, I get writing ideas when I sit there. Alex, you shouldn't say turtle soup where she can hear you."

"Does she have ears?"

"Of course she has ears."

"Sorry, Diana. Get Stephanos!" She gets up.

"Where to, Alexi?"

"I'm taking the *Indiana Jones* guys on a walk around the island. It's the first time anyone's ever asked me to show them real island life."

"So I'll see you at *Kyria* Kassoula's."

"*Malista.*"

"Don't forget to take Al Fresco with you."

Tula comes down from the terrace with an armload of shards. She's looking grimy and distraught. She dumps the pieces into a burlap sack. Then she steps over Diana, busy with toast, and sits down.

"Too bad about the pot," I say.

"The pot?" she shrugs. "*Afto to paleo pragma?*" That old thing?

"Like . . . two thousand years old?"

She nods.

"It's priceless," I tell Monika softly. "We'll have to rescue the remains."

"*Ti krima tin Stella mou,*" Tula says emphatically. And begins complaining that her daughter's not in the play. *Ham sa,* I breathe all through it.

Then I explain that there's only one female role in this play, my mistake, and the music teacher's just right for it. "But Stella *is* in the play," I tell her. "She's part of the chorus."

"*Aye!*" she yells, and clamps her mud-streaked hands over her ears. Just as Arabella's mama would be doing (may be doing; who knows for sure?).

Tula pours some coffee into Alex's abandoned cup and downs it like a shot of tequila. "*Kai Vienoula tragouthei! Dhen to pistevo!*"

I turn to Monika. "She can't believe that Vienoula's singing. Let's scrap the chorus. You could teach them some dance moves instead."

Tula puts a filthy arm around my shoulders.

"The doctor Theo, *prepei na su voithei.*"

"*Entaxi,* Tula *mou. Efharisto.*" I jump up. So does Monika. She follows me into the kitchen.

"What was that?"

"She's begging me to get Dr. Theo's help with the chorus."

"If you can find him."

"*Dhen birazi,* Moni *mou.* With those acoustics, a chorus of jackals could walk off with a Grammy. I'm going to call the magazine."

It's a hot day; everyone's windows and doors are open. Women are bent at their ovens, hanging out wash, feeding babies; men are washing up at sinks, pulling off shirts, shooting dice; young children are playing on cool kitchen floors. You can see the insides of everyone's life on a day like this. I stop along the way to greet Georgos the sandal maker and Theo the baker, two old men with no Broadway aspirations. Christodolous is sitting outside on the stoop playing backgammon with his brother. He gets up and crushes me in his bony arms because he thinks I saved his life. I wish I had the vocabulary to set him straight.

Only four callers at *Kyria* Kassoula's so it looks good for an afternoon sail. Except the mayor is one of them, a very long-winded man. "We elected him to stop him making campaign speeches," Nikos once explained.

"*Saraki*," he greets me, "How you are? He goes well the play?"

"Very well, Vassili. Are you getting a new car?"

"I am calling insurance now. Four times."

"Four times now?" I might as well come back tomorrow.

"*Oxi, oxi.* Four times before. Because they say no insurance for a car in the water. Crazy."

I try to think if my own policy covers fish in the transmission, snails on the seats.

"But it's really a case of theft . . . stealing. Maybe you should have your lawyer talk to them."

"My lawyer . . ." He actually scratches his head. "*Thavmasia!* You are smart girl!" Which he repeats to our little gathering. Then he cancels his call and walks out repeating "Lawyer, lawyer."

My call comes through first. I take this as an auspicious sign that (1) the editor will say yes to the watercolors, and (2) fate approves of Monika.

"Is Molly in editorial there?" I shout to the magazine operator. She gives me Holly in advertising.

"Holly, I asked for Molly, but don't put me on hold, it could last forever."

"No I'll just transfer you."

"NO DON'T! Please. I'll be talking to fish. It's Sarah, calling from Greece. Pick up another phone and ask Molly if she'd like some beautiful watercolors to illustrate the article I just sent her. I'll hold."

"Well, if she's not at lunch . . ."

"Thanks." *Guru om, guru om* . . . But mantra is not really prayer. I switch to "please Lord may she be there." Meanwhile I notice that my three companions callers are all mumbling and running their fingers over their prayer beads. It's Alexander Graham Bell who belongs on *Kyria* Kassoula's altar.

Holly comes back pretty fast—only two thousand drachmas—with Molly's "Yes. She likes the idea. But we need them soon. Mail them to us by the end of the week."

As I'm paying up, Alex comes walking in with the crew of the *Indiana Jones*.

"Hey Sarah! Wow, a phone! Does it take quarters? What time is it in South Bend . . . L.A. . . . . Sausalito?" I hold up my hands.

"Hi, everybody. Listen. Whatever time it is there *now* is not the point. Do you have stuff to read?"

"Maybe we should come back," says Terence.

"Actually this is a good time. It's usually a lot more crowded."

"Then let's wait," says Jack. "Maybe Alex will tell us the history of Pharos. How about it, Alex?"

"Sure," says Nurse Ellen to the owner of the independent movie studio.

"Good idea," I say. "See you all later."

In a way I'm sorry I'm not staying to hear the astonishing, hair-raising, wholly fictional gospel of Pharos according to Alex. Maggie Smith move over.

56

"Do you mind if he's here again?" Alex walks into St. Christopher's with Jack. He's shed his nautical blues and is wearing the Nantucket red Bermudas and T-shirt that blend in so well with the sauce at Republican barbecues. The T-shirt is tight, short sleeves rolled way up. It tells us Jack has a gym at all his locations.

"It's OK with me if it's OK with them."

The cast is assembled for our final run-through. Only the Chihuahua is missing because Stephanos threatened to shoot her and we believe him. Then Maria Milos would kill Stephanos and the show would move to the jail. I see Sophia clearing the first course. Costas is scraping plates. It can only be days before he proposes to her.

"Listen, everyone, would you like to have our American friend here tonight? He'll go if it makes you nervous."

Ha!

"*Kathiste, kathiste!*" Sit! they all cry.

"*Efharisto.*" Jack smiles. "Break a leg."

Only a fool would try to translate that.

"OK. Before we begin I'd like to talk to you. First I'd like to thank Costas for getting the whole set here today. I'd say it's a miracle but St. Christopher's has been deconsecrated . . ." This gets way too a big a laugh if you're one of the multitude waiting for his doors. "And Tina for getting all these costumes for us. You look like Arcadians now. And I'd like to thank you all. You've been working very hard and I'm very happy. Tonight, you just have fun. If you forget a line, look over at Vienoula, she'll read it out. Unless we get into big problems we aren't going to stop. We're going to do all the music, so everybody who's singing have a glass of water. Monika will do a warm-up with you before we start. One more thing: Now that we have wings—those places off the platform—be sure not to talk there; the echo will drown out the people on stage. OK. Have a good time!"

"Any questions?" Alex steps forward. Nice touch.

"Do I really need this thing?" Caliban's trailing a lot of green gauze and Tino, seventy-five years without a tail, is having trouble adjusting.

"I'll trim it . . . a lot," says Tina.

"These sandals look weird. Can't I wear my Nikes instead?" says Ariel.

"No. But you can be barefoot," I say.

"I can't see," says the king of Naples, his crown sitting neatly over his eyes.

"Trim his head!" shouts the duke of Milan.

"It fits me!" Stephanos booms over the laughter. "I can be king!"

"Places, everybody!" I shout. "We'll fix any costume problems when you're in the wings."

Two hours and three acts fly by. The Baptist remembers his line. So does Gerasimos. My D-string snaps during "Where the Bee Sucks" and I sing on with just the violin. A sail breaks loose during the storm. The sailors curse (but that's in character) and fight their way out from under. Ariel's wing gets caught on Prospero's staff causing him to spin and crash into Miranda who trips Ferdinand chopping wood. Kindling scatters. Diana, who's here auditioning, gets loose and lost during the banquet scene. (Alex finds her later in the baptismal font; impossible.) Tina's helpers sew nonstop. There are no injuries, no tantrums, no fits of burping. I notice I can't hear Arabella in the choral parts—probably it's her beaded veil, and Vienoula's way too busy prompting to sing. We'll leave her at that for the run.

"Let's take a break," I say at the end of Act III. There were ravenous looks during the banquet scene. "But please stay in costume; it's just a short break for coffee and sweets."

Theo comes over with a piece of cake. It's not the one the caryatids are serving. "I told Maria you think she's a saint," he says. He hands me a glass of retsina and raises his own glass. "*Stin filia*, to friendship." He smiles.

Thank you, Theo *mou*," I say gratefully, and give him a quick kiss. "Do you think it's going well?"

"*Thavmasia*! –wonderful. You have a job every year."

"*Efharisto poli*. I'm having a great time. But who knows where I'll be next July."

"We give a party for the first night," says Sophia, with Costas beside her.

"We like to do that," says Priftis's wife.

"Why don't you do it together?" says Theo.

"I make my famous pasta," Arabella crows, her veil thrown back.

"I'll bring the wine," says Petros, at her side.

"Petros '99 !" Alex signals behind their backs.

"Let's have the party aboard the *Indiana Jones*," says Jack. He has his arm around Alex's waist.

"Yes! yes!" everyone instantly agrees. Never mind they've just survived a shipwreck.

"*Now my charms are all o'erthrown. And what strength I have's mine own*," Prospero intones just before midnight. Captain Jack jumps to his feet and applauds. Priftis hugs Evdhomada, Costas hugs Sophia, Al Fresco jumps on Stephanos, and then everyone hugs everyone. Takis picks up his bouzouki. Tino opens the bottles of retsina icing in the baptismal font. I look at my notes to the actors and tear them up. Nothing there that would spoil Will's sleep.

Alpha has stayed open to celebrate, and we do.

57

"Opening night and nothing to wear," says Alex between bites. We're having our last second breakfast before the reviews. Nothing in print, of course; but among the two thousand inhabitants, the ratio of critics to audience is roughly one to one. Diana's on the table, along with a platter of apricot pancakes Monika has whipped up from the apricots Tula brought this morning. "Delicious, but she needn't have bothered," Alex says after a forkful. "She's won the war."

"Why don't you shop for something?" I say.

"Oh sure. A nice floral shirtwaist off Leonidas's truck."

"What's all that in your closet?"

"Rags."

There's a knock at the door. "Come in!" I call.

"I was passing by and I couldn't help overhearing," says Tina. "Come over after breakfast, Alex. I'm sure I have something you can wear. Oooh, what are those!"

"Apricot pancakes. Monika's making them. They're sublime," I add, because I see she's actually considering them. "Sit, Tina. I'll get you a plate."

In the kitchen, Monika's piling up a second stack. "Come eat with us, Moni. We're serving Tina some serious calories. She might explode to a size 6."

"Is that a good thing?"

"Think of the hand-me-downs."

We all pour on the syrup and dig in. It takes a while before anyone can speak.

"Cleopatra had a beautiful sequined gown in last season's show," Tina says to Alex. "Very slinky, with a low back. I think it'll fit you. It's a good thing you sunbathe naked." She gets up to leave.

"Well what about us?" I say. "We'll look like her galley slaves."

"Come along with her," says Tina. "There's plenty of stuff." She turns at the door. "Those pancakes, Monika. Bring that recipe to London. I'm coming this winter."

What was that? Is there water in my ears?

"Slinky, with a low back. I like the sound of that," says Alex, feeding Al Fresco with one hand and Diana with the other.

"One last chorus rehearsal at noon," says Monika, getting up with the empty platter.

"But what about Tina's?"

She turns back. "I'm happy with what I've got."

Cleopatra and her dog and I watch her depart.

"Mmm . . . ," says Alex gaily. "London in the winter. Everybody's getting on board. By the way, Jack's asked me to sail with him when he leaves. He's taking two weeks to do the coast of Turkey."

"What did you say?"

"Anchors aweigh!"

"Really?"

"Really." She leans across the table. "You're not mad are you? I know how much you want to go there."

"Not at *all.*"

"Good." She jumps up. "I'm off to Tina's!" Al Fresco opens the door and they're gone.

Monika comes back out while I'm still absorbing this.

"No one else's behavior makes any sense," I say.

"Why should it?"

She stands in a pool of blue sunlight framed by crimson bougainvillea. "Where's Alex?"

"Gone to wardrobe. Soon to return as the queen of the Nile. I just wonder what Al Fresco will be wearing."

"She's going to look fabulous. I can't wait to see Arabella's face! Aren't you going with her?"

"No."

"Why not?"

I look like I'm thinking it over, but it's just an act.

"*Ik ock,*" I say as I get up and come toward her. "I'm happy with what I've got."

She takes a step back.

"But how do you know that, *Saraki*?"

I reach out and put my hand on her heart. "Because I am That," I tell her. And I feel my landing gear bang into place.

Classic Greek Recipes

remastered by Ana Espinosa

In truth, Elena, Lukia, the Marias, and their friends on Pharos never write recipes down. And as for their measuring techniques, let's call them spontaneous and variable, as in "a little handful," "makes enough for the whole family," "maybe add some nuts." Ana Espinosa, our editor-in-chief, has remastered seven Greek favorites using actual measures and adding her own inspired touches and embellishments. To put it diplomatically, these recipes are every bit as delicious as their 1,500-year-old ancestors.

Maria Milos's Tiropitas
(Individual Cheese Pies)

Makes about 60 *tiropitas*

1 pound goat or sheep feta

¼ cup whole milk

2 eggs

scant ¼ teaspoon freshly grated nutmeg, or to taste

2 tablespoons curly parsley, finely chopped and firmly packed

8 ounces Parmigiano Reggiano, finely grated

8 ounces filo

1½ sticks unsalted butter, melted

To make the filling: Chop feta until well crumbled. In a large bowl, whisk together milk, eggs, and nutmeg until mixed. Add the parsley, Parmigiano Reggiano and crumbled feta to the egg mixture. Combine well. Refrigerate for one hour.

To make the *tiropitas:* Preheat oven to 350°F. Thaw filo according to instructions on the package. Place the filo on the counter or on a baking sheet large enough to hold the stack. Cover the filo with a sheet of waxed paper and place a damp kitchen towel on top of the waxed paper. (If the filo gets dry, it will crack and become unusable.) Gently remove one sheet of filo at a time. Working rapidly, brush each sheet generously with melted butter. Cut each sheet into roughly 3 x 10-inch strips. Use a small spoon to form spoonful mounds of filling. Place a mound of filling on the bottom of the filo strip and fold a corner of the filo over the filing, forming a triangle. Repeat the triangle fold until you reach the end of the strip. Place the finished pieces on a half-sheet pan lined with parchment paper and bake for 20 to 25 minutes until golden brown. Serve hot from the oven.

Tips	• Filo usually comes in 1-pound packages. Cut the stack in half and refreeze half.
	• Keep the melted butter warm in the top pan of a double boiler so that it is easy to use throughout your preparation.
	• Uncooked *tiropitas* can be frozen.
Embellishments and variations	You can use other cheeses in combination with the feta, such as blue cheese, a vibrant manchego, or any other tangy cheese you favor. Using cottage cheese in place of some of the other cheeses will yield a milder flavor. For a heart-healthy substitute for butter, you can use olive oil or an olive-oil-and-butter mixture.

Elena's Baklava

Makes about 36 pieces

For the pastry:

6 cups coarsely chopped walnut halves

1 teaspoon cinnamon

½ cup organic cane sugar

1-pound package filo, thawed

1½ cups (3 sticks) unsalted butter

For the syrup:

1 cup honey

1½ cups organic cane sugar

1½ cups water

2½ teaspoons lemon juice

1 teaspoon finely grated lemon zest

1 teaspoon finely grated orange zest

1 cinnamon stick

3 cloves

To make the pastry: Preheat oven to 350°F. In a large bowl, toss together the chopped walnuts, cinnamon, and ½ cup cane sugar until combined. Place the thawed filo on the counter and cover with a sheet of waxed paper; place a moist kitchen towel on top of the waxed paper. Melt the butter and discard the foamy milk solids on top.

Butter the bottom of a half-sheet pan. Gently remove one sheet of filo at a time and place on baking pan; brush generously with melted butter. Repeat with 6 more sheets. Spread half of nut mixture on filo and drizzle some butter on top. Place 4 more sheets of filo on top of nut mixture, brushing each sheet with butter. Add the rest of the nut mixture. Layer the remaining sheets of filo one at a time, brushing each with butter, until all sheets are used. Sprinkle a little water on top with your fingers and brush to even out. Trim the excess filo around the pan. With a sharp knife or pizza wheel, cut the baklava into serving-size triangles or squares. Bake for 10 minutes, then lower heat to 325°F and bake for 35 to 40 minutes until golden brown.

To make the syrup: While the baklava is in the oven, mix all the syrup ingredients in a saucepan. Bring to a boil over medium heat, then lower to a simmer for about 10 to 15 minutes, or until the syrup is thickened and coats the back of a spoon. Remove cinnamon stick and cloves. Allow the syrup to cool until just warm. When the baklava is out of the oven, allow it to cool for 5 minutes, then pour the syrup evenly over the baklava. The baklava should cool at room temperature, allowing the syrup to settle in for at least 6 to 8 hours. Do not refrigerate.

Tips	• It is best to buy walnut halves and chop them by hand. • Keeping the melted butter in the top pan of a double boiler makes it easy to use throughout your preparation.
Embellishments and variations	You can use almonds or pistachios in place of walnuts. Or substitute 1 cup cranberries for 1 cup walnuts.

Maria's Kourambyedhes
(Butter-Almond Cookies)
Makes approximately 4 dozen

1¾ cups almonds

3½ cups flour

½ teaspoon baking powder

1 pound unsalted butter, softened to room temperature

½ cup powdered sugar

2 large egg yolks

1 teaspoon vanilla

1 shot cognac or whiskey

3 cups powdered sugar for dusting

Preheat oven to 350°F. Toast the almonds lightly, until golden, and chop to a medium-fine consistency.

Sift flour and baking powder into a medium bowl and set aside. Cream butter in the bowl of a mixer, using the paddle attachment, at medium speed for about 5 to 8 minutes, until soft, pale, and creamy. Add ½ cup powdered sugar and combine well, then add egg yolks, vanilla, and liquor. Mix for 10 minutes, until very creamy. Add the chopped almonds and combine well. Set the mixer to its lowest speed and slowly add the sifted flour just until it is incorporated. Remove dough from the mixing bowl and place it on a counter. Knead dough by hand for about 5 to 10 minutes. Dough should be soft and pliable.

Line the bottom of a cookie sheet with waxed paper. Make round dough balls (about 1 tablespoon of dough each) and flatten slightly. Space the cookies an inch apart and place the cookie sheet in preheated oven. Bake for 15 minutes, until pale golden. Remove cookies immediately from the cookie sheet and place them on a wire rack. Allow to cool for 5 minutes and sift powdered sugar generously on top. The *kourambyedhes* should be completely covered in powdered sugar. Cool at room temperature and serve.

Tips	• Place a sheet of waxed paper underneath the wire rack to catch excess powdered sugar.
Embellishments and variations	For a sumptuous taste, try adding 1 teaspoon lemon or orange zest.

Lukia's Zucchini Fritters
Makes about 12 fritters

1 pound small green zucchini
Salt
1½ teaspoons finely chopped shallots
3 tablespoons plus 1 teaspoon olive oil
1 teaspoon finely chopped dill
1 teaspoon chopped chives
1½ tablespoons finely chopped lemon zest
Salt and pepper to taste
¼ cup flour
1 large egg, whisked

Shred zucchini on a box grater. Salt zucchini and let stand for 20 minutes. Drain excess moisture with a cheesecloth or press well over a wire colander. Zucchini should be fairly dry.

In a small sauté pan, sauté shallots in 1 teaspoon of olive oil until golden. In a large bowl, mix shallots, dill, chives, and lemon zest with the zucchini. Add salt and pepper to taste. Mix in flour and egg. Heat 3 tablespoons of olive oil in a large sauté pan over a medium flame. Make soupspoon-size dollops of the mixture to form patties (about 2 inches in diameter) and cook until firm inside and nicely browned on each side. Add more oil to the pan as needed, until all fritters are done.

Tips	• This is a great summer recipe, when small zucchinis are fresh from the garden or farmers' market.
Embellishments and variations	Mix ¾ cup of Greek yogurt with 3 tablespoons chopped red pepper and 1 teaspoon finely chopped mint. Add a dollop on top of each fritter.

Elena's Gigantes
(Giant White Beans)

Serves 4

1 cup dried *gigante* beans

3 cups water

1 fresh or dried bay leaf

Salt and pepper to taste

7 plum tomatoes, seeded and cut in half lengthwise

5 whole garlic cloves

2 tablespoons olive oil

½ cup extra-virgin olive oil

1 medium shallot, finely minced (2 tablespoons)

1½ teaspoons grated lemon zest (from 1 lemon)

2 teaspoons finely chopped fresh thyme

¼ cup finely chopped parsley

Rinse beans over a strainer. Place them in a medium bowl with water to cover and soak overnight or at least 8 hours. Drain and place in a medium pot with 3 cups of water. Add bay leaf, salt, and pepper and bring to a boil. Reduce heat to low and simmer for about 1½ hours or until the beans are tender. Remove from heat and discard bay leaf. Reserve ½ cup of liquid and drain the beans.

While the beans are cooking, preheat oven to 325°F. Line a baking pan with parchment paper. In a medium bowl, toss tomatoes and garlic cloves with 2 tablespoons olive oil. Add salt and pepper to taste. Place tomatoes in a baking pan cut side up. Spread garlic separately in the same pan. Bake for 30 minutes, then remove garlic and peel. Bake tomatoes for another

1½ hours or until they are somewhat dry. Remove from oven and allow to cool slightly. Then place tomatoes and garlic in the bowl of a food processor and pulse for a few seconds.

Heat ½ cup extra-virgin olive oil in a large skillet over medium heat. Add minced shallot and cook until slightly browned. Add cooked beans, lemon zest, and fresh thyme. Add the tomato mixture and cook for 3 minutes while mixing well. Add salt and pepper as needed. If the mixture is too dry, add a tablespoon or two of the reserved bean water. Sprinkle parsley on top before serving.

Tips

- If *gigantes* are unavailable, large lima beans are an excellent alternative.

Stella's Dholmades
(Stuffed Grape Leaves)

Makes about 48 *dholmades*

2 cups of water

1 cup basmati rice

1½ teaspoons cumin seeds (preferably whole)

1 medium onion, finely chopped

1 tablespoon olive oil

2 teaspoons dried oregano

Pinch of cinnamon

½ teaspoon freshly ground black pepper

1 teaspoon salt or to taste

1 pound very lean ground beef

¼ cup dry red wine

2 tablespoons tomato paste

½ cup pimento-stuffed olives, well drained and thinly sliced

⅓ cup golden raisins

½-pound jar of grape leaves

2 cups low-sodium beef broth

1 cup water

Lemon wedges

For the filling: In a medium pan, bring 2 cups of water to a boil. Add rice and lower heat to a simmer. Cook for about 20 minutes, until done, and reserve. While the rice is cooking, in a large sauté pan toast cumin seeds over high heat for about 1 minute, until lightly toasted and fragrant. Remove from pan and grind in a spice mill. In the same pan over medium heat, cook chopped onion in 1 tablespoon of olive oil until browned. Stir in ground cumin, dried oregano, cinnamon, black pepper, and salt. Add ground beef, stirring while it cooks completely. Add wine, tomato paste, sliced olives, and golden raisins. Mix well and cook for 10 minutes, stirring occasionally. Remove from heat. Place in a large bowl, mix well with rice, and set aside.

To prepare the *dholmades:* Preheat oven to 325°F. Remove grape leaves from jar and drain. Place them in a large bowl filled with water and rinse gently. Over a large colander, drain leaves well again. Place one leaf, vein side up, on a cutting board or work surface. Place a scant ¼ cup of filling in your hand and press together into a ball, then place the ball in leaf center. Fold the bottom of the leaf over the filling. Fold in sides and roll firmly. Place each *dholmada* in a deep-dish baking pan. Repeat until all the filling is used.

Pour 2 cups of broth and 1 cup of water over *dholmades*. Place another baking pan or oven-proof plate on top to weight *dholmades* and keep them submerged in broth while baking. Bake for 25 minutes or until leaves are tender. Remove from oven and drain liquid. Serve with lemon wedges.

Tips	• Use fresh grape leaves if available and blanch in boiling water before using. • Ground cumin is OK, but it is not as flavorful as freshly ground.
Embellishments and variations	The beef mixture filling can be used for stuffed peppers or with cabbage leaves. Or serve it over rice as an entrée.

Sarah's World's Best Coffee

Makes 6 cups or mugs

There are no secrets to making the world's best coffee. You need: *The right beans*—fair trade, organic, stored in an opaque container with a tight lid. *The right water*—cold, fresh, pure. *The right filter*—a high-quality unbleached cone with micropores and thick seams. *The right grind*—#5–6 for a cone filter, #9–10 for a coffee press. You'll probably have to experiment with your grinder.

> whole French roast coffee beans, enough to make 9 tablespoons when ground
> whole Vienna roast coffee beans, enough to make 3 tablespoons when ground
> 42 ounces of cold fresh untreated water (7 ounces per cup)

Heat the cold water to a boil. Meanwhile, fill a Thermos or carafe and 6 coffee cups with hot water to warm.

Mix French and Vienna roast beans together, then grind. If using a coffee press (aka French press), the grind must be coarse enough to avoid sediment. If using a cone filter, the grind must be fine enough that water pours through continuously but does not stream through.

Measure 2 level tablespoons of coffee per cup into the filter or the bottom of the coffee press. (Most coffee measures hold exactly 2 tablespoons.) If using a filter cone, be sure to fold down the seams gently.

Fill the filter with just enough boiling water to cover the grounds and let them settle. Slowly pour the remaining water into the filter to release all that great flavor. If using a coffee press, use the same method, initially just covering the grounds. After filling, let the lid sit on the press for a minute before serving. Empty the hot water out of the warmed coffee cups or Thermos/carafe and add the freshly brewed coffee. Serve. Expect your guests to propose to you.

Tips	• Boiling water is essential. Many home cof-feemakers don't get the water sufficiently hot to extract the best flavor. • A true burr coffee grinder releases more fla-vor from the beans than a chopper. • If you're traveling and don't have a grinder, Starbucks and other brands' #5–6 grind works for cone filters and #9–10 grind for a coffee press. Pack your own filters—you don't really need all those socks.
Embellishments and variations	No matter what quantity of coffee you make, the ratio of French to Vienna remains 3/1. If 7 ounces per cup makes too strong a brew, add a little more water to the pot. You can always dilute coffee, but you can't make it stronger.

Greek Terms

a

adio: good-bye

akro'asi: audition; interrogation

amesos: just now coming

b

bonatza: dead calm weather

c

café: coffee

cafedaki: a small cup of coffee

d

dhen birazi: don't worry

dhio: two

dholmades: stuffed vine leaves

dhoxe sto Theo: thanks to God

drachma(s): the currency of Greece

e

efharisto: thank you

efharisto para poli: thank you
   very much

elate na dheite: come and see

ella: come, look

ena leptaki: one little moment

entaxi: OK

episis: ditto

etsi ketsi: so-so

f

fasoulakia: green beans

fourno: stove

ftohi: poor

g

galactoburiko: milk and custard cake

gigantes: lima beans

gliko, gliki: sweet

gravura: Greek Parmesan

grigora: quickly

h

harika na se dho: happy to see you

harika: the short form

hronia polla: literally, many happy years; the Greek version of happy birthday

i

I panghia mazi sou: may the Virgin be with you

k

kafedakia: a little cup of coffee

kala, *kalo, kali:* fine, good

kali orexsi: bon appétit

kalimera: good morning, good day

kalispera: good evening

kathiste: sit; plural, also formal singular

kato: down

katse: sit; singular informal

katzika, katziki: goat, goats

kephali: head

kima: wave

kolokithia: zucchini

kori mou: my daughter

kourambyes, kourambyedhes: shortbread-sugar cookie, cookies

kyria: miss, madam

kyrie: mister

m

malista: of course

melanouri: bream

melitzana salata: eggplant salad

metrio (for coffee): with a little sugar

meze, mezedes: appetizers

mou: my; may be used as a term of endearment

n

na ta ksana pumay: till we meet again

nai: yes

nero, neraki: water, a small glass of water

o

octopodhi: octopus

ouzaki: diminutive of ouzo

ouzeri: bar

oxi: no

oxi, efharisto: no, thanks

p

parakalo: please

pedhi mou: my child

platia: town square

poli: very

portokaladha: orange juice

q

quattro formaggio frittata: four-cheese frittata

s

sargoss: a kind of fish

siga: slowly

signome: excuse me

sketto: black, no sugar

sosto: right, correct
spanakopita: spinach pie
stin yiasou: to your health

t

tarama: fish roe
taramosalata: fish roe salad
Tetarti: Wednesday
thavmasia: wonderful
thelete ligo? would you like
   some ___?
thelis, thelete: would you like
   (singular and plural)
ti? what?
ti kanis?: how are you?
ti krima: what a shame

ti thelis na peis? what would you
   like to drink?
tiropitas: cheese pies
trellos: crazy
tsipoura: a kind of fish

v

vlakas: fool

y

yasoo: hi; more properly transliterated
   as *ygeia sou/ygei sas*—literally,
   health to you
yiayti? why?

Acknowledgments

This book is born of the grace of my gurus. My gratitude to them is endless.

It is dedicated to my mother, Sam, instigator of dreams.

I am immensely grateful to the ground crew of brilliant, opinionated, indefatigable friends who got this baby to fly: Ana Espinosa, Catherine MacDonald, Marilynn Preston, Jennifer Priestley, and M. Elizabeth Reed. They always knew we'd have liftoff if they loved and shoved me long enough, going all the way back to typewriter ribbons.

Thank you Gaia Franchetti for your sublime artistry. Thank you editor-in-chef Ana Espinosa, for making everything better.

Thank you Miss Wilson, seventh grade Reed School, for falling me in love with words; Colonel Fagin, Camp Kennolyn's riding instructor and my first spiritual guide, for teaching me and all us impressionable campers that religion is simply how we treat one another; Francis St. John, Headmaster of the Barlow School, who knew I was a writer before I did; and Mademoiselle Nadia Boulanger, for inexplicably accepting me as a music student even after hearing me play the flute.

Thanks to the whole talented Tell Me Press team, including Jeff Eyrich, Lisa Clyde Nielsen, Ian Nielsen, Paula Brisco, Linda Loiewski, Jeff Breuler, and inspired publicist Gail Parenteau. Thanks also to Demetra Merikas and Margaret Merikas for their culinary help and inspiration.

And thanks to Robin Williamson, lyricist of "Maya," for putting into twelve words what I'm trying for in seventy thousand.

Thank you William Shakespeare, *sine quo non* of this work. And then there's Tolstoy, Dostoyevsky, Borges, Woolf, Yourcenar, and Nabokov, whom I haven't actually met but who convinced me that fiction writer is preferable to ski bum, folk singer, coffee vendor, and anything that pays well.

This is a work of fiction. If you recognize yourself, your acquaintances, your boat, or your place of business, you have more imagination than I. As to events, it deserves mention that coincidence is the mother of misunderstanding.

Barbara Bonfigli
Santa Fe